Second Hand Curses

By Drew Hayes

There are legends you will not find in any book of fairy tales. Such stories were not meant to be passed on to children, nor were they of the sort any proper scribe would write down. These tales were whispered between close friends over many drinks, the kind of rumor that most disregarded immediately out of general propriety.

In the tales of fairy, the lines are crisp and clean. Good on one side, evil on the other, and all that lies betwixt the two is conflict. At least, that is how it is supposed to be. Some stories spoke of those who straddled that line. Who lived for it. Who loved it. They who were neither knight nor dragon, damsel nor witch, villain nor hero.

These are the tales of the Bastard Champions.

The Tale of the Lost Slipper

"And what happened after you lost the shoe?" Jack asked. He was wearing his client face, radiating confidence and just a touch of swarthy danger as he listened to the straw-haired young woman's tale. One could say many things about Jack, though few that Marie or Frank hadn't already uttered, but the fact remained that he had the touch when dealing with people. At least, when dealing with the sorts of people who put themselves in the kinds of situations that necessitated meeting Jack.

The girl swallowed hard and glanced out the small window of her cottage. Sunlight shone on the garden outside, and the sounds of birds could be heard even through the walls. No doubt she was yearning to be out there, in the sun, away from such sordid discussions. Such desires were understandable, but ultimately futile. The sun would set, and when the moon rose her troubles would return. Better to sacrifice time in the sun now and face the darkness with some preparation.

"I ran home. The carriage was a pumpkin again, so I couldn't very well take that. By the time I got back it was nearly sunrise. I thought it had been a wonderful night. Then, the next evening…she returned."

"Let me take a guess," Jack said. "Told you that it was time to pay your debt. Said you'd be going with her, maybe she even dressed it up a bit by making the place sound nice. Of course, that's all nonsense. You're going to be a slave, at best."

The woman nodded, her eyes beginning to fill with tears. "After…after I told her I wanted to stay she got angry. I think she would have forced me to come, but for some reason she couldn't."

"Your deal was incomplete." Frank's tone was deep and somber, slipping out from the robe and hood that hid the majority of his features. At the sound of his voice, their young client jumped the smallest bit. "A Feystian bargain is a complicated piece of magic. Until your wish has been fully granted—in this case I'd assume winning the prince's heart—she cannot take possession of you."

"Too bad there are royal emissaries all over town looking for the mystery woman he danced with," Marie muttered. Unlike Frank, Marie wore no robe, only simple, functional clothes that bore a minor shape-changing enchantment. Not that the spell was discernible with the naked eye. Much like Marie's own gifts, it remained unseen until it was needed. "You must have left one hell of an impression."

"It was a magical night," the girl replied. "We were true loves; I knew it the minute our eyes met."

Jack didn't say it, but he suspected that this girl's adoration for the prince, and his for her, had also been supplemented by fairy magic. True love certainly existed, it just didn't seem likely that she'd cast this kind of bargain and end up meeting hers. But even if the love were the genuine article, it didn't help them. True love could do a lot, but contracts were contracts no matter how one looked at them.

"After she showed up, that's when you started doing a little research and asking around," Jack said, moving the conversation back on target.

"Yes, but no one would help me. Everyone I spoke to told me I had made my bargain and they couldn't lend aid." Her hands shook intermittently as she talked. "But the fairy kept returning, and now I think she might be helping the prince find me. I was frantic to find a solution, so when someone told me about you…"

"It's fine, we're not the folks people come to unless they're frantic in the first place." Jack leaned back in the chair, keeping his body language as relaxed as possible. "Technically speaking, you're in the wrong here. You made a deal, and the fairy has upheld her end of the bargain. What you're trying to do is welsh, which puts you on the side of the wicked. That means while you may not have the Narrative set against you, it certainly isn't on your side. No noble knight is going to lift a blade for that situation. Lucky for you, Cinderella, we don't give two dragon scales about whether you're on the side of good or evil. All we care about is the color of your gold. And after hearing the entirety of your situation, I think we can come to an arrangement."

"I…I don't have much. My stepmother and her daughters control most of our wealth, and even that is paltry compared to what it was when my father ran the farm."

"No, you probably can't afford us." Before she could panic, Jack flashed a comforting smile and continued. "But the prince could, easily. I imagine his newest sweetie will have access to plenty of gold. More than enough to cover our paltry fees."

"I thought the fact that I wasn't with the prince was all that was keeping me safe right now." Cinderella's eyes had stopped flowing with tears; now they were wide in confusion.

"That's what we call a temporary solution," Jack explained. "Sooner or later, he'll find you, and when he does we both know that sweet love will take over. As soon as his heart truly belongs to you—*poof.* No more clause in the contract."

"So what can you do? Do you have a way to break the contract?" Cinderella leaned forward, unaware of the view she gave down the top of her dress. Jack noted her breasts with clinical appreciation, but kept his demeanor professional. Greed trumped lust in his hierarchy of sins, and besides, she was as innocent as a doe in fresh snow. Jack preferred women with a bit more wit and spice.

"No one can break a fairy contract," Marie said. "At least, no one we've run across yet."

"Too true, I'm afraid there is no getting out of the contract," Jack agreed. "There are, however, longer short-term solutions that we can employ."

"Like what?" Cinderella asked.

"Like don't worry too much about the specifics. We'll handle the details. All you need to do is give us a few days to lay the groundwork and, of course, reimburse us for materials after the job is done. Meaning no meeting the prince until three days from now, at the soonest, understand?"

"I can do that," Cinderella promised. "My stepsisters have been petitioning him to come and let them try on the shoes, but I can hide in the root cellar if it comes to that."

"Please do. Until then, we'll head to our temporary headquarters to get preparations under way."

* * *

The "temporary headquarters" was a cheap tavern not far from the castle. There was ample food and ale, along with recently vacated rooms now that the ball was over, which made it as nice a place as they could hope for. Often their travels left them without even a roof overhead, which meant having warm food and cold drinks was the epitome of luxury, at least so far as Jack was concerned.

"There's a rat fighting a cat in the corner." Marie's voice was uninterested as she watched the battle casually, no sign of the disgust one might have expected at such a display so close to her food. When she'd first joined them, Marie had been a bit more prone to blanching, but after more than two years with Jack and Frank, very little surprised or sickened her anymore.

Jack looked over and grinned. "Two copper on the rat."

"The cat outweighs him by several pounds, and is evolutionarily designed to be better at this manner of combat." Frank, as usual, saw things analytically by nature.

"No question, but the rat looks like he's got guts."

"Very well then, I accept the wager," Frank said.

That done, they turned back to the large parchment that Frank was scribbling on. In his meticulous handwriting were a list of supplies, some basic designs, and an estimation of cost for the assembled components.

"This would be so much easier if we could kill fairies." It was a comment Marie tossed out any time they worked a fairy job. Or if someone mentioned fairies. Or, sometimes, apropos of nothing. Marie *really* didn't like fairies, with fair reason, and their near immortality was an ever-present bother to her.

"Bloody things are made of magic. It takes a weapon of mythical power to actually slay them," Jack reminded her. "Which we can neither afford, nor find."

"I know. Just saying."

"If fairies were so easy to kill, then they wouldn't require special tactics to deal with, and that would mean our services would be in less demand," Frank pointed out.

Jack drummed his fingers and took a long draw from his stein of ale. "Never looked at it that way before. Suppose in a way we're lucky they're such tough little pests."

Marie narrowed her eyes and glared at Jack. "Oh yeah, I feel like the damn luck dragon of Dagil."

"Just pointing out that some of our most lucrative jobs come from dealing with the unfair folk. On that note, how tough will it be to get the cage built?"

"Based on the level of industry in this town, I anticipate that it *can* be accomplished in three days," Frank told him. "That assumes, of course, that we're willing to pay for a rush job and that I pitch in with the assembly."

"Hmmm." Marie and Frank could both see the wheels turning in Jack's head. It was a time-sensitive job, and Cinderella would only be able to hold out for so long. At the same time, Jack loathed spending more than he had to. Of course, since he was passing on expenses to her anyway, it didn't really make a difference. In fact, it represented one more place he could pad the bill and sneak a little extra in.

"Rush job sounds about right. Make it so." Jack reached the decision that Marie and Frank had both seen coming from a kingdom away. "While you handle that, I'll take care of the botany aspect. At least the gal already has a garden; that will make concealing the circle easier."

"And what should I be doing during all of this?" Marie asked.

"You handle resupply. After that last gig, we're low on too many of our tools. We need iron, silver, herbs, rations, and every half-decent potion you can get your hands on. That'll take a lot of negotiating and haggling, and you're our business expert."

"I would also like the materials to construct more of my powder," Frank added. "I'm nearly out after we had to destroy that tunnel."

"Make a list." Marie's eyes glowed yellow for the barest of moments, the pupils half-forming to slits before she re-asserted control. While Marie was annoyed by supply runs, the truth remained that only she among them had both a formal education on the value of various wares and could sling diplomacy and terror in even measures. "I'll get started shopping in the morning."

"Excellent. We all have our duties, now let's save Cinderella. By the by, Frank, you owe me two copper."

Sure enough, in the corner the cat had scampered away with blood on its flank while the rat stood there, triumphantly daring anyone to try to shoo it from its perch of victory.

"That is not the way logic dictates the fight should have ended." Frank pulled two copper pieces from the coin purse tucked discreetly inside his tunic. His hand stretched briefly into the light, revealing pale skin and a patchwork of stitches that ran across it.

"Guts matter." Jack held out his own palm and gleefully accepted his winnings with a beaming smile. From copper to gold, Jack had never met the coin he didn't like.

* * *

Planting elderlillies was a far from fast-paced or glamorous job, yet Jack still treated the process with as much care as he would a sword fight to the death. The devil was in the details, and Jack preferred to keep his devils restrained, especially when he planned on threatening them. He measured the distance between each flower precisely, being certain that the roots were connecting beneath the recently turned topsoil. The first time he'd made one of these, Jack had gone so far as to make the petals touch, but over the years he'd learned a root link was more than enough to fulfill the magic's requirements.

"What are you doing?" The voice was guarded, as though its owner expected Jack to pull his blade and draw blood at the slightest provocation. He looked up from his work to find a dark-haired woman staring down at him. From the side of the cottage he saw another of similar appearance, though that one seemed to prefer keeping her distance. The young woman before him was comely, and while she lacked the radiant glow of Cinderella, she still possessed enough charms to draw a common man if the need were upon her.

"That depends on how much your sister told you," Jack replied. Cinderella had warned Jack that there was little love lost between her and her family, and it wasn't hard to see why. Their client was extraordinary, and compared to Cinderella, her siblings were mundane. The ordinary often loathed the exceptional, tried to grind it in the dirt until it became like them.

"She said there was some kind of monster that's been coming to the garden, and you lot are helping her with it."

Jack was surprised; Cinderella had spun a tale that was true while still concealing her own scandal. Perhaps there was more cunning in the straw-haired lass's mind than he'd given her credit for. That would be something to watch for, when the time of payment drew near.

"Then you've got the gist of it," Jack said. "My companions and I are specialists of a sort. We handle monsters."

"You don't look like a knight or a prince," the woman replied, eyeing him up and down. His dark hair was damp with sweat under the midday sun, and his hands were stained with dirt from digging in the garden. More than that though, Jack simply lacked the aura of regality one associated with such bold men. He took no slight at her words; after all, she was quite right.

"That would be because I am neither." Jack stood from the ground and gave his back a long stretch. Common though he was, Jack still knew how to turn a smile and add a twinkle to his eye. He was good-looking, though not great, but with the additions of confidence and charm he could often make a receptive woman forgive his less handsome features. "I am simply a man who has gained bits of practical knowledge here and there, and uses them to make a living in this strange, cruel world."

"By planting flowers?"

"You'd be surprised at what a circle of elderlillies can hold, under the right conditions." Jack's ever-present smile widened as he moved closer to the young lady and took a slight bow. "I'm Jack, by the way."

She curtsied. "Truffetta. Mayphera is the one hiding behind the corner. She thought you looked dangerous."

"And you disagreed?" Jack asked.

"No, I thought she was spot on," Truffetta said. "But I don't always dislike danger. Sometimes it can be downright fun."

Jack nodded, his smile shifting into a knowing smirk. "That it can."

* * *

Marie and Frank were settling in for dinner at the tavern when Jack burst through the door. He scrambled to their table and grabbed Frank's ale, draining the whole thing in seconds. Only when that was done, and Frank was glaring at him unhappily, did Jack begin to speak.

"We've got a problem."

"No, I assumed you were rushing in here and stealing Frank's drink because everything was going so swimmingly," Marie said. "How big a problem?"

"About as big as it can get." Jack was badly winded, which was saying something since he spent more time outrunning danger than most men spent under the sun. If Jack was short of breath, he must have raced from the cottage to the inn in one long sprint. "Cinderella met the prince this afternoon."

"Oh, for the love of… It's still a day early. How much clearer could we have been with the girl?" Marie's eyes glowed again as she tossed up her hands in frustration, nearly knocking over her own tankard in the process.

"To be fair, it wasn't entirely her fault," Jack replied, settling in at the table's open seat. "Her stepsisters had been petitioning for some while to be seen, and when the prince showed up Cinderella followed our instructions by beating a hurried path into the root cellar. Unfortunately, the prince somehow knew there were three girls living there, and forced her stepmother to bring Cinderella up. As soon as they saw each other…well, you both know how these things go."

Frank leaned in, his scarred face still furrowed at the sight of his stolen drink. "And how, exactly, did you witness all this? I highly doubt the prince allowed an outsider, let alone one as dirt-covered as you, to sit in on the ceremony of trying the shoe."

Jack cleared his throat and adjusted his collar ever so slightly, inadvertently bringing a purple mark near his collarbone into view. "I snuck in and listened, of course. Keeping a close tab on the client is a very important part of the job."

"Based on the mark near your neck and the flush in your skin, I would wager you were already inside the cottage when the prince arrived. Perhaps you heard the entire conversation while crouched in a closet hoping desperately not to be discovered," Frank surmised.

Jack opened and closed his mouth several times; however, no worthwhile lies sprang to mind, so his tongue lay silent as his lips flapped. Jack's tongue was a willful thing with a reputation to maintain; it couldn't be bothered offering up half-baked fibs that none would believe.

"Really, Jack?" Marie shook her head. "With the doe-eyed girl who's lovesick and terrified all at once? Have you no shame?"

"How dare you!" Jack said, clutching his chest. "The very idea that I would engage in such relations with a client. Do you think that little of me? Of my dedication to what we do? Of my professionalism?"

"It was one of the stepsisters, wasn't it?"

"Dammit, Frank, you are not helping me here."

"I wasn't particularly trying to," Frank admitted. "The girl, however, I do think we should try to assist. Did you manage to get the elderlillies planted before you went off trying to sow your own seeds?"

"We didn't… The prince interrupted… Yes, I got the flowers planted." Jack made a mental note never to steal Frank's drink again. Clearly it left him cranky, and Frank was far too smart to deal with when he was annoyed.

Although far from pleased, Marie seemed somewhat mollified by the news. "That'll hold the fairy through the night, if we can get her in it. But our girl is going to be pricked on a spinning wheel come sunrise, unless we get an iron cage."

"The two days I've had were enough time to commission the work and begin construction. But there is no possible way we could fit a fairy in what I've completed thus far. Nor is it sound enough to hold one as long as we'd require." Frank looked out the window to the afternoon's waning light. "There's roughly an hour to sunset. With Marie's help and about half the night's time I could reshape the current piece, perhaps slap together enough to make a complete enclosure, but I doubt we'd be able to fit a fully grown fairy inside it."

Jack drummed his fingers quietly along the table. "That was pretty much what I'd expected. Dammit all, we need more time. Or a smaller fairy." The drumming halted as a look came over Jack's face. Marie and Frank knew that look very well. It was the one that arrived when they were in tight spots, and usually preceded ridiculous amounts of danger. This was the look that meant Jack had an idea, and even the greatest monsters in the darkest forests gave pause at the sorts of ideas that sprang from Jack's oddly crafted mind.

"Since Cinderella was discovered before the agreed-upon time, it's technically a breach of our contract. Might be best to just cut our losses and go.

But I might have an inkling of something that will work. It's a bit of a long shot, and if it doesn't work then we are going to have a *very* angry fairy on our hands come morning."

"Knowing what Cinderella is staring down, I'd say a long shot beats the hell out of her being dragged off to serve at some fairy's feet," Marie said. It was the answer they all knew she'd give before the asking. Much as Marie loathed fairies, she felt for their victims even more strongly. Given her body's extreme reaction to any severe change in temperament, it was an understandable, if not always pragmatic, sentiment.

"Plus, I paid for the metalwork in advance," Frank added. "So in order for us to recoup our significant expenses we need her to survive." Frank's own heart lined up more with Marie's attitude than the fiscal one he'd voiced, but he knew which of the two arguments Jack would hear the louder.

"In advance?" Jack spoke the words as if they were ancient curses that would summon forth the vilest of demons.

"And for a rush job." Frank could already see where things were heading; he added that one last bit to hurry them along.

"Well then, Marie is right, we can't simply let Cinderella be seized. After all, she's our client and we have a duty to uphold. I'll handle getting the fairy in the ring of elderlillies while you two will have to make use of as much of the night as possible. It's going to be tough, but I know one thing for sure: Marie is going to *love* this plan."

As Jack began to speak, a gleefully wicked expression spread across Marie's face, the sort that made other patrons uncomfortable when they looked at it for too long. Jack's words certainly held true; his was a plan that Marie might have chosen even if safer options were available.

* * *

The girl was waiting in the garden as Ajiana landed, her soft slippers resting delicately on the grass. It was the least this troublesome wench could do, after failing to seal the deal on the night of the ball and forcing Ajiana to run hither and thither to complete their contract. For once, it seemed, Cinderella had decided to make the mature decision and accept her fate. It a wise choice; Ajiana would have caught her effortlessly even if she tried to run, and then taken the inconvenience out on her new slave's flesh.

Cinderella was facing away from the soft grasses where Ajiana had set down, gazing at the cottage that she would never see again. How humorous, to know that the girl was pining for the very place she'd begged the fairy to deliver her from only a few evenings prior. There was no turning back for her now; the deal was complete. The girl had won the heart of a prince, with a bit of nudging from Ajiana's wand, and had tasted true joy on the night of the ball. She'd gotten her wish; now came the time for payment.

"Pleasant of you to wait for me," the fairy said, stepping across the many flowers dotting the garden's landscape. Were she prone to observation, Ajiana might have noticed that many of these hadn't been present in the days prior, or that one type of flower had been planted in a large circle. Such worries were for lesser creatures, however. Ajiana was a light fairy, a being of pure magic. She had no need for fear or worry. She was immortal and powerful; what care had she for newly planted flowers?

At the sound of Ajiana's voice, Cinderella darted forward, racing toward the cottage without so much as turning back to face the fairy. Ajiana muttered an assortment of swears under her breath, then gave chase. She moved with the speed of the winds and the nimbleness of a dandelion upon the breeze. In no time at all she'd closed the gap between her and her prize. Ajiana reached forward to grab the girl, the first step in claiming and breaking her.

Instead, inches away from where Cinderella now stood, Ajiana's hand struck an invisible barrier. Her fingers slid across the mystic membrane, trying to push through but finding it completely unyielding. With a small bit of effort, Ajiana tried to destroy it with a curse, only to find that her power had no effect.

"Elderlillies under sky of night may bind a fairy of the light." This voice didn't belong to the woman she'd been pursuing; it was young, male, and full of an arrogance that set Ajiana's teeth on edge. He emerged from the shadows of the cottage doorway, wide smile gleaming in the moon's soft glow. As he moved forward he set a hand on Cinderella's shoulder and glanced down at her. "Good work tonight. You've done your part; now we'll take things over. Go into the root cellar with your family, and do not emerge until we come for you in the morning. No matter what you hear, stay put. Understand?"

Cinderella nodded, eyes moist and hands shaking from the terror of what she'd just done. Jack released his grip, and she fled inside the cottage. Her hurried footsteps down the cellar stairs could be heard echoing through the night, even as this young man moved closer to Ajiana.

"So, then, you would be Ajiana, Cinderella's 'fairy godmother' who made her a deal she should have refused. Suppose you were banking on her not knowing there's only one fairy who owns that title, and *she* doesn't bother with peasants."

"And you would be the amazing fool who thought to buy the girl time by binding a fairy. Let me guess, unrequited love interest? Perhaps you're a farmer's son whose heart she stole in childhood and you see this as the last chance to win her away from the prince?" Ajiana glared at the man, trying to cast through the barrier and finding not so much as a hiccup charm would pass its border.

"Come now, you have to be able to do better than that. You fairies are supposed to be able to see a person's deepest wishes. I'd assumed that meant you had a modicum of skill in reading people. Do you truly take me to be some lovesick farmer's son, one who happened to know the secret to trapping fairies?"

Ajiana looked closely and realized that, no, he was not some simple bumpkin on a hopeless quest of the heart. Farmers didn't generally wear swords, especially ones as long and thin as the one strapped to his side. They also didn't move like cats across a branch, each step graceful and certain. More than anything, though, they didn't have eyes like this man's, full of knowledge, humor, and a touch of ferocity.

"Who are you?"

He bowed in a deep, measured gesture. "Jack, surname withheld for my own safety, though many monikers have been laid upon me throughout my travels. I am the founder of the Bastard Champions, a small group of scoundrels who handle situations like this one in exchange for coin. There, now we are properly introduced."

Ajiana kept watch on him as she began walking around the circle of elderlillies, trying to feel for a way out. "I'm impressed you knew about this little bit of magic, Jack the scoundrel. It's old magic, so much so that I nearly forgot it existed. However, dear boy, perhaps you should have done a touch more research in your endeavors. While this ring may hold me for now, it will have no effect once the first rays of the sun light this land."

"Well, of course I knew that." Jack walked over to the cottage and leaned against the wall, slowly lowering himself into a seat on the soft grass. "It's right there in the rhyme and everything."

"Then you know that once I am free of this circle, all you will have accomplished is to raise my ire at Cinderella and put yourself in harm's way. I'm a reasonable fairy, though. Break the circle now, and I'll let you off with only a minor curse. Perhaps the inability to say people's names, or eyes that can no longer discern faces." Her fingers kept pressing the barrier, finding not one weak point she might be able to turn into freedom.

"Tempting, but there's a flaw in your logic," Jack replied. "If we deal with you before sunrise, then I get no curses, and Cinderella pays her tab for us saving her."

Ajiana threw back her head and laughed into the night, a noise like high-pitched songbells being played in a graveyard. When she was done, she looked back at Jack, twirling a strand of her long purple hair through her fingers. "Deal with me? You would seek to *kill* a fairy? A being of pure magic? Tell me then: what precious, well-guarded weapon of legend have you brought to accomplish this? Perhaps you wield the lance used to slay a hundred swamp dragons, or maybe the Lady in the Lake asked you to take up her blade? Ah, but wait, you are clearly neither a king nor a knight, which means you would never be entrusted with either, or the handful of other weapons that might be able to accomplish such a lofty goal."

"Quite right you are," Jack agreed. "Even if I could get my hands on such a weapon, I have no doubt it would refuse to be wielded by one such as I. No, I'm all too aware that killing a fairy is beyond my reach."

"Then let us make a deal." Ajiana's lavender eyes softened, and she allowed herself to cast the young man a lingering glance. Fairies were as beautiful as they chose to be, and while she didn't carry on like some of the others, Ajiana had taken the time to form quite a comely body and a striking face for herself. "Perhaps I can be convinced to offer you a true reward for my freedom, rather than a reduced curse."

"And no doubt you would fulfill the contracted reward, followed immediately by the sort of curse that lasts through generations." Jack seemed insultingly unmoved by her advances. "Besides, it's not as if you have me at a disadvantage. I already told you, you'll be dealt with before sunrise."

Ajiana snapped, perhaps a touch out of wounded pride in addition to annoyance. "Then pray tell, Jack, how will you 'deal with me' as you claim? You cannot kill me, and this prison of flowers will only hold for a few more hours. What possible way does a self-sure fool with a touch of knowledge have to 'deal with' a fairy?"

"Iron."

At Jack's word, Ajaina's blood grew as cold as the metal he'd named. She hid her surge of fear, staring at him with a leering gaze to mock his stupidity. "Iron cannot kill a fairy."

"No, but it can hurt them," Jack said. "Wound them, too, even cause injuries that take time to heal. They do all heal, of course, because as you've said fairies are immortal. But iron also binds their magic, so if you lock a fairy in a sealed cage composed entirely of it and bury the cage underground…well, while that fairy might not be dead, she is unquestionably dealt with."

"You…you would lock me, a fairy of light, away like some common pixie!" Though she was yelling, what Ajiana really wanted to do was whisper. Such an idea had never occurred to her. That wasn't how things were done. To vanquish was one thing, but this young man with the unceasing smile was talking about countless years of imprisonment. It was wretched, vile, and wrong. If Ajiana had spared a moment in her frantic scramble of thoughts, she might have reflected on the fact that in her home were no less than ten girls to whom she'd done exactly that. But fairies, at least fairies like Ajiana, were not known for their introspection or their morality.

"No, actually, I won't. See, that's what we do with most of the fairies like you we come across, but unfortunately Cinderella was discovered early, bringing you here before the cage was ready. Which means we had to think of some…less conventional means of sealing you up."

Ajiana heard something coming down the road. It was an animal, and it was running on all fours, but she couldn't imagine a horse heavy enough to make steps that echoed like this one's. Jack heard it, too. He rose from the ground and walked over to peek around the side of the cottage.

"That would be my partners. Before they get here, I want to offer you a bargain. A contract, if you will."

"Doubting that your scheme will work?" Ajiana snapped.

"It's risky, but that's no different from most things we do." Jack shrugged, and Ajiana realized that he wasn't lying. This madman really did things as preposterous as caging fairies with such regularity that he seemed almost bored by the whole thing. That, more than anything said so far, made Ajiana afraid in the core of her being.

"Anyway, I'm offering now because once Marie gets here she'll never let me do it. The girl deeply dislikes your kind, and I can't say I blame her. Still, I feel like this method is going to be messy on top of being quite barbaric, so I think it might be best for everyone if I at least tried to give you an out."

Jack walked up to the edge of the elderlillies, only a few inches and one magic barrier outside of Ajiana's grasp. "Here are the terms: in exchange for your freedom you will void the contract of Cinderella and every other person you've even taken. You will swear to never use magic again, save only for a single spell to return those imprisoned to their homes. You will never speak of the bargain to anyone, nor make any effort to see retribution exacted through others. Lastly, you will never communicate with another fairy in any way for the rest of your life. Oh, and if you have knowledge about the location of any greater fairies, throw that in for good measure."

"You truly are mad." Ajiana stared at him in unabashed shock. "What you ask would all but unmake me as a fairy."

"Precisely." Jack glanced off beyond the cottage, where the sound of the impending beast was growing closer. "Do we have a deal?"

"Absolutely not! I'll deal with your cage, and one day I'll get free. When that day comes, I will find you, or your children, or your children's children, and I will exact a revenge more horrible than you can imagine."

"I already told you," Jack said. "You aren't just getting a cage. You get something special. But that choice was yours to make, and you've done so. It can't be said that I didn't try to find a compromise."

The pounding steps came to a halt, and Jack gave his captive a brief smile before heading to the other side of the cottage. "Ho!" he called to someone Ajiana couldn't see. "Were you able to get enough iron shavings?"

Ajiana swallowed hard, but said nothing. These people couldn't kill her. She had nothing to fear. She wouldn't let go of her contracted servants, or her magic. She would drag Cinderella back home and spend years torturing her for daring to involve such people in their business. The minute one of them stepped in here she would curse them halfway to the pits and use that one as leverage to get her freedom.

That resolve lasted only until she saw the man round the corner with the barrel on his back. In spite of the towering beast with glowing yellow eyes that walked only a few feet behind, dragging an entire cart of supplies, the pale man was the most terrifying thing Ajiana had seen that evening. Though he moved on mismatched limbs and looked at her with stolen eyes, she sensed what he was the moment her gaze fell upon his form. Before she even saw the scars, or the dragon's iris in his left eye's socket, Ajiana knew she was doomed.

Fairy magic held no power over those already dead.

* * *

Cinderella and her family did as they were told. It had been difficult talking them into trusting her, but seeing as she was now on her way to being the princess, her stepmother and sisters seemed eager to appease her. Perhaps they hoped it would assuage any feelings of retribution she might harbor at her years of horrid treatment. Whatever the reason was didn't matter to her in the moment, only that they followed orders, which they did. They stayed in the root cellar during the quiet. They stayed there when the shouting began. They stayed when the shouting turned to screams, unearthly wails that they prayed never to hear again but would haunt their nightmares for years to come.

They even stayed put when a sound like a carriage crashing through a wall tore through the night, and their home shook precariously over their heads. Mayphera began crying then, soft silent sobs as tears streamed down her face, but she made no movement to flee. If anything, the others kept their eyes away from the exit, certain that what lay on the other side was not a thing they cared to witness. Some time later, the door to the cellar was pulled open and Jack stood there, his presence wordlessly assuring them that everything was okay.

Cinderella was the only one who could muster up the courage to speak.

"Is it...is she gone?"

"Most of her. Frank and Marie should have all the leftovers bagged soon."

"Beg pardon?" Cinderella stared at the smiling man, and for the first time she stopped to ask herself, in the fits of panic and desperation just what sort of people she had brought into her home.

"Probably better if you don't know," Jack said. "Let's merely say that Frank is an expert in some…unusual technologies, and that we found a way to deal with your fairy problem. The main parts of her, anyway."

"You caged her?" Cinderella began walking up the stairs with Jack, her mother and stepsisters keeping a long distance. Even Truffetta, who had seemed so keen on him just the day before, watched with uncertain eyes at every step her stepsister's savior took. When Jack had merely seemed dangerous in a roguish, charming sort of way it was one thing. Now, after hearing the screams and feeling the house rattle, there was no allure in the danger he represented.

"That's essentially correct." Jack paid no mind to the fearful glances coming from the others. He'd been on the job for many years; he understood how most people reacted to seeing what his team did. "Given Cinderella's untimely discovery, we had to use a bit of an unconventional method, focusing more on certain pieces of her than binding the whole, and blowing each bit off took some time, so we ended up… Forgive me, perhaps I'm going too much into the details. Regardless, the sun has risen and none of us is dead, so it seems to be holding."

"Then…it is finally over." Cinderella felt a tremendous weight lift off her shoulders, and for the first time since she'd danced with the prince at the ball she allowed hope to enter her heart. That feeling was quickly snuffed out as Jack clamped a powerful grip on her shoulder. Cinderella did not yelp, but she did let out a small involuntary squeak of surprise.

"No." Jack locked eyes with her. His smile dimmed, although never quite vanished, and Cinderella saw the weariness in his face that he hid with the endless grin. "What we have done today is a stall, nothing more. Fairies are immortal. Eventually, someone will free her, and when that happens her wrath will be a thing of horrific splendor. This is far from over, Cinderella. But, if we are all very fortunate, we will be long dead by the time she is freed."

"What if she comes after our children then? Or others of our lineage?"

Jack released his grip on her, and began walking out the cottage's front door. Cinderella followed, noticing the ramshackle cart situated in the road. On it, the one who wore a large cloak to hide his face and had stitches running across his arms loaded the last of what appeared to be three iron containers. They were rough and misshapen, clearly crafted with either hurry or apathy by their smith, but they seemed solid. Each was roughly the size of a basket, and Cinderella couldn't imagine how a fairy could be fit into one of the small containers. Then she remembered Jack's word, *leftovers*, and a chill ran through her despite the warm morning air.

"When she gets free, she will undoubtedly come for those of our line," Jack said at last, surveying the loading being done on his cart. "Which means we have only three options. The first of which is to have no children, to let our lineage die out entirely. As a future princess, I doubt that choice will appeal to you or your eventual husband."

Cinderella nodded. Life at the castle was surely wonderful, but she was not so removed from royal politics that she didn't understand the need for an heir. Even were that not the case, she could not imagine spending a life with the man she'd already fallen in love with and not bearing a child.

"Your second choice is to make sure they know what is coming. Prepare your children, and see that they know to prepare theirs as well. Keep iron and elderlillies nearby, and, if one of you should fit the calling, perhaps take hold of a weapon that can slay a fairy. Of course, as time goes by the threat will seem less real. Within two generations, it will be regarded as a silly tale their grandparents used to tell. That leaves us with one more option."

From behind the cottage, Marie came around carrying a medium-sized sack. Cinderella saw the damp stain across its bottom, and made an instantaneous decision to believe that it was from the morning's dew in the grass. She didn't stop to wonder why the dew would impart such a dark hue; it was a question for which her mind could likely not bear the answer. Not now, not after so much already.

"What's the third option?" Cinderella's voice came out scarcely above a whisper as she saw Marie load the sack into the cart along with the iron containers.

"We hope that when that day comes, there are more people like me and mine to deal with the problem." Jack turned around, and when he did she saw that his smile had brightened once more. "If you'll excuse us, we have some things to bury. We'll return by the next new moon to collect our payment. I trust that will be suitable time?"

Cinderella nodded, perhaps more fervently than she needed to. Jack had done nothing to try to scare her, had gone out of his way to keep her from seeing anything truly terrifying. Yet still, now that the danger was past she wanted him gone. Him, and his strange friends. There was no doubt in her heart that she would pay his fee, if for no other reason than she longed to be rid of him and to put this whole nightmare in the past.

Of course, that would never truly happen, for Jack's words were those of wisdom and experience. He had spoken true when he told her it was not over, and for the rest of her life Cinderella would always start, just a touch, at the sound of wings.

The Tale of the Caged Women

"This is ridiculous," Marie hissed under her breath. She twirled the parasol in her hands carefully, doing all she could to appear incompetent and uncertain. It was a difficult series of emotions to convey through the movements of a glorified umbrella, but she tried nonetheless.

"Shhh." Jack leaned out a few inches from his perch behind a barrel in the alleyway. He was there, ostensibly, to intervene if anything should go awry. That was true, in the sense that Jack might be able to suppress minor problems without alerting the whole village to their presence. If things should take a turn for the truly troublesome, then Marie would be forced to intervene, and her presence was not a thing that anyone was likely to miss. That would mean losing their lead, and she had no inclination to go back on the hunt.

Marie turned and looked down the long stretch of deserted road. It was hard for most to see with nothing more than starlight to guide them, but to Marie the world was as crisp and clear as if the sun were shining right overhead. This part of the curse lingered about her, much like her heightened sense of smell or increased strength. It was a constant reminder that no matter how she appeared, she was far from an ordinary woman. Turning her gaze to the alley where Jack's barrel was located, she saw clearly that he'd leaned out too far and made himself visible, even to one without her night vision.

"Get covered." Marie turned the parasol in a way that she hoped would keep any would-be watchers in the forest at the road's edge from seeing the movements of her mouth. "It's bad enough that you've had me walking this same stretch for half the night; if anyone spots you, then we're as good as discovered."

Jack hurriedly tucked himself back behind the barrel, vanishing from sight so quickly it was as if he'd never been there at all. He was the better choice for a job like this one; Jack had a gift for slipping about in places meant to hold him. Unfortunately, of the three, Marie was the only one who fit the criteria enough to make a useful decoy, so she was stuck parading about in a frilly dress and a garish parasol, hoping to draw the skulking eye of some yet unseen villain.

She pivoted on her heel and turned away from where the forest met the road. This was ludicrous. Even if she had spent a week in the village as a traveler, talking freely of how she loved to go for midnight strolls when sleep evaded her, no one would possibly believe she would be out walking this long. Any criminal with even a modicum of sense would see her here, then stop to observe, quickly realizing that she was lying in wait for their arrival. Marie didn't care what Frank's theory was, there was no way someone would take such obvious bait. For once, her pale companion was going to be proven—

"Dammit." Marie heard the hoofbeats storming up from her behind her and winced internally. They were coming too fast to be a traveler, and it was too late at night for the foolish young men to be holding races, which meant only one thing: Frank was right yet again. It wasn't that she begrudged him his keen judgment; it was merely that he could be such a pain about it when doubted, and Marie had very vocally questioned this plan from the beginning.

After waiting long enough to where a normal woman would have finally noticed the hoofbeats, Marie spun around in time to see the cloaked rider atop a black horse bearing down on her. She let out a high-pitched screech, nothing like the call she used when actually meeting an enemy head on, and then made a show of trying to run away. Her clumsiness here was not as feigned as she'd anticipated, since Frank had insisted she wear the clunky high-heeled shoes popular with noble ladies in the area. Marie made it about ten feet forward before she felt the powerful arm close around her torso, scooping her effortlessly off the ground as the horse rode by.

No sooner was she grabbed than the rider slung her over his horse's back, into a leather mechanism that coiled around her. The rider pulled a strap tight and it sealed Marie in, to where she could scarcely move, even with her strength. With a single fluid motion the rider hooked the strap onto his saddle, then fastened a golden lock in place. Just like that, Marie realized she'd been captured.

Dirt was still drifting through the air in the spot where Marie had been taken, her parasol left precariously in the road. Jack scooped it up once the rider was out of sight, twirling it nimbly in his hands as he stared into the empty night. While many might have been fearful about the kidnapping of their companion, Jack was elated.

The first part of the plan had gone off without a hitch. Now, if Frank was able to track them, they could have Marie sprung by morning. Of course, if the criminals managed to evade Frank's watchful eye, or tried to get too fresh with Marie, then she'd have to liberate herself. Jack truly hoped that wouldn't be the case.

The reward paid double if the criminals were brought in alive.

* * *

Marie's ride was not a gentle one, as her kidnapper favored haste over comfort in his effort to get her as far away from town as possible. He'd turned only once to face her, stuffing a rag in her mouth as she feigned distress with wailing screams. Honestly, she was thankful for the gag, it was far less annoying than having to keep up her prattle all through the ride. Besides, it meant the kidnapper wasn't paying her any attention, and that made her job far easier.

As they rode through the night, Marie would periodically kick a small latch hidden in the thick heel of her shoes. Each time she did so, a small metal ball would drop from a compartment in the footwear, falling to the ground, all sound muffled by the powerful beats of the horse's stride. Though these balls were little more than shined spheres, Frank assured her that he would be able to track her so long as she left a reasonable trail. Aside from the ones in her shoes, she also had spheres stuffed in the sleeve of her dress, since they'd had no idea exactly how she'd be restrained. It was a risky strategy, that was certain, but one that had the chance of paying off the best if it succeeded.

It was nearly sunrise when the horse finally began to slow. Marie wiggled her head around, noting that they'd gone quite deep into the forest. Large, ancient trees wound around them, and the sound of a stream could be heard not far in the distance. The rider continued forward, following a narrow path of stone that ran along the stream's side, winding down a half-hidden slope. It was only when the horse passed through a grove of massive tree trunks that Marie caught sight of what had to be their destination. The mouth of a large cave loomed before her, previously invisible through the foliage and now impossible to miss. The rider let out a high-pitched whistle, the first sound she'd heard leave his mouth aside from breath, and he pushed forward across the rocky terrain.

When they entered, Marie saw another man in dark clothes, but he was holding a well-made bow and watching the path to the entrance fervently. Her mind raced, realizing that their entry system was one of both recognition and a password, or passwhistle in this case. That showed the sort of forethought she wasn't used to encountering from mere ruffians. This lot might be a step above the usual crowd. She hoped they were, anyway. Dealing with mere humans always felt a touch unfair. At least the magical foes had a fighting chance.

Her rider dismounted easily from his saddle, thick black boots thudding at they struck the cave's stone floor. He reached over to the cord that bound her and unlocked it, then took it in his hand and kept the grip tight. With his free hand, he produced a single worn dagger from under his cloak. To his credit, he didn't do anything so overt as pressing it to her throat. The mere act of drawing it was enough of a threat.

"I am going to release you." His voice was old and rough, a stark contrast to the youthful strength and energy he'd demonstrated in her capture. "Do not attempt to run. We have no desire to mar your body, but we will choose less profit over letting you escape entirely."

That was all the preamble he gave before Marie felt the bond holding her grow slack, and discovered she was able to move freely once more. She used this freedom to lift herself off the horse and get carefully onto the ground. It required a concentrated effort, because her arms had gone numb and she had to pretend to cower. Technically, now that she knew where their hide-out was, the assault could begin, but she'd promised Frank and Jack a day's peace before catching up with her. Besides, not even Marie wanted to pick a fight when her enemies were braced for it. She preferred the element of surprise, for the brief moments she could grasp it.

The kidnapper roughly grabbed her shoulder and began marching her down one of the cave's tunnels. It twisted as they walked; only torches lit at periodic intervals made it possible for those without her gifts to see. Marie appreciated the torches as well; she didn't fancy having to stumble about in these shoes to mask her night vision. Within a few minutes the tunnel opened up once more. This chamber was large but contained, the tunnel being the only visible way in or out. Inside it was a massive metal cage, one that was far too large to fit through the tunnels. Marie knew that either made it magical or meant it was assembled on site, and she was hoping for the latter. Magical barriers could be a bit tricky to deal with.

Aside from the cage, the only other things in the room were a third man in dark clothes, though this one wore no cloak over his scarred face, and three young women inside the cage. Their tired eyes took in Marie's arrival, but none made any attempt to scream or yell at the kidnapper. Marie had been to more than one prison in her time, and she knew the look of those who had lost the last vestiges of hope. Deep in her gut, a growl tried to rise, but she pushed it down. Now was not yet the time. She needed to know exactly how many there were, and to see if other girls were waiting down a different tunnel.

"Got another," her kidnapper said.

The jailer nodded, picking up a large wooden club and walking to the cage's door. He glared at the girls inside, watching for the slightest sign that one of them would dare to make a move for freedom. None so much as twitched, but still his gaze remained on them as he unlocked the door and pulled it open. Marie felt herself being shoved forward, and she nearly lost her footing as she stumbled across the cage's threshold.

A loud clang filled the air as the door was slammed shut behind her, followed by the sound of the lock being turned. Reaching up, Marie carefully extracted the rag from her mouth and dropped it on the ground. Silence had been a useful tool for her capture, but now she required the use of her tongue. There was much she needed to know, and precious little time to learn it. Either her friends would show up, or her bubbling anger at these men would overflow. Whichever event started the chaos, there was no happy ending for the men who had been stealing these girls.

Marie intended to see to that personally.

* * *

"There." Frank pointed over Jack's shoulder, gesturing to a small twinkle of light reflecting from the ground. They trudged across the damp grass of early morning until they reached the object. Frank bent down and picked it up, cradling it between pale fingers as he examined the sphere. "Definitely one of mine. She went this way."

"I don't how you can spot those things," Jack said with a shake of his head. The shuttered lanterns Frank had built were great for directing beams of light across the ground, which made spotting the balls quite simple in the night. Now, though, with the sun shining down around them, it was more difficult to find the spherical breadcrumbs that Marie had left behind.

"I've got an eye for details," Frank replied. "Besides, these are more confirmation than anything. The trail isn't a subtle one. The only reason I couldn't find it without Marie was how well-traveled these woods are. It's crossed over three different fresh trails just since we've been tracking it."

"Place gets a lot of foot traffic for a village off the nearest kingdom's roads." Jack had also noted how many of the shops in the area seemed to conspicuously avoid advertising their wares, and the way that many of the locals avoided looking at him or Frank. Jack had a lingering hunch that this place had a booming industry in the sorts of things no proper kingdom would allow to be sold, which was why they'd called in the Bastard Champions instead of sending for some knights to deal with the kidnapping. Jack's company didn't care about what was being done behind closed doors; they merely took the job and asked no questions beyond what was relevant.

"It does seem to be a surprisingly busy little hamlet," Frank agreed. "Which, I suppose, is why someone thought they wouldn't miss a few of the many maidens frequenting the streets."

"Makes you wonder though, why do they need so many? They haven't been going after princesses, or any royalty for that matter, and scooping up girls at random means they must not care about virgins." Jack tapped his foot on the dew-laden grass as he scanned the trail ahead. "Five girls, counting Marie, snatched up in less than two weeks. To grab that many, and have no concerns about origin or magical potency, there aren't a lot of explanations that bode well for that."

Frank had evidently been harboring similar thoughts. "Either the girls are food, meant to be sold into slavery, or being used for a ritual that simply demands a vast amount of sacrifices. Though it is always possible for there to be another option we have not considered, those are by far the most likely explanations for such a series of crimes."

"Thing is, in any of those situations, I'm not sure why the town would care if we bring the kidnappers back alive," Jack said. "Why not just pay for their extermination and the return of all the girls who are still breathing?"

"Because in all of those cases, it speaks to the kidnappers likely being hired middlemen. The mayor probably wants to find out who paid for their services in the first place, to make sure they look elsewhere for their supplies next time. And, of course, it's possible that he wants to make examples of these men, to discourage any who might entertain ideas of a similar enterprise."

Jack thought back to the squirmy little man with the dark eyes, the mayor who had hired them. Frank was right; Jack could easily see that man using captured criminals as examples, letting horror stories of their fate spread through the land as a natural deterrent. If his town really was dealing in the sort of dark magic supplies Jack suspected, then he'd certainly have the resources to accomplish some hellish punishments.

"Maybe you're right. The criminals had better hope we have to kill them."

"Indeed, it might be the best outcome for all involved," Frank agreed. He slipped the metal ball into his pocket and headed down the path once more. It would be rude to keep Marie waiting longer than necessary.

* * *

Jailer, as Marie had begun to think of him, stared into the cage for a moment, then went back to polishing his sword. He didn't pay much attention to his captives, not unless they actually started getting near the cage's door, which had left the women free to talk amongst themselves. Unfortunately, Marie had quickly realized that there wasn't much she could get from the other captives. All three had been snatched from the street at night, but in the panic of it they hadn't been able to absorb many details. The only one who seemed to have any presence of mind was Lily, a brunette in a torn green dress.

Lily was the one who confirmed Marie's suspicions about the kidnappers, There were, in fact, only three that any of them had seen: Jailer, the one who was keeping watch over the girls; Sentry, the man who guarded the front with his bow; and Snatcher, the man who grabbed the girls and brought them in. Beyond that the girls knew almost nothing. Sometimes new women were brought in, sometimes one of them was taken away. The men never spoke to them, never did more than occasionally throw in some bread and water skins. Marie knew this tactic well; they were trying to break their captives down by placing them in a void. Without anything to grip onto, not even the changing of the days, mental deterioration was inevitable.

All of this swirled through Marie's head as she rested against the back of the cage, eyes locked on Jailer. He was strong—the thick, knotted muscles in his arms spoke to that fact—and from the way he carried himself Marie wagered he'd seen a fair share of combat. None of that would matter once she got free, of course, but it could make breaking through the metal restraint more difficult. There was also the risk that, if he were smart, he'd try to grab one of the others as a hostage rather than fight her directly.

"Thinkin' of trying to seduce him?" Lily sauntered over and plunked down next to Marie. She was far from a noble, speaking with the sort of habitual twang that spoke to a life amidst the farms and fields of the land. Probably new money, by Marie's estimation; perhaps her beauty had caught the eye of a well-off merchant.

"Since I'm not shiny and made of metal, I doubt I'm his type." Marie nodded to the impressive armory of weapons stored near Jailer, which he was carefully tending and polishing one by one.

"Smart call. Shayana already gave it a try on the first day," Lily said. Off in the corner, Shayana turned away from her conversation with Rohesia at the sound of her name. She was quite a beauty, with cinnamon-colored skin and a bust that her dress could scarcely contain. If she hadn't made any headway with seduction, it was safe to assume that Jailer wasn't so easily swayed. Lily gave her fellow captive a small wave, and the other two resumed their hushed discussion.

"Only thing that gets a reaction from him is makin' a run for it. Had a girl try that when she first got here; wasn't pretty. He stabbed her leg, then the others came for her not long after. She never stopped cryin' long enough for us to even get her name."

"And you have no idea where they took her to?"

"Like I told you earlier, they aren't exactly forthcomin' with any information. Lucky to get a snort out of any of them on the best day."

Much as she disliked these men and what they were doing, Marie had to admit they behaved like professionals. The guard, the silence, the cage, even the kidnappings; all of it was handled with exceptional proficiency. And yet…something was still off to her. The men had this intelligent system set up, yet Snatcher had still been dumb enough to fall for her little act. Jailer seemed more than aloof; she got the sense that he was not even interested in them as living beings. Perhaps Sentry was the mastermind behind it all, but if so then why give himself the worst job of the lot? It was as if they were all following instructions, which meant there had to be someone who gave those instructions in the first place.

"If you don't mind my sayin' so, you're taking all of this awfully well. Most of the others were inconsolable. Cryin' and carryin' on for the first few hours, if not days. You seem more put out than scared, and bit miffed about it at that."

"My kingdom was not a peaceful one," Marie lied. Save only for skirmishes and long-standing animosity with a neighboring land, her kingdom had been, and she dearly hoped still was, one of the safest, most peaceful kingdoms in all the lands. "While I may not have been in this precise situation before, I have dealt with enough trouble to know the wisdom in keeping my wits about me. What about you? Those two could barely muster up more than a few words, but you've been downright coherent."

Lily lifted her arms, taking a long stretch before answering. "Similar thing, I suppose. Grew up in a farmin' village. Had a witch near our town border, not a powerful one, mind you, but she was strong enough all the same. Anyway, we let her be and she sometimes sold us a few potions if the need was great. 'Course, you can't have a witch without her attractin' a few goblins and trolls, not to mention the odd knight bent on slayin' her. Made for a pretty chaotic village, so I'm not so unfamiliar with dangerous trouble."

"What brought you from there to this city?" Marie asked. It was the first thing she'd said to Lily that hadn't been based around gathering information for the job. Marie couldn't help it though; she'd taken a shine to Lily. The woman's simple but sturdy philosophy was endearing, plus it was nice to have someone to pass the time with.

"Believe it or not, I was runnin' an errand for that very witch. She needed some specific supplies they sell around here and she hates leaving her cottage, so I was chosen to be her helper this year. Isn't a bad job, really, she's nice as long I'm respectful, plus she provided me with some fancy duds. Says no servant of hers can be seen in a state of disrepair." Lily looked down at the ripped and dirty dress. "Imagine she'll be bothered by the state of it when I finally get back home. Not to mention the fact that I lost her supplies. Maybe I'd best hope they sell me off after all. Last thing I need is to run afoul of a witch."

Marie's head jerked up halfway through Lily's story, her eyes straining as she cocked her head to the side. By the time Lily was done speaking, a wide smile had crossed Marie's face. She rose from her perch, then offered a hand to help up her fellow captive.

"Sorry to break it to you, but I'm afraid you'll just have to go home safely and explain things to her. Now get behind me, things are about to get interesting."

* * *

Frank lowered the small silver object from his mouth, then stowed it in a pocket sown onto his robe. "If she heard it, then she knows to start a ruckus in two minutes."

"And if she didn't hear it, then you and I are about to charge an empty cave like a couple of fools," Jack pointed out.

The two of them were tucked behind the last of the large tree trunks before the path opened up into a wide, unobstructed walk to the cave's entrance. Gleaming in the light of the setting sun, only a few feet from them, was one of the silver spheres Marie had dropped. If Frank had doubted his tracking skills, that alone would have confirmed they were on the right track.

"It's definitely not empty." Frank was peering carefully from around the trunk, analyzing everything his gaze fell upon. "There's someone at the front of the cave, crouched down and not moving. A guard is my guess, probably with a bow from the way his arms are positioned." Frank's left eye, the one that could never be mistaken for human, glowed slightly as he stared across the wide space and peered into the cave's depths. Jack didn't particular understand how the dragon's eye allowed Frank to see the heat put off by people, nor did he care to. He just knew that it came in awfully handy in moments like these.

"Right, then, archer guarding the front. Assume there are more on the inside, but that one will be our first obstacle. Think you can hit him?"

Frank shook his head. He reached down and pulled one out of his small, slender, dangerously sharp daggers. "Too far away and they are mostly concealed. My chances of success are practically non-existent unless they're drawn out."

"Which means I'm up." Jack checked his boots, pants, and shirt to make sure everything was tied and tight, then took a good grip on the rapier strapped to his hip. The last thing he needed was it swaying about and knocking him off-balance at a critical moment. "If they're any good with that thing, I won't be able to get too close, so don't hesitate if you get the shot."

"Do I ever?"

It was a fair point, so instead of replying Jack merely took a deep breath and stretched his legs a few times. When all of his stalling tactics were officially exhausted, and he realized Marie would be starting up her own jailbreak soon, Jack sprang into action.

He leapt out from behind the tree and dashed forward immediately. As he ran, he kept his eyes trained on the mouth of the cave, scanning for any hint of movement that might offer a half-second's extra warning. With every step, he calculated, imagining being the person with the bow, seeing a stranger leap out and make a charge. First there would be surprise, but it would quickly fade. After that it was a matter of drawing the bowstring tight, taking aim, and—

Fwip! The sound of the arrow whistled past Jack's ear as he jerked to the left just in time. It was a quick reaction, faster than he'd expected. That meant he was dealing with someone skilled, and it would only get more difficult the closer he drew.

Jack's boots danced across the rough path as he surged forward, zigging and zagging at just the right moments to avoid being impaled. The second and third shots came quickly, but Jack was still able to move completely out of their way. The fourth arrow came only after he'd crossed the halfway point in his charge, and sliced a hole in his shirt as it narrowly missed his flesh.

The world seemed to grow silent as Jack continued forward. He could just make out the silhouette of the person firing at him, his bow pulled taut as he tried to get a bead on Jack. There was no more time for calculations or planning. From here on, it would be a battle of pure speed. Either Jack's reactions or the archer's attacks would prove to be the faster.

Shot number five came so close to Jack that he felt the wind ruffle his hair. Number six took him in the edge of his shoulder, spilling a trickle of blood that oozed down his arm. The seventh shot would have taken Jack in the center of his gut, but he twisted to the side at the last moment and let it sail past. Unfortunately, this move slowed him down, and meant that arrow number eight would almost certainly hit its mark.

As Jack wheeled about to try to regain his speed, he noticed that the archer was no longer perched in a perfect position, but was now slumped over. From the tip of his forehead, a single gleam of metal jutted out.

"Got him." Frank was standing several feet behind Jack, his other blades still clutched in his hands. "Nice job, decoy."

"One day," Jack grumbled as he checked the wound on his shoulder. "One day, someone else is going to be put on drawing fire duty. I can't be the only one who does this job."

"But you're so good at it," Frank replied, giving his a friend a smile that would have sent other men cowering in fear, but only told Jack that the quip was meant in good spirits. Despite his visage, Frank was easily the kindest of the three. "Besides, we all know you live for that sort of thing."

"True, but that doesn't mean I also want to die for it. Not unless the payout is worth it. Now let's hurry up. That took longer than I thought. I'd hate for Marie to gut the rest. We're already one down."

Frank nodded, and the two hurried toward the mouth of the cave. Jack's concern was a perfectly reasonable one. They'd given Marie the signal to go wild. If they didn't arrive to coordinate her aggression then it was quite possible that not a single kidnapper would remain when she was done.

* * *

"When you say interestin', do you perchance mean that you're contemplatin' a jailbreak?" Lily asked, whispering as she pulled herself up from the floor.

"That's exactly what I mean. But it's going to be…chaotic, so try to stay back. I don't want any of you to get hurt." Marie reached down in herself as she spoke, easily finding the presence that dwelled below the surface. At the merest brush, her inner beast roared with excitement, and Marie felt her skin tingle in a mix of anticipation and magical metamorphosis.

Lily looked her new friend up and down, then glanced at the cage door where Jailer was sharpening a wicked-looking set of daggers. "Suppose, just suppose, that the door was unlocked when you did whatever you were thinkin' of doin'. Would that be helpful?"

Marie turned her attention from the door to Lily, who met Marie's gaze with a coy grin. "I might not have been totally forthcomin' about my relationship to that witch. It's possible that she's taught me a trick or two along the way."

A grin that exposed her now sharp, large teeth spread across Marie's face. If Lily was an apprentice witch, that would make things go much more smoothly on their end. Not to mention it explained her unusually calm demeanor. Frank and Jack wouldn't like it; they generally avoided dealing with or going against witches, but they weren't the ones in the cage. Marie had a bit more of an open mind, at least where witches were concerned.

"That would help quite a bit. If you could also make sure the other girls don't get too near Jailer before I'm done, I'd be very grateful."

"Pretty sure I can manage that," Lily replied. She turned toward the door and began muttering a series of syllables beneath her breath. Marie could hear the words just fine, but they were utter gibberish to her, falling out of her head only moments after entering her ears. When the muttering finally stopped, Lily looked to Marie and gave a small nod.

It was still risky to trust a witch, apprentice or otherwise, since, if Lily was lying, Marie would be caught off guard. Of course, since her original plan had been to slam into the gate at full speed, nothing would be terribly changed if the door turned out to still be locked. It would just slow her down, but with someone as combat-savvy as Jailer seemed, that loss of speed, especially if unexpected, might prove dangerous. There was nothing to be done for it, though. Whether Lily was honest or not, Marie had to break through that door. Her friends would be arriving any minute, and she wasn't going to let them hog all the fun.

Her first steps were light and dainty, as Marie's frame was smaller than her personality implied. As she gained speed, she also gained size, not to mention fur, teeth, and claws. In the short span of time it took to race from the back of the cage to the metal door, Marie the woman vanished and Marie the lumbering monster took her place, its tremendous stomps echoing throughout the cavern and down the winding tunnel. Jailer looked up in time to leap to his feet and put his blades at the ready. That was all he managed before Marie lowered her head and charged through the door, which flung open and slammed to the side. It was a tight squeeze, even with her head down, and Marie warped the edges of the cage as she barreled through.

Jailer wasted no time, coming at Marie with a flurry of slices that very nearly took a chunk out of her leg. She wheeled back, getting her bearings after the charge. Jailer pushed forward, determined not to let her recover. Marie's assessment had been spot on; Jailer was indeed a skilled combatant. He practically danced through the air with his blade, spinning and slicing like a top gone mad. The man was undeniably fast.

Unfortunately for him, compared to Jack, Jailer might as well have been standing still. Marie's eyes easily tracked his movements, sliding her bulk to the side with more grace than a creature her size should possess, rapidly learning his attack pattern in the span of seconds. As Jailer pushed forward with another series of slices, Marie saw her opportunity and struck without hesitation.

A single punch into his ribs sent Jailer hurtling through the air and smashing into the cavern's wall. Only Marie could hear the sounds of his various bones snapping, but even so she didn't relent. Jailer had scarcely hit the ground before Marie was quite literally on top of him. She crushed his legs with a single mighty stomp, and was rearing back to deal the killing blow when she remembered that they were going to be paid more if the men were captured alive. Carefully lifting her foot off the shattered remains of what had once been Jailer's legs, Marie held up a claw and motioned to Lily.

"Stay here." Marie's voice was closer to a growl than words, but Lily nodded, so it seemed she had gotten the message. Until Marie knew all the kidnappers were handled, she didn't want the other women roaming about. She was about to head down the cavern when she noticed that Jailer's eyes were milky white and rolled back into his head. Leaning over, she listened carefully for the sound of his heartbeat, only to find that it had ceased. It was aggravating, but sometimes enough pain was able to kill someone outright.

With hurried steps, Marie made her way down the tunnel. Jack and Frank had almost certainly killed Sentry on the way in, which meant Snatcher was now their only hope for getting the bonus. She just had to get to them before they killed him, too.

* * *

Jack spotted the cloaked man sprinting down a large tunnel as he rounded a bend in the cave. He pursed his lips and let out a sharp whistle to get Frank's attention, then motioned to the tunnel. Despite the seeming inevitability of impending battle, Jack's hand merely held his rapier in place, rather than drawing it. He tried never to unsheathe his blade before all diplomatic options were exhausted, as a rule, because he found that once weapons were out the chances of talking through a problem all but evaporated. Of course, he also didn't like to run with his sword out, since there was the very real chance of falling and skewering himself. Even Jack's most idealistic attitudes were tainted by necessary practicality.

The footsteps of the sprinting man echoed through the tunnel as Jack and Frank gave chase. Their prey was fast, and clearly quite motivated, but his pursuers were tireless, one metaphorically and one literally. As they raced across the smooth stone floor, a new noise greeted their ears, one that caused Jack and Frank to push forward even faster. Through the tunnel screamed a mighty roar, one not associated with any natural beast in the land. For most, it would have been terrifying and unfamiliar, but they knew that sound as well as they knew the warmth of the sun on their backs.

Jack and Frank came around a corner to find Marie in all her hairy glory, the sprinting man clutched firmly, but carefully, in her mighty paws. With one glance at her eyes Jack knew she was still in control, and a wave of relief washed over him. He really hated to give up extra reward money.

"This seems well in hand," Jack announced. His voice was a bit winded, but still quite merry as he surveyed the scene. "Frank, what say you and I go tend to the maidens while Marie eats her fill."

"W...wait!" The man yelled, his voice not nearly so calm as Jack's. "You're going to let her kill me?"

"Don't see a reason not to. The ladies are right there in the cage behind Marie, so we don't need you to tell us where they are, and the reward pays out for your return dead or alive. No reason to bother the city with jailing you, especially when I'm sure our dear girl here has worked up an appetite. Besides, you can't very well try to swear vengeance on us if you're dead. Killing you seems like the most logical option, when all the facts are weighed." Jack began walking toward the cage again, his lazy smile out of the cloaked man's vision.

"Please! I can tell you things! Who hired us, where we sent the girls!" The man was panicking now as he stared at the wide, sharp teeth that filled Marie's mouth.

Jack's own grin stretched as he heard the cry for mercy. Had they tried to interrogate this man directly, he'd have seen his value and clammed up immediately. Making him think he was worthless, save as a snack, put the interrogation on an entirely different level, one where their prisoner was desperate to tell them what he knew in the hopes of saving his life. Sometimes

Jack marveled at how situations that were intrinsically the same could be seen so differently by people, merely based on the angle by which they looked at them.

"We were paid to take you lot out and recover all the girls you had. It's not in my contract to go save the ones you already sold off, and I don't do any work *pro bono*."

"Hold on Jack," Frank interrupted, perfectly on cue. "If we bring him back alive they might be willing to pay us to go save the rest of them. They were quick enough with the gold on the first job; with proof of our skill I'd wager we could fetch a higher price this time around."

Jack ceased his walking and turned, allowing both Frank and the man in Marie's grip to see the expression of furtive contemplation on his face. He was quite proud of this expression, and he practiced it in a mirror nearly every chance he got. It was meant to convey apathy mixed with the slightest undercurrent of interest. He felt it essential to be able to dangle hope without actually making someone feel certain of their survival.

"I suppose there might be some merit to that, assuming these other maidens you took can still, in fact, be rescued." Jack turned the rest of the way around and met the cloaked man's eyes. "Tell me, my good kidnapper, are these young women you snatched in the dead of night still alive?"

"I…I don't know for sure," he stuttered. "We were never told where they were going or what they were being used for. We were just given instructions by our employer and told to deliver, not ask questions."

It was an honest answer, Jack had no doubt of that. If the man were going to lie, he'd have surely done so in a way that offered him a better chance of survival. Plus, it told Jack something he'd already suspected: this went deeper than just three men and a cave.

"Then let's start with what you do know," Jack replied, all but slithering across the floor as he kept his gaze locked with the fearful man's eyes. "If you can tell us who, or what, your employer is, then that will at least give us an idea if the maidens can be saved. A witch or warlock will have used them for parts already, while a lonely monster might be keeping them locked away to look at before ultimately eating."

The man in the cloak swallowed hard. "She'll do terrible things to me if I tell you."

"Then don't tell us," Jack said, spinning around on his heel. "You were the one who wanted to trade information for your life in the first place. If you've decided the deal isn't worth it then Marie can have her snack and we can be on our way." It was a risky move, but he had to keep their prisoner off-kilter. The moment the man thought he had leverage, everything would change.

"Wait! Yes, I want to talk! Please. The woman who hired us, and the others like us, she wasn't a witch or a monster. She was the Blue Fairy."

It was a good thing that Jack was facing away from the captive, because not even he was able to hide the look of shock that shattered his composed facade. Behind him, he heard the man gasp for air as Marie involuntarily tightened her grip on his torso. Frank was likely the only one of them to keep a neutral expression, since he was used to maintaining a stoic, composed front.

Jack finally spoke after a few seconds of uncomfortably tense silence. "Frank, strip him and bind him. When that's done, get Marie her enchanted clothes so she can change back. I'll talk to the girls while we figure out the logistics."

As much as Jack loathed the idea of giving up extra gold, it paled in comparison to the idea of letting a lead like that slip away. The Blue Fairy was one of the most powerful fairies of light in existence, one of the five lieutenants beneath the true Fairy Godmother herself. The Bastard Champions had been hunting them all for a very long time, and now, at long last, they might finally be on the trail again.

Of course, they had to finish the job at hand first. There were contracts to fulfill, after all.

* * *

Marie herded the other girls through the forest path, making sure they all stayed together and out of danger. It wouldn't do to have someone getting hurt, or worse, with the town so close that they could practically smell the baker's shop. The going had been rough at first, especially when Shayana and Rohesia realized that they wouldn't be able to ride horses on the trek back. As they drew nearer, spirits began to rise, thankfully, and Marie had gone from trying to keep them moving to forcing them not to rush stupidly. Just because they could see the village didn't mean they were out of the forest yet.

"If you don't mind my askin', what exactly are you goin' to tell the mayor about what happened to us?" Lily had drawn close to Marie as they walked. She wasn't whispering, instead she was acting as though her conversation were utterly banal, which was a more useful trick to keep it from Rohesia's always-perked ears.

"The truth," Marie replied. "We were able to rescue you, but all of the kidnappers were killed in the process. Jack and Frank stayed behind in case any others returned and sent me to bring you back and collect our fee."

"Now I might be a simple girl from the farms, but that last gent didn't quite seem like he'd truly given up the ghost just yet."

"He's dead," Marie assured her. "From the moment he decided to deal with the Blue Fairy, he's been dead, even if he didn't know it at the time."

A particularly thick pile of brush forced them to stop talking and focus on getting through the rough. Marie was thankful to be back in her normal clothes, and not just because of the fact that they would shift with her. Dresses had their place, but it wasn't out in the woods, taking on all manner of creature that came at her.

"Is this Blue Fairy really that bad?" Lily asked once they were through. Back on the proper road trodden by horses and carts, the village sprawled out before them, open and inviting, making promises of safety that every woman now knew it could not deliver.

"She's not the sort you want to trifle with."

"And what is it you plan on doin'?"

"Trifling." Marie smiled at the apprentice witch, regarding her warmly. It was nice to find another like herself, a woman whose peaceful appearance belied the current of danger running underneath. "But that's sort of my job. Besides, we're after some big things, the sort that only the strongest of fairies are capable of, and we'll do whatever it takes to see that hunt through. Even if it means running after someone most wise folks spent their lives avoiding."

"Then I wish you luck." Lily surprised Marie by grasping her savior and pulling her into a tight hug. "I owe you for your help gettin' us out, and I don't forget my debts easily. If you ever need a hand, you can call on me to lend it."

"I'll keep that in mind." Marie squeezed her once back, then the hug ended and the trek back into town resumed. She didn't say it, didn't even want to think it, but with the path Lily was on there was a good chance that the next time they met, it would be as enemies. Not all witches were evil, or at least they weren't ambitious with their wickedness, but more often than not all that power corrupted them from the inside out. Still, Marie allowed herself to hope that Lily would be one of the exceptions.

After the last few days, Marie could use a pleasant thought to hold onto.

The Tale of Rats and Blood

The Bastard Champions had encountered many scowls in their days, to the point where they considered themselves to be connoisseurs of the expression. As they sat in the stiff chairs, too aware of all the eyes in the room on them, they noted that the Sheriff sitting across from them, on the other side of the massive desk, had an exceptional scowl etched into his weathered face. Not the best any of them had encountered, but certainly an effort that spoke to a dedication to the craft and a man who had clearly spent time in a mirror honing his art. That bold scowl shifted its attention among them for some while, until an aide stepped through the door and handed the Sheriff a stack of pages. He perused them for several moments before setting them down on that over-sized desk.

"Mad Jack. Laughing Jack. Grinning Jack. Deathless Jack. Jack the Nimble. Jack the Quick. Jack the Perpetrator who did...*what* with a candle stick?"

"In my defense, I did warn the gentleman to jump or it would hurt more." Despite the tension in the room, or perhaps because of it, Jack's smile was as wide and bright as usual, if not more so. This hadn't exactly been the plan going in, but they'd still ended up right where they wanted to be. Sometimes, when they were in private, the group referred to this as a "Jack Special".

The Sheriff and his mighty scowl were not impressed by the flippancy, letting out a brief grunt before turning back to his pages. "Looks like you've blazed quite a trail across the lands. That's a lot of aliases for one man, and something tells me I've barely even scratched the surface."

"I'm the sort who leaves an impression," Jack said.

"Which makes it all the more interesting that neither of your companions are turning up similar rumors. Tell me, why do I have a stack of pages with names for you, yet nothing mentioning either of these two?" He motioned to Frank and Marie, who were sitting silently. These were the moments where they leaned on Jack, since he had a knack for getting people to talk. This strategy also came with the risk of having to fight their way out of the room if he pushed things too far, but Jack's odds tended to be around fifty-fifty, so it was better than nothing.

"They're the quiet sort, can't you tell?" Jack's smile deepened. It was one of the many tools he used to keep attention focused on him, allowing the others to work more easily.

Another grunt, followed by the shuffling of papers. "Here's what I know: we caught you three trying to ride into Deverton with a prisoner bound and gagged over the back of a saddle. He's not talking yet, so I have to get your story first, but this could end with you facing some serious charges."

"That man is a kidnapper and a criminal; if you allow one of us to go speak to him I assure you a full confession will be made. You can even use a truth potion on him beforehand if you fear corruption," Jack offered. "But he is also not our real concern. He met with a person here some months back, a middleman for the target we're actually after. We're passing through Deverton only long enough to go to their meeting place, ask around for who saw our stranger leave, and follow his trail. If we're allowed to go to work this very moment, we can be out of your town by sunset."

The Sherriff was only paying half attention to Jack as he looked through more of the pages, eyes darting to Frank and Marie as he no doubt tried to pin down who they were. It was a largely futile endeavor, as Frank had little history in this land and Marie's true identity would never be suspected of keeping this sort of company. As it turned out, however, he did find *something* in his perusing of wanted posters and rumors. "Well lookey here. You three, you wouldn't happen to be the outlaws known as the Bastard Champions, would you?"

Murmurs ran through the other men in the room, the guards here to watch over these three strange prisoners. Jack paid them no mind. It wasn't as though their company name was a secret; if anything he was happy to hear it being spread about. More notoriety led to more jobs, and being able to charge a higher fee for them.

"Outlaw is a strong word. I think you'll find we've never been proven to have broken a single kingdom's law. That's why all those pages you're holding that mention me don't actually call for my arrest. And yes, we are indeed the Bastard Champions, a group of problem solvers who will tackle nearly any task, assuming one has the gold to afford us."

They expected more muttering, maybe a few laughs, but the shift of mood in the room took even Jack by surprise. Suddenly, faces grew hard and somber. Even the Sheriff's mighty scowl seemed uncertain as he leaned forward.

"*Any* task?"

"Within the confines of a kingdom's laws, of course." Jack's smile said he knew this was tripe just as much as every guard in the room. To Jack's thinking, laws were just rules passed by the powerful, and he'd never been much of a fan of rules.

"You any good at tracking?" The Sheriff's scowl was beginning to fade as something new took its place, interest tinged with…hope? "Tracking things not meant to be tracked, maybe?"

"We have some excellent tracking skills available to us, but our world is a long, sprawling place with many people and magics. Perhaps you could be a touch more specific, and we can tell you whether or not we'd have the skills to do what you ask." It was as polite a way as possible to tell the Sheriff to dole out the details or let the matter drop.

Slowly, the Sheriff laid the pages down on his desk and stared at the trio. He was evaluating them, looking in their eyes to see if he trusted them. It was a much briefer affair than normal, mostly because not long after meeting eyes with Frank he turned away. That was to be expected; Frank's eyes were disconcerting, and not just the dragon's pupil in his left socket. The crystal blue right eye was almost just as bad, simply because it was so beautiful that it clearly had no place on his patchwork face. Whatever the Sheriff saw in them, evidently it was enough to keep the spark of hope alive, because with a heavy sigh he began to explain.

"The rats came a month ago. Big, mean bastards that chewed their way into cellars and ate everything they could find. We tried poison, traps, even sent a rider into the nearest kingdom to pick up some magic potions, but none of it worked. Then the piper showed up. Promised that for a handful of gold he'd clear out the entire town. We agreed, with the caveat that we only paid for results. Sure enough, he put that flute to his lips and within an hour we were free and clear. It felt like the Narrative had sent us a miracle. Then he came back."

The Sheriff paused for a moment, his face turning red as poorly hidden anger welled up. "He had some muscle with him this time, and he demanded far more than what we'd agreed to pay. Said that was just to play the flute, marching the rats away costs extra for every step. We told him to piss off, obviously, and that he'd get nothing from us. That night, some people heard the flute again. It wasn't until morning that we realized what had happened. All of the town's children were… He took them away, somehow. Stole them in the night. Now he wants even more gold or he says he won't give them back."

Up until the end of the story, Jack was feeling quite good about their situation. Tracking down a con man who had no more protection than a few goons and a rat-flute would be relatively easy. It was in the final words of the tale that they hit a snag, however. Children had been brought into the equation, and while Frank didn't stiffen up, tap Jack on the knee, or give any other outward sign, Jack knew his friend was staring at him with those mismatched eyes. Now that Frank knew children were in trouble, they *would* take this job. Frank was easily the least-demanding member of their team, but this was a point he was famously inflexible on. The trick was to negotiate a proper price out of the Sheriff before he knew they'd have to do it for free if needed just to keep Frank happy.

"Interesting," Jack said. "I heard a rumor once about something similar down in Hamelin, although it was long done by the time it reached my ears. I assume you've already sent people out looking for the children?"

"The best trackers we have," the Sheriff confirmed. "They came up empty. All the trails were obscured. A horde of rats had trampled over most of the forest, wiping out any hints as to where the piper and the children went."

"And how long until he wants his money?"

"Less than a week left. We've been trying to scrape together what we can, but we're a small hamlet. There's only so much gold to be found."

It was a tight time frame, but if the piper was relying on rats to obscure his trail that meant he probably didn't have any better, more magical, options. Hunting him down should be doable, even if it did mean their delay. Still, getting out of here without bloodshed would be nice, and if they could add some gold to their pockets in the process all the better.

"I believe my associates and I can be of some help, so it looks like we can come to an arrangement," Jack said after careful consideration. "We'll even be willing to do it for the shockingly low price of a mere hundred gold, along with the return of our prisoner and any help you might be able to lend in tracking our target."

The Sheriff blanched visibly, and whispers flew around the room. "A hundred gold? That's two-thirds of what he wants to just hand the children back."

Jack was a bit shocked to hear that the piper was offering such a low-ball price. A hundred and fifty gold for an entire town of children was far less than he'd expected. Perhaps the piper took a town's fiscal capacity into account when making such demands. "Two-thirds the price, and it comes with the added benefit of getting the head of the man who stole your children delivered to you, on a platter or a pike, your choice. Sounds to me like quite a bargain."

From the side of the room came a brief scoff. A guard with red hair and what seemed to be a permanent sneer, far less refined than the Sheriff's expert scowl, was glaring at Jack. "They're just more liars and thieves, Sheriff. We can't trust them. We'll not get ourselves out of this by casting our lot with rogues and monsters." The guard tilted his head toward Frank, who instinctively pulled his hood and cloak further over his scarred flesh.

A low, deep rumble filled the room for an instant. Most would have called it similar to a dog's growl, but only because they hadn't been deep enough into the woods to learn what the real beasts sounded like. It ended quickly, as Jack stood from his chair and looked the guard straight away in the eye.

"Scoundrel, actually."

"What?" The glare had been replaced by confusion, not the first man to have such a reaction when talking with Jack.

"I prefer the term 'scoundrel'. 'Rogue' has a connotation associating it with illegal acts, whereas scoundrels are more looked upon as generally unsavory rather than outright lawbreakers. We still do ignore the rules, you understand, just not with the same professional dedication as a rogue would. Now you, good sir, tell me about yourself. Are you perhaps the son of the local mayor, or this fine sheriff's second in command?"

"N-no. I'm a guard." Everyone in the room was beginning to look uncertain, save for Marie and Frank, who knew exactly where this was heading.

"Ah. So no strong political or financial connections then? You're not a man with influence, just an honest fellow doing a hard job for well-earned pay?" Jack's smile had taken on something of a gleam, a warning sign that too few knew to heed.

The guard puffed his chest out a bit, finding his nerve and staring Jack down. "That's right. I'm no one fancy; I earned this position through my own hard work."

"Fantastic." In a blur of motion Jack pulled a dagger from the guard's belt and sliced it across his throat, stepping out of the way as the guard began to clutch his bleeding neck and panic. Instantly the other guards drew their swords and knives, pointing them at the nearest member of the trio.

"Calm down," Jack ordered. "I sliced the skin of his neck, but went no deeper. While it will be tender, he'll be fine, assuming this town has a half-decent apothecary or alchemist. Understand this, though: that was the only warning you people get. My friends and I don't *need* to help you. We could walk out of this room and ride away without so much as a glance back. You need *us*, not the other way around, and for so long as that's true I expect you to treat my friends with the respect they deserve. The next person who whispers the word 'monster' around any of us will find out why none of the kingdoms that spread word about us actually put out warrants. Because none of them wanted us back in their lands."

He dropped the dagger, which plunged into the floor and quivered in place for several seconds. That done, Jack took his seat once more, meeting the Sheriff's now-furious eyes. "We are considered to be too dangerous to have around, if you can believe that. Now please tell your men to sheathe their weapons. I'd hate for this lovely town to suddenly be absent its law-enforcement personnel."

There was a long moment where none of the three knew if they were about to have to fight their way out or not. Not that they would have blamed Jack if it came to that. They'd all heard that word too many times, and none was inclined to tolerate it any more, even less so when it was directed at one of their friends. Finally, the Sheriff motioned to the guards to put their tools away.

"Much as I want to lock you up for that, you've just proven yourself to be a scary man. Scary, and hopefully useful. Sixty gold, the return of your prisoner, help finding out which direction the man you're after went, and the ability to walk freely out of here despite assaulting one of my staff. That's the best offer you're getting, so I suggest you take it before we clap you in irons."

In any other situation, Jack would have kept haggling. The advantage of force the guards thought they had wasn't really there, and it would be easy to demonstrate that. But they were going to have to take the job anyway, which meant walking away was off the table. The longer he haggled, the greater the chance of the Sheriff figuring that out, and once he did all of Jack's leverage was gone.

"I suppose that will do. Rescuing children is something of a public good, anyway. Very well, Sheriff, I accept your offer on behalf of my company. Now tell me everything you know about this piper."

The Sheriff began to recount the tale in more detail as several guards stooped down to help the bleeding one up from the floor. True to his word, Jack had slit no more than the skin, though one wouldn't have guessed it from the quantity of blood dripping down the guard's tunic. The others ushered him out the door, where he paused only long enough to throw a hateful glance in Jack's direction. To his surprise, Jack had twisted around in his seat and was waiting for the glare, meeting it with that constant grin.

The guard's anger faltered as fear reasserted itself, and he quickly excused himself from the room. Rage was well and good, but Jack was a man who could smile after nearly slitting a man's throat. No one wanted to see what sort of cheery smirk would be there if he cut deeper next time.

* * *

In assessing a hostage situation, the first step was to determine if the hostages were more likely to still be alive, or already been killed. This was vital, as keeping them alive required resources like food, water, and sufficient isolation to keep anyone from finding them or hearing their cries for help. All of these were elements that could be tracked or accounted for, and narrowed down the number of potential hiding places with easy access to the town. If the hostages were assumed to be dead, on the other hand, all that was needed was a large enough hole in the ground.

By Frank's estimations, the children were more likely still alive than dead. Kidnapping was one thing, bad as it was, but wholesale slaughter of an entire town's children was unnecessarily risky. That was high-league evil, the sort that would draw down brave knights or turn a farmer who'd lost his child into a hell-bent avenger. The Narrative existed for moments like those, using them as a catalyst to create new adventures, and if the piper had lasted long enough to pull this scam more than once then he was probably smart enough to avoid calling down that kind of attention.

Sitting in their room at the local inn, Frank pored over a map of the surrounding area. The Sheriff had, to his credit, provided them all the tools they requested for the job in short order. He didn't like them, or trust them, and that was fair. Between getting scammed by the piper and Jack almost opening up a peon's jugular, Frank imagined in that man's position he'd be wary of trusting strangers, too. Yet he'd still handed them all that they asked for without hesitation. He was desperate, and given the stakes, that was the correct emotion to feel. If the town lost their children, they'd be out for blood, and if the piper couldn't be found they'd blame the Sheriff for failing to bring him to justice. Desperation could be useful down the line, although Frank would leave pressing that advantage to Jack. For his part, Frank never really enjoyed dealing with people much.

The door to the trio's room opened briefly as Marie ambled in, pulling off her cloak and tossing it onto a chair. "I sniffed up and down the forest, and all I could smell was rat. No wonder they couldn't figure out where that piper went. He didn't just cover his tracks; he covered every set around this whole town."

"Clearly he's done this many times before and perfected his tactics." Frank's pale finger ran down the map as he evaluated each potential hiding place.

Some had water, some had isolation from the roads, and some were in fertile enough grounds to hunt, but few had all three factors. What was worse, the town guards had already checked out the spots that hit all three criteria and come up empty-handed. They were missing something, some element to the scheme, and Frank hadn't hit upon it. Yet. "Jack still down in the bar working the locals?"

"Chatting the ears off some miller's daughters when I passed through. I hope he remembers to pump them for information after pumping them for pleasure."

"Jack has his vices, but none of them are more pronounced than greed. The job has gold attached to it, so he'll make it his first priority." Although Frank didn't say it, he also trusted that Jack would work hard on this because he knew it mattered to Frank. The man was a self-admitted scoundrel and made no bones about it, but he came through when it mattered. When it mattered to Frank or Marie, anyway.

Marie gave a terse nod. "I know he will, I just wish he'd put a little more urgency into things. Since you're still looking over that map I've got a hunch you didn't find anything either, which makes Jack turning up a lead our best hope. As for me, I'm going to go find a garden and pick some pleasant-smelling herbs. That damned rat smell is coating the entire forest, and it got stuck in my nose. I feel like I can practically taste the cursed things."

With those words came the flash of insight Frank had been hoping for. His eyes widened as he stared at the map, looking at it with fresh eyes. "The rats. We forgot about the rats."

"No, we very much didn't. I *just* complained to you about them," Marie reminded him.

"Not like that." Frank stood up, bringing the map over to Marie and setting it down on the nearby table. "What are the three components to holding a prisoner in secret?"

"Food, water, and isolated shelter." The words came instantly; Marie had worked nearly as many of these jobs as Frank had. "That's what you're looking for."

Pale fingers traced the map's roads and features, searching for something new. "Exactly. And that's what the town guards were looking for as well, yet they came up empty. Because we forgot that the piper has demonstrated the skill and capacity to use his rats in more than one way. First, he obviously sent them into the town, setting up the need for his aid. Then he used them to cover his tracks when he stole the children. So why not use them once more, in another capacity? They may not be tasty or particularly nutritious, but you could still live on cooked rat for quite a long time if you had to."

"The bastard is using the rats as food, so he doesn't have to worry about hunting or buying supplies." Marie snapped to the idea quickly; she was often quick on the uptake. "So all he really needs is isolated shelter and water to keep the kids alive."

"Exactly. And once we rule out the places that the guards already searched, that leaves us with a few high-potential targets." Frank pointed to four spots on the map in rapid succession, tracing a path among them. "If we leave at first light, we should be able to scout all of them before the day is done. Narrative-willing, we may be in time to save those children well before the deadline."

Marie clapped him gently on the back. "That's some quick thinking. Now the only question is whether or not Jack will be in any condition to wake up by first light."

Frank smiled slightly. It had nothing on Jack's unfailing, disconcerting grin, but it was a touch unsettling all the same. Although, given the crisscrossing of scars on his face, there were few expressions Frank could make that didn't disturb people.

"That sounds like a problem for Jack more than us. Remind me to get a bucket and water ready tonight in case he tries to sleep in tomorrow."

* * *

The first location was empty save for a few rabbits, and all they found at the second potential holding site was a grumpy bear who cursed them out for waking him up. As they approached the third site, however, Marie held up a hand to slow their pace. Tentatively, she stepped forward, craning her neck and sniffing deeply from the air.

"Rats. Lots of rats have been through here." A few more steps and sniffs forward then Marie paused again. "I'm also getting people. Men, not children. And the unmistakable scent of treated leather, like you'd use for armor."

"Interesting." Jack followed Marie's steps, moving more quickly and quietly than she had, making his way past her until he reached the apex of the small hill they were climbing. Peeking his head over, Jack briefly scanned the area before making his way back down. "Looks like an ambush. I guess they figured out someone would be able to track them this far."

From deep within Frank's throat came a heavy noise, something between a groan and a growl. "But no children?"

"None that I could see," Jack replied.

"Still not smelling them either," Marie confirmed.

Their opponents were smart, which was troublesome, and experienced, which was an outright pain. They'd played this game before, so they knew most of the moves that could be made. Clearly Frank wasn't the first to figure out the idea of using rats for food. So they'd laid a trap to catch whoever came calling, likely as a tactic to gain more hostages or rob the people of hope. At this point, Frank had to assume they had other contingencies in place as well; he'd be a fool to think otherwise after seeing how well they ran this scheme. Outthinking his opponents would take time, a resource that dwindled more with every passing hour. There was another way, however, even if it wasn't Frank's favorite. He and the others could do what no knight or guard stumbling across these people would have; he could use ruthlessness to handle things more expediently.

"If the piper is down there, take him alive," Frank commanded. "In fact, take as many alive as possible. Just in case our piper isn't with them, I may need to use duress to discover his location."

"We could try to bluff them, see if they're dumb enough to give us what we want without knowing they've betrayed their leader." Jack sounded confident in the plan, and for good reason. It was one of his favorite, and more successful, tactics.

Frank still shook his head, even as he was bending down and taking the carefully fastened sack off from around his back. Inside was a black leather bag not quite like anything else in all the kingdoms. "Too dangerous. One of them might sense danger and get away, giving them time to move, or get rid of, the hostages. We hit them hard, get them all, and then go from there. I'm not in the mood to play nice." From the bag Frank removed a pair of small shining blades of a shape unfamiliar to nearly all people in the land, as well as a few more sharp implements. Once those were stowed on his body, he tucked the bag away under a nearby tree until he could retrieve it. There were delicate pieces in there, the sort that would be a pain to replace if they were damaged in battle.

By the time he was done Marie's eyes were yellow and her teeth had turned sharper. She wouldn't fully shift until they were in position; that beastly form of hers had little capacity for stealth, but already the anticipation of battle had awoken the creature's bloodlust. Jack, on the other hand, was still unarmed; the rapier at his hip remained in its scabbard.

"Is there an issue we need to discuss?" Frank asked.

"No, I'm in. Just waiting until we get a little closer. You know me; I like to be in the moment when I start things off."

"Good. How many are there?"

Jack craned his neck back toward the hill, mentally recounting the men he'd seen hidden amidst the trees. "I spotted five, so let's assume around ten since some were probably out of my line of vision."

"For the stink, that sounds about right," Marie said.

Ten men, armed mercenaries most likely, specifically waiting for a group just like theirs. Ten waiting, trained killers against the three of them. The poor bastards, it was so lopsided Frank almost felt a twinge of guilt. Then he remembered the kind of man these flunkies were protecting and his glimmer of empathy was snuffed out. They'd made their choices that brought them here, and now they would face the consequences.

"Remember," Frank reminded them. "Leave a few alive. The first one probably won't talk, but the ones I make watch will."

Jack carefully put his hand on his rapier's hilt, though he didn't yet pull it from the scabbard. "I guess today we find out which of these goons are lucky, and which ones get captured alive."

* * *

Weser stirred from his sleep slowly, climbing out from the land of dreams with considerable effort. It was a welcome surprise; usually he slept horribly in the wild, preferring the comfort of his soft mattress and fine sheets. But luxury did not pay for itself, so such sacrifices were necessary from time to time. Not much longer now and the town would pay, they always found a way to pay, and Weser would have enough gold to live off for at least a year, perhaps two if he was less free with women and drink. So a year then, at the most.

Trying to rise from his bed, Weser found that his arms and legs were heavier than normal. Putting some effort into it, he managed to lift his left leg several inches before it was halted. Peeling his eyes open, Weser glanced down to see shackles binding his legs and arms to the bed where he'd fallen asleep. That was disconcerting enough, but far worse was when he caught a flicker of movement from the corner of his eye. No one was allowed in here except during emergencies, and even if one arose all of his men would know better than to linger about. And they certainly wouldn't have shackled him to his bed.

"Hello? Who's there?" With more time to think or a clearer head, Weser might have come up something a bit more probing, but he was working with what he had in the moment.

"Ah. You're awake." At the sound of the voice, Weser felt his stomach drop toward his feet. It was impossible to say precisely why; there was no threatening tone in the words. Some part of him simply recognized it as off. Wrong. A thing that should not be. And that thing had him clapped in irons.

"I warn you, stranger, I am not a man to trifle with. My wealth affords me a private force that will hunt you to the shores of the Endless Sea if you harm so much as a nail on my finger."

"No, you *had* a private force. They, or at least the ones you had set to ambush anyone who came looking for the children, are no longer in your employ. Some have ceased to breathe, and others decided there were things they valued more than loyalty to you. They were kind enough to point us in your direction, eventually."

It was the calm that bothered Weser the most. This voice was bordering on placid, its wielder was so calm. There should be tension in his tone, especially if he just murdered a mercenary squadron and captured their leader. If he was truly calm in a moment like this, it meant he had encountered untold numbers like it before, and that was very bad news for Weser. He did still have one card left to play, however, and it was a big one.

"So you killed off my men? Impressive, certainly, but I trust you can figure out what will happen to a town's worth of children without someone getting them food regularly. Starvation is an ugly death, I've seen it firsthand, and it would be a shame to sentence so many innocents to such a fate. Free me now, and we can talk terms. I'm not an unreasonable man; I can still be moved to release them for a fair price."

"Bold. Very bold. Trying to swing your leverage about as if you're the one in charge. It's an understandable move, but a wasted one. You will tell me what I want to know. The only question is whether you'll do so in time or not."

At last the speaking figure stepped into view. He was holding a bottle with a tube of some strange clear material poking out the bottom. Lifting it up, Weser's captor hung the thing carefully from a hook fixed in the ceiling, one that hadn't been there earlier in the day. As he did, Weser caught sight of the man's hands from under his expansive robe. They were terrible things, pale and scarred, yet to watch them move was impressive. The fingers possessed an inhuman grace that was fascinating while being repulsive in an oddly contradictory manner. Delicately, the hands ran down the clear tubing until they reached the end, where a small needle had been attached. In a motion so quick Weser barely caught it, the needle was plunged into the skin on his arm, and liquid from the bottle began to flow into him.

"What is that? What are you doing to me?"

"Don't worry, this will help keep you alive," the man told him. Despite the assurance, Weser found the concept very worrying all the same. He'd have protested, but the man kept going. "You were still asleep when we first drugged you, and I needed time to make preparations. Now, at last, we are ready to continue. Tell me, pied piper, where are the children? I know you won't listen, but I urge you to heed my advice: take this chance. You will tell me eventually, and you will curse yourself for not doing so at this opportunity."

Weser was, for a moment, actually tempted to tell this man all he wanted. The detached way he went about this process was unnerving, as if he really didn't care what it took to make Weser talk. But it was obviously a bluff, a bit of theatre meant to scare him. Knights and princes were the sort who came after missing children, and none of them would ever stoop to something as base as torture. When the bluff failed, the bargaining would begin, and Weser had no intention of trading his leverage for a dungeon cell.

"Children? I can't seem to recall at the moment. You know how the forest is, and I have no sense of direction."

"So be it." The robed man stepped out of view again, and when he returned he was carrying a small table. Lying on his back, Weser couldn't see much. The only bit that was easy to spot was an hourglass. That, and a few brief shimmers of metal reflecting light from an unseen source. His captor carried the table down to the end of the bed, perfectly in Weser's view, and set it down. "This hourglass counts down thirty minutes. After every answer, I flip it over and we begin anew. My prediction is that you'll tell us what we want to know by the third turn, but perhaps you'll be smarter than that."

From the table, the man lifted a piece of smudged coal in one hand, then began to roll up Weser's right pant leg with the other. "Do you know why you're going to tell me where the children are? Because I understand the value of patience. The gain in going slow. Jack and Marie are both impulsive; they'd rip an arm from your socket or stab you in the lungs to start things off. But I understand that taking away something essential at the outset will make you feel despondent, as though you have nothing left to lose. You'd be wrong, but by the time you realized that it might be too late. So I'm not beginning with something truly necessary to your way of life as a piper. I'm staying away from your hands, and eyes, and the lower instrument every bard is fond of having others play, at the outset. I want you to understand the stakes first. I want you to feel the slow, crushing terror of realization as you grasp what's happening. Because once you do, you'll talk. You may prefer death to jailing, but I promise you don't have the fortitude to face the fate I'm offering."

Moving with that same grace, the hand smeared coal marks down the front of Weser's right ankle, just above the foot. When that was done, he set the coal aside and wrapped a heavy cloth around Weser's shin, a bit above the line he'd drawn. The cloth was drawn tight, painfully so, and pulled into a knot. It felt like his foot was already starting to fall asleep, and with every step in this process Weser's certainty that this was all a show waned more and more.

"What…what are you doing?"

"Cutting off the circulation so you don't bleed to death. I've got a pan heating over your fireplace to cauterize the wound, but this will make sure I have enough time to work in. Too much blood loss and you'd pass out, which wouldn't serve either of our purposes well."

There was no more denying it now, this man meant to either cut off Weser's foot or convince him that was the plan. Eyes wide, Weser began to struggle, pulling against the shackles with what little strength he could muster. Dammit, why did his body still feel so heavy? Was this lunatic using potions, and what was that the liquid running from the bottle to Weser's veins?

"You can't do this!"

"I can. I have before. I'm going to again." Still calm. Still deadly calm.

"You can't, though! That's not the way this works. The Narrative leads champions to fight people like me. You…you're a monster!"

For the first time, those scarred hands fluttered as the hood craned upward. Weser's captor stepped out of view briefly, making his way around the bed. When he appeared again, it was directly over Weser's face, giving him a glimpse into that hood that he dearly wished he hadn't gotten. The face was scarred up and down, but horrifying as it was it had nothing on those eyes. That burning, clearly non-human eye in the left socket was bad, yet it was the blue one in the right that bothered him more. There was sadness in that eye, deep and unspeakable. The sort of sadness one who has seen, and done, horrendous things might carry with them.

"You're right. About almost all of that. From what I've heard, the Narrative didn't used to work this way. The Endless Sea used to, presumably, be truly endless. But times change, and perhaps the Narrative is changing with them. I have my theories, though none I've been able to prove yet. And you're right, piper, I am a monster. Not for the reasons you think, but it doesn't change the fact that it's true. The problem is, you're a monster too. You steal children in the night and threaten to kill them if not paid. I think as far as the Narrative is concerned, you and I pitted against one another is a wash. Two monsters fight each other in the woods, no knights need intervene. Which brings us to the one thing you were wrong about: I *can* do this. And I will. If I had to kill the whole town to get the information, I would, and without a moment's hesitation."

The face leaned forward, until it was so close Weser could feel the breath on his face. He shut his eyes, trying to purge the face from his mind.

"I will never fail another child. My sins are already too heavy to bear."

A small drop of something fell from onto Weser's forehead, the unexpected drip causing him to open his eyes and look upward. There, on the patchwork face before him, was a small line of what appeared to be tears, running from the blue eye down the scarred cheek.

"Are you…crying?"

"Part of me is. Perhaps the only decent part I have. She mourns for you, piper. She mourns for what I am about to do to you. Sometimes, that would give me pause, make me reconsider my actions. Today, however, I know I must see things through."

Pulling himself upright and out of view, the stranger walked back down the length of the bed, to where the table and Weser's exposed foot were waiting. He pulled a gleaming handsaw from the table, inspecting it carefully before turning back to face Weser.

"I'll flip the timer when this one is finished. Once I start, you're going to be tempted to tell me whatever I want to make it end. Feel free to lie, if you like, but know one thing: this all ends when my friends return and tell me they've found the children, not when you speak up. So if you give us a false location, the only person you'll be hurting is yourself. I imagine the loss of time sending them on a wild chase will take up quite a few turns of the hourglass."

A prepared lie died on Weser's tongue at the words. This didn't end until after the children were found…but he'd stashed them some ways out. How fast were these friends? How long would it take them to check out his story? Maybe there was still a bargain to be made. He opened his mouth to speak, but the stranger in the hood pressed the edge of the saw down, right along the coal marks that had been drawn on Weser's ankle.

"One last thing. I have no interest in hearing you beg or bargain, so whenever you're speaking to say something that isn't telling me where the children are, I'm going to work faster. So choose your words very carefully, because I'm quite adept at this kind of task. It's a family tradition."

* * *

Dusk was lingering at the edge of the horizon, but the smiles of the townsfolk were shining so brightly the sun may as well have been right overhead. All through town square parents were scooping up their children in big, powerful hugs that tried to convey the sense of terror and loss they'd felt at being separated from one another. Deep down, in a part of his heart rarely touched, Jack felt the slightest flutter of homesickness. It had been a long time since he checked in, and next time he was in the area he would see how things were going.

Absent from the touching display was Frank, who'd holed up in a dark room almost as soon as they'd finished bringing the children back. Days like this took a toll on him, even if he liked to pretend otherwise. Despite the appearance, it was generally agreed upon by Jack and Marie that Frank had the kindest heart of all three of them. Curiously, that didn't mean there were lines he was less likely to cross; rather it meant that Frank could do truly horrible things when the occasion demanded it. Frank was the sort who would put another stain on his soul before he'd let an innocent suffer.

Out of the corner of his eye, Jack spotted the Sheriff ambling over. Marie was across the square, and Frank was missing, so perhaps he wanted to try to get the jump on Jack when there were fewer people to fight. Or he simply wanted to chat. Jack dismissed neither possibility as he watched the large man lumber his way across the poorly paved stones of their square. When he arrived at Jack's side he halted and didn't go for his sword, which seemed like a good sign to start things off.

"All of the children are here and accounted for." The Sheriff was beaming, waving to people who were shouting their thanks to him. Jack wasn't sure the tale this fellow had spun, nor did he care, but it was apparent the Sheriff had painted himself into a heroic role.

"My people and I may be many things, but we aren't the sort who take on jobs we can't handle," Jack replied.

"Yet I can't help noticing that the son of a bitch who actually did all this is nowhere to be seen. Happy as these folks are right now, sooner or later they're going to remember that someone actually stole their children in the first place, and at that point I'd better have a body to hang. Any insight as to what I should tell them?"

"The truth." Jack often found that to be the best answer to any question, although there were certainly ways to frame or structure the truth that made it more advantageous to the speaker. "Tell them that the piper is not a sight appropriate to put in front of children, so we left him where he was. I assure you, unless he's got incredible arm strength or some magic potions tucked away, he won't have gotten far. I'll be happy to give you his location once my people and I have our prisoner back and our investigation is complete. Can't have you not needing us just yet, it wouldn't be prudent."

A long sigh slipped out from the Sherriff's beaming face. "About that prisoner of yours…seems someone slit his throat this morning. And they didn't stop at the skin. Came in to find him dead as can be. I'll look into who did it, but as you might imagine there are a lot of suspects. I'm happy to keep my word and turn him over to you, if you want to haul a corpse down the road."

Reaching into a pouch on his side, the Sheriff pulled out a modest bag and offered it to Jack, who accepted. With one brief shake Jack knew that the sack was full of gold coins, and while he didn't get the exact number from one jingle he knew it was at least close to what they'd agreed.

"I felt a bit bad about what happened to your prisoner, and I don't think I want bad blood between us, so I spent the day talking to folks, seeing if one of them remembered the man meeting with anyone. One of the barkeeps did, said your gent met with some figure in a black cloak with red trim a few weeks back. No description, but the mystery person went north. I've got a stable master who saw that rider leaving town. Wish I had more to give, but it seems that's all we've got."

Jack appreciated the gesture. Not as much as he appreciated the gold, but still. Inclined as part of him was to start slicing his way through the guards of this town for daring to touch someone under his protection, ultimately the act would cost more than it gained. Best to put this place behind them, give Frank some distance. He'd be better when they were on the road again. It always took a day or two's ride to shake these situations from his mind.

"Thank you for your efforts," Jack said. "And for prompt payment. We'll leave behind a map with the piper's location at the inn just before we ride off. One word of advice though, if I may. Send only men with strong stomachs. What awaits them is not for the faint of heart."

The Sheriff's head dipped into a nod as he stared at Jack, worry clouding his eyes even as he kept smiling for the townsfolk. "I'm grateful for what you three did. Truly I am. All the same, I think I'd prefer if you were out of here as soon as possible, and you didn't come back anytime soon. You three don't quite fit right in these lands."

Tucking the sack of gold carefully away in his larger bag, Jack let out a brief chuckle before turning toward the inn. "Trust me, Sheriff, we are keenly aware of that fact. One could even say it's how we make our living." Jack walked away without another word. They needed to leave this place as quickly as they could. Eventually the good humor would wane and people would start thinking too hard about the sort of monsters they'd let into their town. Better to be gone before that happened, vanishing under the safety of nightfall and riding north with no real idea where they were going.

A cloaked figure headed north wasn't much to go on, but there were a lot of towns and kingdoms in that direction. Jack was sure they'd find a way to turn a profit, no matter where their journey led next.

The Tale of the Angry Frog

Conversing with magical animals wasn't especially dangerous, per se, but as a rule the Bastard Champions didn't do it much for the simple fact that it was boring. A goose with the power of speech might seem as if it would be interesting, but that ignored the fact that it would only want to talk about goosely things like bread and swimming. In practice, it was best to treat talking animals like strangers one passed on a road: give a polite nod to acknowledge them and then pointedly avoid any further engagement.

The frog that had hopped up while they were watering their horses was different. For one thing, she gave a proper introduction without once mentioning her favorite type of lily pad. For another, there was a subtle humanity in her speech that most animals lacked. The most important reason of all, though, was that she spun one hell of a story.

"So you dropped a ball into this pond, met a frog who claimed to be a prince, kissed him, and turned him human," Jack said, quickly packing her ten minutes of talking into a few brief bullet points. "And then a few seconds later, *you* turned into a frog?"

"That's the long and short of it." The frog was currently sitting perched near the edge of the pond, close enough to be heard but with an easy escape route in case they got too close. She was wary, and they could respect that, especially given her diminutive form. "He bolted right away, pausing only long enough to tell me that the curse could be passed on with another kiss. I have no idea if he was ever a prince or not, or he was the one who first got this curse. All I know is that it's been nearly a week, so my kingdom must be in an uproar. Unlike him, I'm not lying when I claim to be royalty."

"Royalty who cared so much for a toy that they were willing to kiss a frog?" Marie asked.

"The ball was a gift, thank you, I consider it a keepsake more than a toy." The frog seemed a bit testy at her tone, bristling as best an amphibian could. "And I kissed him because it's the obvious thing to do. If someone is in need, you help them. Freeing someone from a curse when all it costs me is a single kiss? I'd be a heartless beast to do otherwise."

"Or you'd still be a human," Jack pointed out.

"I won't feel bad about doing the right thing. That ruffian already stole my human form, far worse if I allowed him to take my humanity as well." The frog let out a loud croak of indignation, after which her eyes quickly went wide. "Pardon me, those are hard to stifle."

Frank and Marie looked over to Jack, who was eyeing the frog carefully. Marie might be able to smell her way across an entire forest blindfolded, but no one could sniff out a lie like Jack. He took a tentative step closer to the frog, lowering down onto his haunches. "You seem to be telling the truth, madam. Might I inquire as to who in the royal family you are?"

Another croak, this time without an apology, as the frog began to look nervous. She didn't want Jack to know who she was. Marie could practically see the internal conflict as the frog weighed trusting them too much against the fact that they at least acted as though they believed her. If the frog ever wanted to be human again, it would need aid, and there were only so many people who would come through this area, let alone believe her tale on top of it. And even if the frog didn't know it, she was probably in the presence of some of the most capable helpers she was likely to find. The coincidence of it all made Marie's hair stand on end, as it often did when she sensed the Narrative's hand guiding things. There was no helping it on this one, however. She was duty bound to aid royalty, and her own opinion on curses meant she had extra pity in her heart for those struck by them.

At last, the frog gathered up her courage and spoke. "I am Princess Vasilisa, of the Revna Kingdom. Aid me, good travelers, in finding my culprit and restoring my form, and ample riches shall fall upon you as a reward."

Jack's eyebrows rose so quickly that Marie nearly swore they caused a breeze. He was, no doubt, imagining the mountains of gold he might receive for returning a lost princess. Marie, on the other hand, knew to probe a touch deeper.

"Princess Vasilisa, it is an honor, but I must ask: how many princes and princesses are in the kingdom of Revna? As I recall, they are a family that emphasizes ample breeding, believing that through great numbers they will sire the strongest possible heir."

"I have…many brothers and sisters," Vasilisa admitted, some of the pomp going out of her eyes. "In truth, I am not considered a great candidate for the crown when my father passes. But I am still of royal blood, and there will be gold waiting for you if you give me aid, I swear it."

Marie didn't doubt that, she just wanted to reel in Jack's expectations a touch. He could be positively pouty when a big payday failed to materialize. "We can pin down the precise number as we travel, as I'm sure Jack will want to haggle with you for some time. To begin with, however, this job actually has two components. You want to be returned to your human form, and you want to find the man who tricked you. Those two do not necessarily need to be intertwined. It would be no trouble to find someone that you could pass the curse on to, then we could hunt for your perpetrator without you staying trapped in that body."

Vasilisa blanched, her green skin paling in a way that Marie was almost certain real frogs couldn't manage. "I would never! Passing along this curse to anyone else would make me as vile as the man who did this to me. I must return him to this form. Him, and no one else."

"Are you truly set on that?" Frank asked. "Surely the dungeons have people sentenced to death. Is it any crueler to turn them into a frog before they're killed? A life is a life, no matter the form it takes, and they have presumably earned their punishment."

This time, Vasilisa was a touch slower to reply. She mulled over Frank's point for some time, pausing only to snatch a fly from the air with her tongue. A look of embarrassment swept across her amphibian face, but Marie tried to pretend she hadn't noticed. As someone with a primal part of her brain constantly whispering inhuman thoughts, she had a measure of empathy for the trouble of dealing with frog instincts. Finally, once the fly was chewed and swallowed, Vasilisa seemed to reach a decision.

"You make a point, robed stranger. If we cannot find the man who turned me in reasonable time, then perhaps I will be forced to take your advice and change someone whose fate is already sealed. As a princess, I have a responsibility to be there for my people. But I won't turn to such a path unless it is necessary. And to make sure you're properly motivated to see justice served, I think your lady was right. We should look at this as two jobs, and you'll be paid accordingly. Let's say one hundred gold for restoring me to human form, and one hundred gold for returning this curse to the man who passed it onto me. Fail to find him, and your reward is cut in half."

Marie was slightly impressed. They'd only met Vasilisa a half hour ago, and already she'd seen right to the heart of how to motivate a third of the team. Debates on morality might be well and good, but by tethering their pay to what they could accomplish, she'd more or less locked down Jack's compliance. He would do, and had done, far more than hunt down some poor sap for the decadent sum of a hundred gold.

"I think that's an excellent starting point for our negotiations," Jack said, the greed in his eyes momentarily outshining his smile. "Frank, grab one of our cooking pots, if you would. The princess will need water to travel in, and this pond has a healthy supply. We'll mount it on my saddle for the ride."

"No." Marie stepped forward, angling herself slightly between Jack and the frog. "She rides with me. I'll stay close enough for you two to bicker, but I'll handle the princess's safety. In case there's a fight, she'd slow you down."

Jack's stare was brief; he didn't need to ask why she felt accountable for seeing this princess home safely. "Very well then, I can hardly protest when our greatest fighter wants to guard royalty."

"Her?" Vasilisa was looking over at Marie, oversized eyes even wider than normal. "She doesn't look particularly tough."

"Marie may lack Frank's insight and my raw speed, but make no mistake, on a battlefield she is hands down the most formidable in our numbers." Jack walked a step closer to the princess, getting lower so that he could approximate looking her in the eyes. "And given your current predicament, I hardly think I should need to lecture you about the importance of not judging things based on how they look, princess."

Vasilisa met Jack's gaze before glancing back to Marie. "My apologies. I fear my manners have rusted in their time spent trapped here."

"Quite all right. I rather like being underestimated. Makes my work easier," Marie replied. "As to the matter of hunting down your man, can you tell us anything about him? A description? A name?"

"I know what he looks like, although it's quite plain I'm afraid, and the only name I have is the one he gave me. It's probably false, like the rest of the tale he spun."

"Still, probably better to know in case he's used it with other people," Jack said.

"Henry. The lying bastard called himself Henry."

* * *

It took roughly an hour for Vasilisa and Jack to agree on a price for their services, one that ultimately was very close to her original offer. Every time he tried to increase the total, she countered by adjusting the ratio. The more gold Jack wanted, the more Vasilisa pinned on him finding Henry rather than restoring her to her natural form. Marie rather enjoyed the exchange; it wasn't often they met someone who had the patience to argue with Jack for longer than a few minutes. Vasilisa had clearly studied the art of negotiation, a tool useful for any member of royalty, and was putting those lessons to good use.

Once the price was set and the bickering died away, they passed the time by asking Vasilisa about her kingdom. The more they knew, the better prepared they would be, and Revna was more remote than some lands, meaning there were fewer rumors to go on. Even Marie knew of them only from a trade alliance, and that had been a few passing facts at best.

Revna was, as Vasilisa portrayed it, a relatively small kingdom with heavy emphasis on agriculture. No diamond mines or grand magical communities to keep them afloat, they were a land of hard workers who had been formed around tending the soil. It wasn't especially grandiose, but the thing about food was that there was always a market for it. Diamonds might wane in value and magic might grow more dangerous than profitable, but people would always be hungry. Because of that, the kingdom was prosperous, if not lavish. It was a far cry from the kingdom Marie had grown up in, yet she could respect it all the same. As time wore on and they grew closer to Revna's capital city, she found herself eager to see the place with her own two eyes. It had been too long since she stood in a proper castle.

Sadly, that would not be their first stop. Frank had hit upon the fact that since Vasilisa was out for a ride when she met her frog and the pond was some distance from town, Henry must have stolen her horse to get back. Tracking a plain-looking man in the capital of a kingdom would be nigh impossible with no leads, but someone riding a royal steed into town would stir up notice. If they could find the creature, they might discover where the rider had gone to. While it was a thin string to pull on, it was the only one they'd found so far. Unless this led them somewhere, there was a good chance Jack would end up with only half pay, and neither Frank nor Marie wanted to deal with the amount of sulking that would follow such a disappointment.

The ride to Revna's capital was a short one, which worked out well. Had it been a long, harrowing journey Marie might have felt a touch swindled once the city came into view. "City" was actually too generous of a term; it looked more like a large village that happened to have a castle in the center. The keep surrounding the castle was substantial, at least, and from a ways out they could hear the sounds of guards doing drills in the courtyard. As Revna had never been known for its massive size or unstoppable army, it was strategy that kept them safe. Being one of the largest food suppliers to all neighboring kingdoms meant going to war with them would mean charging with empty-bellied soldiers, a poor strategy in any conflict. Not to mention all the kingdoms they were still feeding had a vested interest in making sure their supply shipments weren't interrupted.

The modest size of the town and castle were a good reminder that here, land was meant for tending, not building lavish estates.

The first stable they tried ended up with nothing, even after Jack smiled and charmed the clerk, who was pushing a hundred if she was a day, into letting them leave their own steeds for a pittance. At the second, their luck held no better. It wasn't until they approached the third stable, which by this point Marie had a hunch about because these things *always* seemed to happen in threes, that they got a lead. The clerk did indeed remember a man showing up, riding a fine horse despite being dressed in rather damp and common clothes. He'd been looking to sell the stallion, or trade it for a lesser horse and a few coins, but the stable master had suspected something was amiss and turned down the offer. He had, however, traded the rider a set of new clothes in exchange for a few trinkets from the saddlebag on the horse. This revelation incensed Vasilisa to the point where she let out a thundering croak from her pot of water. Annoyed as the princess might be to have her belongings bartered away, Marie was grinning from ear to ear at the news.

For a few copper, less than the rags were even worth but that was Jack, they purchased the abandoned clothes. When Jack was distracted, Marie slipped the man a piece of silver to tell no one about their visit. Better to keep the element of surprise for as long as they could, even if it did come with a cost. With the clothes in hand, they headed to the nearest inn and booked a room. Marie needed some privacy to focus for the next part.

* * *

"What's she doing?" Vasilisa had emerged from her pot of water and was sitting on the edge of the bed, something the inn's owners would likely have been furious about if they knew. Marie, the "she" in question, was seated on the floor, the former frog's clothes stretched out before her. One by one, she picked up each article and held it to her nose, breathing in deeply, separating each scent woven through the fibers from one another.

"Marie has a fine nose," Jack explained. "So good that if she has something with a person's smell deeply ingrained, she can learn that scent and track it halfway across a kingdom. Usually getting our hands on something to smell is the hard part; most people are too careful to leave such items behind for exactly this reason. Well, I suspect they fear dogs tracking them rather than someone like Marie, but the point remains. This Henry fellow is sloppy. He should have traded for new clothes outright and burned the old ones."

Henry had indeed been sloppy. Sloppy, and scared. There were still lingering slivers of his terror amidst the clothes. Marie could smell it there, along with the sweat from the ride, the musk of the horse, and the stink of the pond. The curse changing the victims' clothes along with their bodies was a lucky break for those kissed, but Henry had apparently failed to get fully out of the pond before turning back. The pond-stink was making things harder. Harder, yet not impossible. As Marie breathed deeper, she unknotted the complex aroma and began to lock in on Henry's true smell. Not the fear or the sweat or the pond, his natural odor that would be forever present and impossible to hide. With every sniff, she drew a little closer.

"Vasilisa, tell me something." Frank was sitting at the window, watching the people in town wander past. "If I were a man, a normal man, who entered your town with no money and few items to trade, what would be the easiest way for me to make some coin? We now know that Henry didn't have any assets nearby if he was trading things from your saddlebag to afford new clothes. Sooner or later he'll want for food and shelter. Now, there's a chance he could get those on his own, however even if he has the skill, that will be difficult without proper tools. So for a stranger with little to their name and a quickly emptying belly, what would be the best path?"

"Easy: joining the kingdom's army," Vasilisa replied. "We're always wanting for warm bodies to take up swords; most of our people stick to working the land like their ancestors before them. If Henry can point a blade in the right direction, they'd take him in and start his training. That comes with room, board, and a small stipend as payment. Very small, actually, which makes it all the harder to recruit new soldiers. My father and I disagree often on that policy."

"Tell me about it." Marie mumbled the words under her breath, not quite aware that they'd slipped out as her mind focused on the task at hand.

Jack, in the meantime, had produced a gold coin from his pockets and was twirling it effortlessly between his fingers. "That's why I was never big on civil service. The glory of the kingdom pays for shit, while taking these skills onto the open market can make one very wealthy, if one knows how to apply them."

"In this case, the kingdom's frugality may turn out to be our ally," Frank said. "If the stipend is small enough, Henry won't have been able to save enough to leave, so he'd still be in town."

"And all we have to do to get to him is what, break into an army barracks?" Jack asked. "We're all quite good in a fight, but that seems to be pushing it even for us. Not to mention, I can't imagine the princess here would take kindly to us slaughtering her men."

"You have guessed extraordinarily correct." Vasilisa was staring at Jack with as much malice as a frog's face could muster, which was actually more than one might expect.

Through it all, Marie barely listened, clothes pressed to her nose as she burned the scent into her mind. She could already feel the change hitting her eyes, which was why she was keeping them closed. Doing something this bestial required tapping into the other part of herself. Not fully, as when she was fighting. This was an exercise in self-control as she drew forth only some of the curse. There was a time she'd have never thought such control possible, when suppressing the shift had taken every bit of willpower she possessed and even then sometimes failed. Meeting Jack and Frank had changed that. They were the first ones who taught her to see the curse not as an outside entity, some threat to be repelled, but rather as a piece of who she was. While Marie still burned for the day she'd be free of the monster in her blood, for now she had accepted that it was part of her, a part she could work with once she'd made peace with that truth. Terrible a burden as that inner beast was, it did have a fair share of uses.

With one last deep sniff, Marie set the final garment onto the floor. She sat for a few minutes longer, making sure she could still feel the smell in her nostrils and would be able to recognize it when needed. The time also allowed her to shift her eyes back to normal, which was important. Peasants and villains seeing her nature was one thing, but there could be serious repercussions down the line if a princess knew what she was. Even a princess she'd done a favor for.

Finally, Marie stood, noting that the others were still bickering and debating how they'd go about the infiltration. Clearing her throat to make them notice she was awake once more, Marie nodded to the doorway.

"Let's stop speculating and start hunting. Wherever Henry is, if he's in this town I'm going to find him. We can figure out what to do next after that."

* * *

Frank's deduction was, as usual, spot on. No sooner had they approached the entrance to the castle's keep than Marie caught a whiff of Henry. It was sharp and sour; he'd been sweating a lot. From there, it was a short journey over to the army's barracks for new recruits, with the smell growing stronger every step of the way. Getting around wasn't especially easy. The three of them and their frog in a pot stood out even more than usual around so many people in armor and adorned with Revna's crests, but Vasilisa knew the grounds well enough to guide them. They couldn't get close. There were limits to what a nonchalant attitude and a princess's wisdom could accomplish, but they got near enough to confirm what they needed. From the distance, Frank was able to spot a man matching Henry's description drilling with the other would-be soldiers, and Marie confirmed she could smell him all over the area. Mercifully, Vasilisa didn't think to ask how Frank could possibly make out a person's face from so far away. Explaining the dragon eye would have added a lot of unnecessary discussion to their day, and might very well have led Vasilisa to decide it was better to live as a frog than to throw in with this lot.

"On the upside, this is a pretty easy fix." Jack was smiling, to the surprise of no one, as he watched the guards do their drills from their seat on a stone bench. They'd taken up space in a nearby garden that locals often wandered though, and were far from the only ones watching the show. Evidently watching guards drill was one of the few forms of entertainment people had around here. Reaching over, he tapped the pot gently. "All you have to do is kiss someone, return to your old form, order them to bring Henry before you, and then have him kiss the new frog. Poof, your victim is back to normal, maybe with a few coins in their pocket for the trouble, and Henry is back to lounging on lily pads. No offense intended."

"None taken," Vasilisa said from within her pot. "They're actually far more comfortable than you'd think. I'm afraid I don't intend to kiss anyone else except Henry, though. I've read the old tales, and no magic is endless. There may be a limit on how many times this can be transferred. If I've reached it, then there's nothing to be done, but I won't risk another person ending up stuck in this body."

"Come on, what are the chances that there's only one change left?" Jack looked over to Frank, who was watching some snails crawl along a leaf. "Help me out here."

Frank continued admiring the slow movements for a few seconds longer before responding. "Logically, Jack is right, there's no evidence or cause to think that this magic has limits to how often it can be transferred, or that we would hit those limits right now."

The smile on Jack's face had gone from grin to full-on beaming, but it began to shrink back down as Frank continued.

"However, Vasilisa is a princess. A cursed princess. Meaning we can't dismiss the idea that the Narrative's will is at work here. And from that point of view, running out of power to transfer the curse sounds like exactly the sort of thing that would happen. Perhaps she'd doom some innocent person to life as a frog and in her guilt send out knights to hunt for a cure, inadvertently kicking off untold more adventures. Or the magic would fail and she'd be trapped herself, again prompting the hunt for a cure. The only way this story ends happily is if Vasilisa returns the curse to the man who tricked her, leading to a righteous conclusion."

Smile down to nothing but a slight smirk, Jack shook his head and let out a long sigh. "I hate the thrice-damned Narrative."

"It is a strange creature," Frank agreed. "In my lands, at least the gods people worshipped were usually absentee, or adept at enforcing their will without making themselves known. The Narrative is much less subtle."

In her seat, Marie shifted uneasily. She was never quite comfortable discussing the Narrative as openly as Jack and Frank. It was supposed to be taboo, that's how she was raised, and even after years with these two, the hairs on her neck stood on end when they had talks like this. "Let's focus on the task at hand, gentlemen. Vasilisa won't kiss a stranger unless it's necessary, which means if we want the full payday we have to break into the barracks and force Henry to smooch a frog. Any ideas?"

"It might be possible for Jack to slip in." Frank didn't sound especially enthused by the idea, even as he said it. "That strategy comes with a higher risk than even we consider tolerable, since discovery would mean either imprisonment or fighting his way out. Neither of those situations would be ideal."

"Discovery? Give me a little credit here, I'm silent as a cat at midnight when I want to be." If Marie didn't know better, she might have thought the feigned hurt in Jack's voice to be real.

"And with enough time to study, plan, and map the area I have no doubt you'd pull it off," Frank agreed. "Do you plan to spend that long in this town, though?"

The look on Jack's face said everything. He liked gold and loved adventure, but to put in that kind of work he'd expect far more than what Vasilisa was offering. This was a quick job, in and out in a couple of days at the most, that was how they'd all been looking at it. Committing that much time to the effort…well Vasilisa would have to raise the pay far more than she'd probably be willing.

"Perhaps we *should* entertain other ideas."

"We could try to nab him when he leaves," Marie said. "If he's saving up to go somewhere, he'll have to buy supplies and the like. Vasilisa, how often do the new recruits get time off?"

"If I recall correctly, it's once a month, on the day after the new moon."

"Oh." It hadn't been a bad thought, and Marie still felt it was a solid enough idea. The problem was that they were weeks out from a new moon, and that took them right back to the issue of how much time to spend on this. She would see the job done, it was her duty to Vasilisa, however she couldn't expect Frank and Jack to wait around on the chance that Henry would leave the barracks during his day off.

Rising from the bench, Jack let out a long, theatrical sigh, and began to unbuckle the sword from his hip, handing it over to Frank. "It seems the fastest way out of this is to be straightforward about it. Frank, I entrust all of my belongings to you, and I know exactly how many coins are in every pocket and pouch, so don't go treating yourself to drinks on my tab. Vasilisa, I'm going to ask for a royal promise from you, on your word as a princess."

Peering up from the top of her pot, Vasilisa watched as Jack removed his jacket next, then began pulling out concealed daggers from his belt and boots. "I'll need to hear the request, but if it is reasonable and in my power, then I'll grant it."

"I want you to promise me that upon your return to human form I will be released from all oaths and allegiances to any part of your kingdom, up to and including a pledge to serve in its army. Or, if you don't return to human form, I'll be released after three days' time. Have to account for the potential that the transfer magic has run out, as you suggested."

Marie, who could already see where this was going, let out a soft moan under her breath. There was a chance this wouldn't end messily, but it wasn't an especially good one. "You're going to enlist, I take it?"

"Easier for me to sneak out to you, get Vasilisa, and bring her into the barracks than try to break in. Lower stakes too, since at the worst they'll think I'm a deserter and more likely I can convince them I was out for a midnight stroll. If anyone has a better idea, I'm certainly open to hearing it."

"Take me with you," Marie suggested. "I'm the one who can track Henry's scent if you need to identify him, and it would be good for you to have backup, just in case the need for speedy exit arises."

"You think the army is going to allow me to stroll in with a lady on my arm just like that?"

A croak from the pot brought their attention back to Vasilisa. "Remember how I said that we always need soldiers? That means we can't afford to turn away people with existing commitments. If Marie was your wife, then she'd be permitted to come on the grounds with you. They'd set you in different barracks from Henry, but it would still get you both in the door. Marie might even be able to smuggle me in as a pet, meaning you wouldn't need to sneak out and fetch me."

Marie and Jack locked eyes, a moment of quiet horror passing between them. It wasn't the first time they'd had to play the charade of lovers or married partners, but virtually none of those occasions went especially well. Much as they cared for each other as friends and teammates, the duo were quite at odds romantically. Still, it was their best way in, so it seemed there was little to be done for it. Jack and Marie would don the guise of marriage once more.

"The only thing is, since they're taking on an extra person to feed and house, they won't be quite as lax with the entrance requirements. You'll have to prove some basic competency with combat before they'll let you bring Marie in with you," Vasilisa continued.

Jack's smile, which had dimmed dangerously close to vanishing at the news they'd have to play a happy couple, brightened considerably at the news. "Somehow, I think I'll be able to just barely pull it off."

* * *

The sound of wood hitting flesh would have made Marie wince, once upon a time. Those days were long since past, though, which was a good thing. Otherwise, it might have been hard to stomach watching as Jack nimbly avoided every blow the officer wearing a fancy crest threw his way and paid back the favor by striking the man in his limbs. Jack was being smart about it; his strikes always hit just barely, glancing blows that never came close to the head or torso. If he was too good, it would make the man testing him look bad, and that had the potential to create problems. Plus, standing out that much would draw attention, and that was the last thing they wanted for this job. The way Jack was fighting, he made it clear that he had talent enough to be worth accepting, even with a "wife" in tow, but he certainly didn't seem like someone to make a big fuss over. Just a man with a knack for the sword looking to start a good life for his family.

"He's quite good, isn't he?" Vasilisa was peering over the edge of her pot, watching the demonstration. She and Marie were seated nearby, resting on the ground with their backs to a stone wall as Jack proved his merit. As covertly as possible, Marie lifted a handkerchief from one of her pockets and draped it over the pot, allowing Vasilisa to still look out but with less risk of being spotted. The last thing they needed was word getting back to Henry that someone had brought a frog onto the grounds.

"You should see him when he fights for real. Jack has an abundance of flaws and failings, he'll tell you that much himself, but the man excels at combat. I've never seen him lose a swordfight."

"He's never lost?" Vasilisa sounded somewhat incredulous, which almost made Marie chuckle despite herself. There was something off about that tone coming from a frog under a handkerchief.

"Oh no, he's lost before. Plenty of times. I just said I've never seen him lose a *sword*fight. And I'm sure he's had his share of failure there as well, but before I was around to see it."

Another flurry of motion came from the dirt-covered training area where Jack was being tested. The officer in charge had switched from a wooden sword to a pole. He offered Jack the chance to alter his weapon as well, but Jack shook his head. While Jack would use another weapon in a pinch, he always chose a sword if it was an option. Marie still wasn't entirely sure why, except that he said it felt more natural in his hand.

"You are a curious lot," Vasilisa said. "A gifted sword-fighter with a dire lust for gold, a man who is covered in scars and stitches from the few bits I've seen beneath his robe, and then you, a seemingly normal woman with the ability to track like a hound. And, strangest of all, is how at home you three seem with this. You've all yet to balk once, from hearing about my curse to being told to infiltrate a kingdom's army. I was expecting some amount of disbelief or uncertainty."

Although Vasilisa couldn't see it thanks to the handkerchief, Marie momentarily grinned in a way that was almost Jack-like. "My friends and I know a few things about curses. More than we'd like to, if you take my meaning. As for doubting your tale, well, if you can manage to lie to Jack then you've earned our help. We'd still have to gut you for cheating us, of course, but there would be some respect as we did it."

"Then I am truly thankful that I've spoken nothing but the truth since meeting you." Vasilisa sank down into her pot once more as the match came to a close.

Despite the advantage in reach that a pole afforded the officer, Jack was still able to get in range to land a few hits. This time, however, he allowed himself to take some minor blows as well. Nothing vital, just enough to soothe his assessor's ego by letting him get in a few hits. The test ended with a handshake, and then a hearty slap on the back as the officer welcomed Jack into the fold. Poor fellow, he probably thought he'd uncovered a new prospect with ample potential. Pity they'd be gone before he ever got the chance to learn what Jack could really do.

"That went well." Jack wandered over and Marie rose to meet him. She kissed him delicately on the cheek, in what she hoped came off as a demure fashion. Some affection was necessary for the sake of the ruse, but neither of them would want to do more than was necessary. "We should be set up within the hour. There's a special barracks for couples, one where we get our own room. It won't be much, but it will be private. The general recruits, I just learned, sleep in one massive room with their beds side by side."

Damn. They hadn't exactly been expecting Henry to have a wing of the castle all to himself, but they would have liked it if there was a little privacy to work in. Sneaking into a room was one thing; sneaking into an open building crammed with soldiers was another matter entirely.

"Interesting. Are you thinking of visiting our friend in there, or letting him come to us?" Marie asked. Flush out or infiltrate were their only options if they didn't want this to drag on for days.

"I think we've journeyed far enough, don't you? He can close the rest of the gap and come to us. I was just told I can still leave to fetch any things I brought with me, so I'll pass the word on to Frank. There's more than enough daylight left for him to whip up something that will let us smoke our friend out."

"What are you planning to do, exactly?" Vasilisa didn't raise her head from the pot, but her question came through all the same.

In response, Jack lowered his head and carefully lifted the handkerchief, peering down at the princess and flashing a smile that was probably meant to be reassuring. "You'll find I'm not one to speak in metaphors unless I'm passing along a code. When I say we'll smoke our target out, that is exactly what I mean."

* * *

Henry woke up coughing. While that was a surprise, it had nothing on what greeted him when he opened his eyes. Thick smoke had filled the barracks, and all around him he could hear his fellow recruits coughing and choking for air as they shook off the last of their sleep. It didn't take a powerful mind to jump to the most likely explanation, which was why moments later someone screamed "Fire!" at the top of his lungs. The few men who were still sleeping found themselves roused by the call. One by one they staggered up from their beds, some grabbing for trousers while others ran for the door in bare flesh. Henry was part of the former group, as he had only the one set of non-army clothes and couldn't very well afford to let them burn. Between the smoke, the grogginess, and the desperation it took him far longer than it should have to don a simple pair of pants and a shirt, but eventually he completed the task and ran for the door.

Just before he stepped into the night, Henry thought about how odd it was that there was this much smoke yet he hadn't seen a single flame. The room didn't even feel hot. Then Henry was out the door, into the cool air of the evening. He took a deep breath, filling his lungs to purge the smoke. It was a lovely moment of relief, and also a brief one. The sharp press of a blade in his back cut the joy short, as did the voice whispering harshly in his ear.

"On my word as a scoundrel, I do not plan to kill you this evening. If you come quietly with me and do as you're told, you'll live. Call for help, make any stupid moves, or otherwise cause trouble and I'll plunge this into your organs and toss you back into that smoky room. By the time they find your corpse, I'll be long gone and all you'd have managed to do is get yourself killed for nothing. Nod if you understand."

Between the shock of his awakening and the cold metal that felt as if it could pierce his skin at any moment, Henry could scarcely think straight. One thought did manage to penetrate the fog though: the man with the knife absolutely sounded as if he was willing to kill Henry right here and now. That alone was enough to make Henry's choice for him. He tilted his neck forward, giving the nod, and he felt a hand close on his shoulder.

"Go where I steer you. It's not very far."

Not sure whether that was a good thing or not, Henry complied as the stranger guided him away from the building, still boiling with smoke and without a single flame as the cause. If Henry had been around the next day, he'd have seen the officers uncover a small pot, one formerly used to haul around a frog, that was filled with the sticky residue of a substance they'd never encountered before. Even then, few would ever guess that this simple cooking implement, or rather the concoction that had been crafted in it, was the cause of so much panic.

They walked on, past the barracks, over to a small garden courtyard that Henry had been told was a favorite reading spot of the princess. There, standing by the fountain in the center of the garden, was a woman wearing a cloak. She didn't seem all that scary, but what she was holding in her hands made Henry's blood run cold. This mystery lady was holding a frog, a frog that was staring at

Henry with unmasked fury in its eyes. Not everyone would have been able to read the frog's expression so well, but Henry had ample practice in understanding the expressions of amphibians. Too much practice, really, and he wasn't inclined to get any more.

Henry's feet slowed, and without hesitation he felt the blade begin to slide slowly into his back. "Yes, Henry, it's *that* frog. You stole someone's humanity, and they want it back. I'm sure the idea seems intolerable to you, but keep in mind the other option is death. Or maybe I'll slide this blade through your spine and drag you over there. I wonder how long a frog that can't hop lasts in the wild?"

"Please…please, you don't have to do this." Henry was walking again, keeping his voice low so as not to earn more of the knife but pleading all the same.

"I know. I don't have to do anything. I *chose* to do it, because the princess and I came to a fiscal arrangement."

"I'll pay you more. Whatever she's offering I'll double it. Triple it. Just don't make me go back to that." They were getting closer now; Henry could swear he smelled the pond's stink coming from the frog.

"You had to trade stolen goods for the clothes on your back; somehow I doubt you'd be able to top the princess's coffers."

How the hell did this man know that? How had they found him in the first place? It wasn't as though he was even using his real name during enlistment. So far as the other soldiers knew he was named Heinrich. These were good questions worth asking, but they didn't matter in the moment. All that he cared about was staying alive and keeping his human body.

"You're wrong. I can pay more. I'm a prince, you see, from a kingdom Revna is on bad terms with. I was just trying to make enough to pay for the trip home. Release me, and I will make it rain gold down upon you."

The stranger holding the knife paused, briefly, before the marching continued. "Interesting. You lied quite a bit just there, yet not completely. Sadly, I would have to refuse even if the whole offer was true. One of the few rules my people and I go by: once we take a job, we don't turn on our employer. It would be a short-term gain that tarnished our ability to do business down the line. Long-term thinking, that's how you survive in this world. Like maybe picking a better target than a princess to turn into a frog."

They were almost there now, only a few steps away. Henry was crying silently, afraid to let out a sob lest he lose the use of his legs. "I was desperate. So few people came there, and none of them were willing to kiss me."

"And the only one kind enough to give you aid is the one you betrayed. Save the tears. Even if I could feel pity I wouldn't spare any for you. This is a bed you made for yourself."

And then they'd arrived. Princess Vasilisa was only a few feet away, held by the fingers of this unknown woman. She didn't matter anyway. Neither did the man with the blade. All that mattered, all that existed in that moment, was the frog.

"Princess," Henry said. "I am truly sorry for what I did."

"Good. Then I trust you're willing to atone for it."

No mercy. No forgiveness in those eyes. This night ended for Henry either as a frog or a corpse. Much as he hated the curse, at least he'd have the chance to pass it on again. If he died, then that was the end. Kneeling down, he got onto eye level with the frog. "I am indeed, Your Highness."

There was no preamble or lead-up. Vasilisa was simply thrust forward, her lips hitting Henry's in the span of seconds. Instantly he felt his whole body start to burn as pain overtook him. Bones shrank, muscles vanished or shifted, and his skin took on a new texture. It was over in moments, but the pain lingered on, a reminder that he was now unnatural, a being out of its true form. Staring up from the ground, he saw Vasilisa and the unknown woman looking down at him.

"Your man promised he wouldn't kill me if I came along." Henry knew he was helpless. There was nowhere to run except the fountain, which was hardly an adequate hiding spot. All he could do was hope they kept their word.

"And I won't." As the voice spoke, a pair of strong hands wrapped around Henry, lifting him into the air and then dropping him unceremoniously into a metal container. Seconds later Henry heard a click and he knew his fate was sealed. "But we can't have you cursing more innocent people. Attacking a princess would normally get your head chopped off, so imprisonment isn't the worst deal. If you're nice, she might even bring you some flies."

The cage was handed over to Princess Vasilisa, who peered down into it, glaring at Henry in his new form. "You should get used to that cage, dear Henry. I don't think you'll see the outside of it for a very, very long time."

* * *

In the day it took for Vasilisa to put things in order and arrange for their payment, Jack and Marie canvassed the town, hunting for any leads about a mysterious cloaked figure riding through the area and what direction he might have gone. They got ample leads at first, and it seemed as if the task would be an easy one until they realized that people were talking about Frank, not their mystery rider. To the townsfolk's credit, Frank did cut a rather mysterious figure and he'd been hanging around the castle, so the mistake was forgivable. Once they clarified that it was a mysterious man in a specifically black and red cloak they were after, they were able to narrow things down.

Ultimately, the few rumors that matched the description well had their man heading further north, so that was the direction they opted to keep traveling. Jack seemed a touch bothered by the news at first, although he wouldn't talk about why, and after a pint of ale even that small glimmer of annoyance vanished.

By the time their second day in Revna came to a close, Vasilisa had sent a royal messenger with their gold, along with a proclamation officially releasing Jack from any duty to Revna as a soldier, stating that he had already rendered high services to the kingdom. With their money acquired and Jack not expected to show up for training, the three saddled up on the third morning and headed north, on what they hoped was the trail of their one lead to the Blue Fairy.

"You think she'll tell anyone about what happened?" Jack asked once they were clear of town.

"Her confidants, I'm sure, as well as anyone who might happen to be around the frog. She can't risk someone else getting duped and letting him out of his cage." Marie glanced back down the road, where the modest castle was still in plain view. Part of her had hoped there might be a banquet to celebrate the princess's return, but of course no one knew she'd been missing in the first place. And even if there had been one, they wouldn't have invited her, Jack, and Frank. When the job was done, people wanted them back on the road, traveling to the next town. Marie understood; she'd have done the same if people like them came to her kingdom, but she still would have liked to attend a proper banquet once more. It was probably for the best anyway; the potential for getting recognized inside the castle was too great to risk.

"Pity we couldn't keep him," Frank said. "A frog curse transferred that easily might have been useful, especially if it works on non-humans. We could have had a simple way to deal with whatever powerful foe we get on the wrong side of next."

"And miss the chance to fight someone who's actually worth the effort? No thank you. The princess can keep her frog; all I wanted was the gold." Jack's grin rivaled the sun this morning, as it often did after they came into a large amount of wealth. "But we can get you a pet if you like. There are bound to be some frogs or squirrels on the road."

"I'll have to pass. Animals don't like me," Frank reminded him. "It took weeks to get the horse comfortable enough to let me ride her."

"Then that's their loss." Marie knew how he felt. While dogs and horses were fine around her, smaller creatures tended to bolt as soon as they saw her, regardless of the form she was wearing. Her best theory was that they knew on an instinctual level that she was a predator, and they were prey. Even though she didn't act on those urges unless she was hunting and hungry, they knew she had them. Just one more symptom of her cursed inheritance.

Frank turned slightly in his saddle, affording Marie a brief peek under his hood. "Have you given any thought to what you'll say if you see Vasilisa again? In your other role, I mean."

"Given how long we've been chasing this fairy and how often we've come up empty, I can't say I think it will come up anytime soon," Marie admitted. "But if that happens, then I don't think I'll say anything until she does. It can be our little secret between the two of us."

"Ah, secrets, lighter than gold and ten times as profitable." Jack spurred his horse, picking up the pace, and the others followed suit. "If you do see her again, tell Vasilisa I thought she was quite stunning in human form. Far better than I'd expected."

Frank snorted and Marie rolled her eyes as they rode harder down the morning road. She pushed her horse, picking up the group's pace as a whole. While she'd never admit it, Marie was anxious to put Revna behind them and chase down their lead. After seeing a proper castle, homesickness was burning in Marie's chest and she ached to return to her own land. But she couldn't. Not yet. Not like this.

Not until they found a cure.

The Tale of the Greedy Village

The hamlet of Jacobsville was already bustling as the Bastard Champions rode into town, a curious development that none had expected. This was supposed to be a waypoint, a brief and peaceful stopover on their trek north. It wasn't unheard for places like this to fall into chaos when the Bastard Champions visited, but usually that didn't happen until they'd been there for at least a few hours. This time, however, people were scrambling about the town's square, many holding pitchforks, sickles, or other crude farming implements that were being repurposed into poor tools of self-defense. While they hadn't planning on doing more there than buying more supplies, asking about their mystery rider, and getting some sleep at a real inn, this madness changed things considerably. Where there was panic, there was profit to be made.

The nearest stables were by the edge of town, so the trio made a brief detour before investigating what was going on. After they'd left their horses and made it a few steps away, Jack leaned in to whisper to the other two. "Whatever she's about to do, just let it happen. The woman has a tendency toward the theatrical and she'll be even more insufferable if we don't let her play it out."

Before Frank or Marie could ask what he was talking about, the ringing of a blade being drawn filled the air. Turning, they saw that a woman in a blazing red cloak had somehow managed to sneak up on them and was holding the tip of her sword to Jack's shoulder. Marie was more stunned than anyone else. How had someone gotten so close to them without her smelling the intruder? Taking a deep whiff, she quickly found the answer to her own question. Somehow, most likely with potions or enchantment, the potential attacker had completely masked her own scent. It stood to reason she'd taken a similar precaution to muffle her footsteps. It didn't change their situation on a core level, but the realization that magic was in play did mollify Marie's wounded pride.

"I'm surprised at you, Jack. Getting snuck up on like some common trainee. Master would be disappointed."

"And I'm sure I'd care about that exactly as much now as I did back then." Jack turned his head to the others, unbothered by the blade resting against his back. "Frank, Marie, meet Scarlett. Scarlett, this is Frank and Marie. I asked them not to do anything, but I'd wager you've got about ten more seconds of holding that sword up before they ignore me and tear you apart."

Scarlett's gaze turned briefly away from Jack, taking in his companions for what seemed like the first time. She barely glanced at Marie, while taking her time to examine Frank, or at least the little of him that she could see poking out from under his robes. "I think you mean they would try. Although the hooded one does seem like he'd have interesting talents, it's not as if I came here on my own."

From behind a nearby building crept a lumbering figure. It was a wolf, technically, though its massive size and the level of intelligence in its eyes betrayed that there was far more to it than a simple wild animal. Giving a careful sniff, the wolf turned directly to Marie and let out a low growl. Taking a step forward, she released one of her own, a noise deeper and more primal than any human throat should be able to muster.

"That's interesting," Scarlett noted. "But mine is still bigger."

"For now." Jack turned around to meet Scarlett's eyes, that mad smile splitting his face. "If you're done with the greeting, can we put our blades and fangs away and go see what's happening in the middle of town? I smell gold to be made, and you know how I feel about people getting between me and money."

Scarlett held her blade aloft for several moments longer before pulling it away and sheathing it in a single fluid motion. With her sword gone, she stepped forward as Jack turned, and the pair embraced in a hug that was more affectionate than Frank or Marie could have expected. While Jack was certainly one to show affection when wooing a lass, he wasn't the type to go in for hugs. Especially not with someone who'd pulled a sword on him.

"It's good to see you, Jack." she said, finally pulling away. "I feared you'd gone and gotten yourself killed for good finally."

"Nothing that stuck. Mind calling off your furry comrade? I can't imagine the villagers are going to be calm about seeing a huge wolf in their midst."

Scarlett shook her head. "They have bigger issues on their minds than Peter, but you're right, he would only complicate things for now." Her mouth pursed and a sharp, short whistle escaped her lips. In a blur of movement Peter darted away, past the building he'd hidden behind and into the edge of the nearby woods.

"Jack, perhaps you would be so kind as to elaborate on who this woman is, and why you're willing to tolerate her putting a blade to your flesh." Frank was calm, which seemed good until one remembered that he could use the same tone when dismembering someone for information.

"As I said, this is Scarlett, and I tolerate it because that's how we were taught to greet one another. Our teacher was big on constant vigilance, so we were expected to sneak up on each other at every opportunity. She embraced the lesson a little more enthusiastically than I did."

"Your teacher?" Marie's eyes grew wide, and a smile that could rival Jack's began to appear on her face. Jack, as a rule, rarely talked about his past. All she knew about him before that fateful night in a tavern when she'd met Jack and Frank was that he'd been across the Endless Sea and hailed from a small town in the lands of some unspecified kingdom. "I don't think you've ever told us about any teacher, Jack. Care to elaborate?"

A *tsk* came from under Scarlett's tongue. "Still keeping secrets? He and I trained together for three years and I never learned so much as the name of his home village. Jack has trust issues, you see."

"I trust these two just fine," Jack said, perhaps a bit more quickly than was necessary. "I just don't like dwelling in the past. Those things are over and done. I'd much rather focus on the future. That's where the excitement is. Speaking of, you mentioned that the townsfolk here have something on their mind. Care to fill us in?"

Motioning to the road, Scarlett began to walk forward, bringing the others along with her. They were heading back toward the center of town, where a rabble of farmers and craftsmen were yelling over one another, each certain their idea was important enough to be heard and drowning out the rest of the crowd. It was chaos, with the potential to break out into a full-on riot, and Jack began to mentally increase his initial asking price. Whatever was going on here, it had people spooked, and that meant he could charge even more to solve their problems.

"What else gets the people this stirred up?" Scarlett asked. "It's a witch. Some girl got lost in the woods for a week, then turned up suddenly with sacks of gold in her arms."

Jack let out something between a cough and a squeal of delight, one clearly being used to mask the other. "Sorry, did you say *sacks* of gold?"

"Yes, I did. And as I was getting to, the girl told people quite a tale about helping an enchanted oven, cow, and tree before she got captured by a witch. She was going to be kept as a slave, but found those sacks of gold stuffed up a chimney. The girl tried to run away, got help from the cow and tree, then stuffed the witch in an oven. It wasn't lit, but that's still uncomfortable all the same. Harrowing as her tale was, it wasn't even close to the most interesting part. As she tells it, the sacks she brought back were but a small portion of the witch's fortune. The chimney was filled with bags of it."

"Oh no." Marie put the heel of her palm against her forehead, already aware of where the tale was going but willing it not to be true. "Don't tell me people tried to go after it."

"Of course they did. It was untold wealth in the hands of a presumably captured witch. I'm sure you can guess what happened next."

"A small child who aided enchanted creatures and was taken against her will escaping with spoils is a happy ending for one who deserved it," Frank said. "But the rest of the townsfolk would just be robbing a stranger; the Narrative wouldn't offer them any protection. The only question is: were they killed or captured?"

Scarlett looked at Frank for several seconds, stepping over stones in her path with a fluid grace that almost resembled Jack's. "You're rather quick on the uptake. According to the few scouts who've entered the woods and returned, the ones who went to rob the witch are only captured for the moment, strung up in cages hanging all around her house. We're guessing they're fated for some kind of ritual, or she's using them as bait to lure the rest of the town. Either way, with their friends missing and unknown sums of gold up for the taking, Jacobsville sent out word to every nearby town. Whoever slays the witch and frees the prisoners can keep as much of the gold as they can carry."

"I think they'd regret that phrasing if they knew how much Marie can haul when she sets her mind to it." Jack grinned at Marie, who met his expression with a scowl. She didn't like when he tipped their hand on surprises, even if he did trust this woman. "This situation is somewhat muddled, though. The little girl was clearly in the right, but once people started trying to rob the witch she had some moral ground as well. Not having the Narrative's protection is one thing, we almost never do, but actively going against it is a whole different matter entirely. Those kinds of jobs require very heavy pay, more than some nebulous amount that may or may not be up a chimney."

"A nebulous amount that we would have to split with anyone else involved in the rescue effort," Frank added. "Which looks like quite a crowd from what I can see."

Now that Jack was looking at the scene with context, he understood it better. It was not just fear driving the people to chaos; greed was in the mix, too. They'd probably come from neighboring villages, eagerly seeking their fortune. How hard could killing a witch be if a little girl managed to escape her grasp, after all? These simpletons had no idea what they'd be really dealing with, but Jack didn't have the time or energy to properly caution them.

"With no guaranteed money and the murkiness of the Narrative, I think we should skip this one," Jack said. "I'm fine with hard work, but only if there's a proper amount of gold due at the end. Let's take a day to resupply and rest then get back on the road. Something tells me we won't get much information out of these people."

"I'm surprised, Jack. There was a time you'd have gone off and tried to kill a dragon if there was even the hint of gold at the end of the job." Scarlett chuckled softly under her breath. "Have you gone soft?"

"I like to think of it as going prudent. My time is valuable, as is that of my colleagues. We can't afford to waste it on potential paydays when real ones are waiting down the road. Besides, I thought you'd be glad to hear I was backing out. Less competition for whatever is really up that chimney."

"Less competition is nice, but none would be better." A sour expression crept across Scarlett's face, pinching her forehead and eyes in an unbecoming manner. "I got word that Hans and Greta are coming for this bounty, too, not that I'm surprised. Those two always go for the witches."

Jack stopped in his tracks, a halt so sudden it jarred the rest of the group. His smile didn't dim, as one might have expected, but rather grew wider, a glimmer of what dwelled beneath his constant facade rising briefly to the surface. "Hans and Greta? They're coming for this witch?"

"I imagine they'll be here today, if they haven't arrived already," Scarlett replied.

"Well now, that changes things." Jack looked to Frank and Marie, who were standing stone-faced. They knew where this was going and refused to give him any emotional angles to play against them. "What would you two say about taking this job after all? There's bound to be a lot of gold up there. We can even take some of the pressure off ourselves by partnering with Scarlett. A four-way split isn't that bad."

Frank's jaw fell open and Marie looked as if someone had slapped her with a singing carp, all efforts at stoicism gone. Jack, *their* Jack, was advocating for less gold? True, it was prudent given that they were going up against a witch, one of the most notoriously difficult opponents one could face, but prudence virtually never topped greed in Jack's mind. Something was up. Something big.

"Hey now, I never said I wanted to work with you," Scarlett protested.

"It's an unknown witch in unfamiliar terrain, and we've got competition hot on our heels. You know it's the smart move. Plus, if we work together instead of against one another we have a better chance of succeeding, and I know you want to stick it to those two as much as I do." Jack was so certain it seemed as if the discussion had already ended, and after a brief moment of consideration Scarlett relented.

"Fine, I'll join up with you. But it's a five-way split, not four. Peter gets a share, too."

"I'm sorry; did you say your wolf gets a share?" Marie asked.

Scarlett nodded. "He's smart enough to spend money, so it's only fair he gets paid for his work. Take it or leave it, I'm not budging on that any more than you'd cut your friends out of the deal."

Sure that this would be the end of the discussion, Frank and Marie readied themselves to watch Jack disagree and storm off. Instead, his head slowly inched forward in agreement. "Five-way split it is."

If the initial idea had shocked them, this revelation nearly knocked Frank and Marie to the ground. Exchanging a single look between themselves, the two came to a wordless understanding. Frank stepped forward, clearing his throat to make sure this came out succinctly. It was important to pick one's words carefully when negotiating with Jack.

"Despite this being an unfavorable situation, Marie and I are willing to follow your lead and go after the witch. There is one condition though. You must tell us the whole story, to our satisfaction not yours, of what this Hans and Greta did to incur so much of your hatred. If you're willing to split the gold with more people just to keep them from success, then we'd like to know why. It's the least you can do, given what you're asking of us."

Jack was one of the few people Frank had ever met who could scowl with a smirk still on his face, a skill he was utilizing at that very moment. "I suppose that's fair."

"Say you agree to my terms, Jack. Don't just tell me that they're reasonable."

The scowl deepened, even as the smile widened. "I regret teaching you the art of negotiation, Frank, even though I am proud of how much better you've gotten. Very well, I agree to your terms on the condition that we set out as soon as possible. I don't want those two getting any more of a head start than they might already have."

Another brief look passed between Frank and Marie before Frank responded. "Well then, it sounds like we should get some pitchforks. I believe that's customary when one is hunting a witch."

"Torches, too," Scarlett added. "If we're being proper about it."

"No. No torches." Frank turned away from her, looking out to the forest. "I'm not a fan of torches unless they are absolutely necessary."

Scarlett waited for someone to say something, expecting this to be some manner of joke. When Jack and Marie both stood silent, she took the message and decided to move on. "Pitchforks it is then. Grab whatever you need and meet me by the eastern edge of town. Peter should already have a scent for us to track by then."

"Showoff," Marie muttered, heading down the road again before Scarlett had a chance to ask what in the kingdoms that meant.

* * *

Of all the terrible things people could say about Jack, and there were quite a number of them, he was at least a man who kept his word. So it was that they'd no sooner begun their trek through the woods than he started recounting his previous encounter with Hans and Greta. It had been many years earlier, when he and Scarlett were still under their mysterious teacher's tutelage. They'd been sent to a nearby kingdom under orders to hunt down a witch doling out poison apples. The bounty on her head was sizable, and the risk was great, so he and Scarlett had worked as a team rather than at odds with one another. But that much gold drew more than just them to the task. It also enticed Hans and Greta, or the Witch-Killing Twins as they were known. It wasn't a particularly flashy or creative name, but it got the point across, and that right there summed up Hans and Greta in a nutshell. No flash, no panache, no fun, just hard-nosed and stone-faced work. Jack had disliked them from the minute they first met, and the feeling had been visibly mutual, Scarlett was happy to add.

In the end, Jack and Scarlett had tracked the witch down first. It was a hard fight, one that had drained and wounded them, but in the end they were able to defeat her. While that should have been the end of things, it sadly wasn't. No sooner had the witch been bested than Hans and Greta appeared, striking at the two in an ambush. Jack quite proudly noted that he'd managed to put a scar on Hans's cheek before the altercation was over, but in the end even he couldn't recover fast enough from the witch fight to claim victory. Hans and Greta managed to escape with the witch's body, leaving Jack and Scarlett with nothing to show for their efforts save for an abundance of wounds.

"It would have gone differently if Master had allowed me to bring Peter along," Scarlett said. Several sets of eyes involuntarily darted to deeper into the woods, where a lumbering shape could just barely be seen trailing them. "We were supposed to be learning to rely on just our blades, though, so Jack and I were on our own."

"Jack got robbed? I can't believe it." Marie gave a fake swoon, as though she might fall over at any minute. "I genuinely always thought he'd rather die fighting than part with so much as a single coin."

For the barest of moments, Scarlett's face turned toward the ground. "He very well might have, actually, but I'm ashamed to say that Greta scored a deeper wound on me than Jack is letting on. I was hurt in a bad way, and he broke off pursuit to lend me aid."

"Self-preservation at its finest," Jack said immediately. "If I'd brought you back as a corpse, our teacher would have cut me into pieces and scattered them to far kingdoms. You were always his favorite; he'd never forgive me for letting you die."

While everyone nodded, neither Frank nor Marie particularly swallowed the excuse. Loyalty was one of the founding principles of their team, loyalty to the deals they made, and to one another above all else. Given the number of perilous situations they ended up in, it was vital that they could trust each other, if no one else. Since Jack had founded the Bastard Champions, the fact that loyalty was baked into its structure belied how devoted Jack could really be when he managed to care about someone. Not that any of them would ever point out such a thing. He was entitled to his pride, after all.

"Interesting." Frank held up a hand, indicating for everyone to slow their pace.

"Really? It was a decent story, I suppose, although I feel I've told far better ones," Jack said.

"Not you. That." Frank pointed ahead, deeper into the woods. Everyone else leaned forward, straining their eyes and squinting. Some ways off, barely visible through the foliage, was what looked like some object made of dark metal. That was all they could manage to make out, for while they each had good vision, no one could match what Frank's eye managed to see.

Marie was the first one to break, because she knew Jack wouldn't and Scarlett seemed the prideful sort as well. "I give up, what is it?"

"An oven," Frank replied.

"An oven in the forest?" Marie didn't doubt him; Frank knew what he saw and he wouldn't lie in a time like this. Still, that was a rather strange thing to stumble upon. She lifted her head and gave a deep sniff, searching for the scent of a metal, ash, or burning wood. Remnants of those smells lingered in the air, but now that she was paying attention she caught another as well, coming from the same direction.

"The girl who found the witch mentioned an enchanted oven," Scarlett reminded them. "She said it begged her to take some bread from it, then hid her and ultimately swallowed the witch as thanks. Guess it didn't hold her for long."

Another sniff, just to make sure, and this time Marie had no doubts. "We should be wary. I don't know if it was only the Narrative keeping that girl safe or the witch messed with the enchantment on the talking oven, but I don't think it's on our side anymore. I smell blood coming from that direction. Fresh blood."

"Maybe we could go around?" Scarlett suggested.

All three of the others shook their heads, nearly in unison. It was Frank who bothered to explain their dissent. "We can't. That's not the way these things work. We're on the witch's grounds now, so we have to face her trials. If we try to avoid it, at best we'll never find the witch's lair and at worst we'll run into something far more perilous than an evil oven."

With a long, annoyed sigh, Scarlett began trudging forward once more. "This is why Master told us to never fight witches unless we had to."

"Yet he sent you to hunt one down?" Marie asked.

"Our teacher was a fan of prudence and preparation," Jack replied. "Just because he didn't want us going after witches didn't mean we shouldn't be able to protect ourselves from them. The one we went after was comparatively weak; she'd even stolen the apple bit from some witch-queen to the west."

It was hard not to think about the fact that, while Jack and Scarlett had clearly survived, a "weak" witch was able to wound them enough for someone else to steal their prize. Who knew what sort of challenge this one would present? Then again, it wasn't as if Jack and Scarlett were on their own. They had allies now, powerful ones, and this wasn't the first time the Bastard Champions had tangled with a witch. Granted, they rarely did it intentionally, more often taking on a job without realizing a witch was at the heart of it, but they'd survived every encounter so far. Even if some of them were a little closer than the trio might have liked.

Reaching the oven didn't take long; it was almost as if the forest was leading them toward it. As they drew near, it became more and more apparent that something was wrong with the enchanted object. Rust and stains coated its dark exterior, and the door to its inner fires was warped and bloated. No sooner had they stepped into the clearing then that door swung open, allowing a deep, weary voice to speak.

"Halt, travelers. I am the first of the witch's guardians. You may not go deeper into these woods without my permission. Try, and you will find yourselves here over and over, until your bellies grow empty and your throats crack from thirst. I can only let you past if you feed me. Flesh or novelty, these are your choices."

Jack stepped forward, seemingly unbothered by the idea of bartering with an inanimate object. "Flesh or novelty? Can you expand upon that?"

"Ten pounds of flesh for each person who wishes to pass, or something I have never tasted before. Put one of those into my belly, and the way will clear for you."

Now that they were this close, the smell of blood was thick enough for even those without Marie's nose to pick up. They could also see bits of bone and blood on the ground, as well as a few swords and saws that had apparently broken midway through the process.

"Judging from all the blood around here, I'm guessing more than a few folk have taken the flesh option," Jack surmised. "Does that mean it's hard to find something you've never tasted?"

"Yes. I was once a stove in a royal palace, made by a talented wizard for a king with great appetites. All things I cooked were made better in my belly, and the chefs filled me every day to prepare great and exotic feasts for the palace." The warped door drooped a few inches, as if it were frowning. "Those were splendid days, before the war came and the castle burned."

Jack tapped a finger on his chin for several seconds, then turned to Frank. "What do you think? If we took off your legs that would probably be enough, and I'm sure we'll find some corpses you can butcher for replacements. But you'd be unable to help much until then, and we'd have to drag you around."

"It's not an ideal scenario," Frank agreed. "Perhaps there is another way. Oven, tell me this, does the novelty we feed you have to be considered food?"

"Nay. The witch didn't put such a requirement on me when she laid her curse, so anything untasted would work. However, I have lived many centuries and been used for more than my true purpose. More times than I care to admit, I've had my dignity sullied by being used as storage. And over the past days many have come, using their materials to gain passage. I have tasted much, so novelty is quite a rare thing."

"One more question then." Frank stepped closer, overtaking Jack, and hunkered down a few inches from the oven's door. "Are you happy like this? As a being created to serve others and abandoned, do you find value in this life, or would you prefer to be freed from it?"

"No axe or blade can destroy me, my shell is too powerful, and my insides burn too hot to strike; they melt any weapon before it can make contact."

"I can handle the logistics. Just tell me what it is you would like." Frank's voice was gentle, more caring than they usually heard from him. For the oven, he'd made an exception, and it wasn't hard to see why. The two of them were kindred spirits, in a way. Made for a purpose that was long-since past, trying to find their way in the world.

The oven's door wobbled, as if it were uncertain, before finally responding. "I felt good helping that child, and she told me my bread was delicious. If that were my last memory, I would be happy. But now, what the witch has turned me into… I am an old oven. If there is an afterlife for things such as me, I would like to see my chefs and king once more."

Carefully, Frank reached into his bag and pulled out a red pouch. Immediately, Jack and Marie took several steps back, with Scarlett quickly taking the hint and following suit. With delicate precision, Frank tied the pouch's strings to the front of the oven's door, making sure it would be thrust into the center of the fire once the door shut.

"I can all but promise you have never tasted this before; the recipe comes from across the Endless Sea. It is not the flavor in the pouch that I offer you, however. For our novelty, we offer the taste of freedom. There is but one catch, my friend. Do not close the door until we have begun to walk away. This is all I have of our powder right now. I won't chance giving you too little to see the job finished, but we need to be safely out of range. Will you do that for us?"

"I will. And thank you, strangers. I have little faith that this will work, but I am grateful that you showed me the kindness to try."

There was nothing left to say, so Frank motioned for the others to follow and they began to hurry away from the oven. Moving at a brisk but careful pace, they'd put it well behind them when an explosion tore through the forest with the force of a giant's roar. Scarlett dove for cover, which was in fact a wise reaction, while the others merely paused so Frank could look back to the clearing where the oven had been.

"It worked. The oven is in more pieces than I can count, so unless that wizard who made it was a living avatar of magic itself, the enchantment is certainly broken." Lifting his pale hands up, Frank pressed his palms and fingers against one another and lowered his head. It was a stance they'd seen him take many times, though they never quite understood why. "If there are any gods in this land, please look after what soul that creature had. None of us chose what we are made as, and it did all it could to lead a life fulfilling its purpose."

"What's he doing?" Scarlett asked.

"He's praying," Jack said. "It's a thing people do across the Endless Sea. Although I don't know why he bothers, since he doesn't even believe in their version of the Narrative, things they call gods."

"No, I don't. Not in my land." Frank parted his hands and lowered them back to his side. "But here, in these kingdoms, anything seems to be possible. So why not take a few seconds to try, just in case?"

Smoke was rising from the remains of the oven, acrid stuff that blew through the trees and hastened their departure. With one guardian bested, it stood to reason there were more on the way. Best to get through as quickly as they could, lest anyone else reach the witch first.

* * *

"Force me to the ground, or let my horns skewer your flesh." What had once been a talking cow begging to be milked was now a hulking bull, larger than a natural creature would grow. The horns it spoke of were massive things; they looked as if they'd part a limb from one's body rather than just putting a hole in it. Curiously, while blood soaked the ground, there wasn't a single bit of flesh to be seen. That absence made more sense when one paid attention to the ring of red around the bull's mouth, as well as the bits stuck in its teeth.

Scarlett stepped forward, drawing her blade. "This will be a battle, but if we work together we can drive this monster to the dirt." She turned, expecting the others to back her up, only to find Jack and Frank walking over to the edge of the clearing where they'd met the creature while Marie did some light stretching. "Or you could all leave me to do it on my own, I suppose."

"Don't worry, I can handle this one," Marie said, patting Scarlett on the shoulder. "You go sit with the boys and enjoy the show."

Scarlett still looked uncertain, looking Marie over several times before turning to Jack, who was patting a tree stump nearby for her to sit on. "Are you sure about that? The opponent is quite large."

"I'll be fine. But you don't want to be around here when we get going. I can't promise one of us won't end up running into you." Marie took a deep breath and faced the bull as Scarlett walked over to Jack and Frank. "Just to the ground? Do you need to be pinned or on your back or anything? Because I don't want you getting knocked over and then pretending there were more rules."

"I…no. Just to the ground. That was the witch's order." The bull seemed confused, which was fair. Marie had traveled and fought too much to be considered slender, yet she was hardly an imposing figure, which made it all the more curious that she seemed so confident of victory.

"Well, then, nothing else to do but get properly ready." As she spoke, her eyes turned yellow, and that was only the beginning. From behind, Scarlett let out a gasp as Marie's body swelled, fur and thick muscles replacing her tender flesh. She grew by several feet, upward as well as outward, until Marie the human was nowhere to be seen. In her place was a massive beast with its eyes trained squarely on the bull.

Behind them, in a voice purposely loud enough to be heard, she could make out Jack talking to Scarlett. "See, I told you that yours was only bigger for the moment."

That was the last bit of chatter before the bull charged, intent on goring Marie now that she presented a much larger target. Once, when she was in her kingdom hiding her curse, the bull might have been a true opponent for her. Matching strength for strength would have come down to a struggle, for both were huge and powerful. Sadly for the bull, traveling with Jack and Frank had taught her early on that strength was meaningless if one didn't know how to wield it properly. She'd been forced to learn quickly if she wanted to survive the sort of trouble they got into.

As the bull bolted forward, Marie stepped nimbly to the side, putting herself out of harm's way from the horns. Without pause, she dug her feet into the ground and pushed off, slamming her shoulder into the bull's hind before it could fully pass her. Immediately the bull scrambled, trying to regain its footing and balance, but she didn't give it time. Marie plowed into the bull again, this time catching it in the shoulder. Between the force of the blow and being already off-kilter, the bull went tumbling down, slamming to the dirt with a *thud* that blew away nearby leaves.

"I am…bested. You may pass."

From the edge of the clearing came a polite smattering of applause, Jack and Frank clapping for her while Scarlett stared with an expression of naked shock. Finally, just as Marie finished turning back, Scarlett managed to find her voice once more. "That was incredible. You've been given a true gift."

"No, it's a gift when you have full control over it," Marie corrected Scarlett, her eyes still slightly yellow from the shift. "Mine likes to try to come out at inopportune times, that's what makes it a curse. A handy curse though, I will give you that."

"And your clothes? They merged into your flesh, is that part of this curse as well?"

"That was just good shopping," Jack said. "Had to find someone willing to enchant them, and it cost a fair bit, but they made the point that it would cost less in the long run than buying Marie a new wardrobe every time she transformed. Now let's get going, I'm not sure we want to be here when that fellow gets up."

Scarlett looked to the bull, who was eyeing Marie warily while shooting the rest of them looks of fury. Letting out a whistle so Peter knew it was time to move, Scarlett followed the others as they plunged deeper into the forest.

* * *

"I think we can safely assume that these defenses are new. There's no way a bunch of farmers made it this far into the woods against magical guardians." Jack was eyeing the apple tree, its cursed bark warped into something like a face howling in pain. "The witch must have put them in after the first batch of fools showed up, trying to take her gold."

"To pass me, you must dine upon my poisoned fruit, or snatch one of the leaves from my branches." The tree seemed a little miffed that no one had addressed it directly, the twisted face taking on a slight tinge of frustration. "But my branches are quick, sharp, and thorny. You will not find the leaves to be easy pickings."

Without bothering to debate, or even ask, who should handle this task, Jack shrugged off his coat and wordlessly handed it to Frank. Stretching his arms and legs for a few seconds, Jack walked up closer to the tree's trunk. To get there he had to pass heaps of apples that were too deep of a red to be healthy, knocking a few aside with his boot. As soon as he was within fifteen feet of the tree, the first of the branches shot toward him, the tip on a perfect trajectory with his heart. It was fast, but two of Jack's nicknames didn't involve the words "nimble" and "quick" without merit.

He easily sidestepped the first attack, scanning the branch for leaves before moving in closer. More branches came, some from the front while others tried to swipe him from the side. None of them so much as clipped his clothing, as Jack dodged through them with little apparent effort. They all knew that part was for show. Putting on a display like this one was tough, even for someone like

Jack, but he never liked to let on that anything was difficult. That would have detracted from his image.

After a full minute of dodging branch after branch, Jack finally struck back. His hand whipped out as a limb swung at him, plucking a single green leaf from its hard surface. Instantly the attacks ended, branches going limp as they rose back up to their proper place.

"You have passed my test and are free to proceed."

"Thanks, I figured that out." Jack paused, studying the leaf and the tree. "Should we set this on fire before we go?"

"What?" No one had known for certain that a tree could sound panicked, but they all got confirmation in that moment. "I already told you that you passed!"

"True, however you're obviously under a terrible curse. Wouldn't it be more humane to put you out of your misery while we've got the chance?" Jack asked.

The tree shook, its mighty limbs swaying as though there was a massive breeze running through the forest. "Defeating the witch will end her curse. I rather like being an enchanted tree, thank you very much, and I'll be glad to go back to normal when this is done."

Jack took his coat back from Frank, slipping it over his shoulders. "This one isn't as eager to die as the stove."

"The stove was pulled from its place and purpose long before being cursed," Frank reminded him. "This is a tree in a forest. Safe to say its purpose is still well intact."

"Guess that's fine then. Was just an offer." Jack's gaze lingered on the tree for a moment longer, as if he were still debating setting it ablaze, before calling to Marie and Scarlett. "That's the last cursed guardian we know of. From here on it's either the witch or surprises, so everyone stay ready."

Marie's eyes glowed a faint yellow; she was on the verge of transforming already, while Scarlett let out a series of sharp whistles and received a howl in response. "Peter and I are ready."

No one else said anything for a time, because words held little point. They didn't know for sure what waited next down the path, but there was a very good chance it would be a witch. If that were the case, silence was their greatest ally. Witches were hard enough to fight as it was; the last thing they needed was to lose the element of surprise.

* * *

The screams started the moment their group stepped into view. Men and women, though by far more of the former than the latter, all strung up in giant cages fashioned from branches and woven into the trees. None of them looked well; the best of the lot simply seemed malnourished, while some showed signs of having passed through the trials the hard way. Sick complexions and missing limbs told the story better than words ever would. A few in the cages were already dead, no surprise given the poison and blood loss they had suffered to make it this far. Those who were still alive were rowdy though, and as soon as they spotted potential help they began calling and yelling, begging to be freed from their prisons.

"Idiots," Scarlett hissed under her breath. "If they'd stayed silent, we'd have caught the witch off-guard. It's not like we could free them until she's dead anyway; those cages are clearly formed from magic."

"They're scared and desperate, reaching out to the one source of hope they've found. It's understandable, if a bit inconvenient," Frank said.

Ahead of them, Jack began to pick up his pace. "With surprise gone, our best chance now is speed. We have to get to the witch before she casts wards or spells to protect herself." That was all he lingered to say before taking off like a shot.

The other followed, all of them quick but none quite able to match Jack's raw speed. Well, perhaps save for Scarlett. Despite starting behind Jack, she wasn't letting the gap between them lengthen. If anything, Marie though she might actually be gaining a bit of ground on Jack, although it was hard to tell while bolting through the woods. Even more impressive, Scarlett was whistling as she ran, passing along some kind of code to Peter and getting more howls in response.

Reaching the cabin took little time. Jack didn't even bother to slow down, he merely used his momentum to kick down the door. Waiting inside was a short woman wearing a dark shawl and stirring a cauldron with a long, thick, wooden branch. As Jack arrived she watched with an expression of detachment, nodding her greeting.

"Oh, lovely, more supplies. And these are in good shape, too. You just wait there like a good boy, I'm afraid you'll find the floor enchanted so you can't move even if you wanted to. Once I'm done preparing this, I'll tend to you."

Just as she finished, the others piled in behind Jack, finding their movement slowed until they came to a stop. With one exception, that was. Frank, able to deduce the situation from seeing his friends stuck in place, capitalized on his brief window to surprise the witch. He bolted toward her, so fast that she barely had time to look shocked, before jamming one of his daggers into her spinal column and flipping her up, over, and into her own boiling cauldron.

The witch fell in with a hearty *splash* and suddenly the others found their feet willing to move again.

"How did you do that?" Scarlett asked. "Are you a wizard, walking around with wards of your own?"

"Nothing so grand. She wove her spell to stop any living creature who entered her home. I did not technically qualify."

"Places everyone." Jack was watching the cauldron as it boiled, the bubbles growing more and more violent by the second. "We all know witches don't go down that easy."

The explosion of briny green liquid that burst from the cauldron proved Jack's point well, spraying all over the cabin as the witch tore herself out of the massive pot's depths. Reaching around to her back, she yanked out Frank's blade, the metal growing hot and warping in her grip. When she dropped it, the knife was no longer recognizable as the deadly instrument it had once been. They waited as she emerged, fully aware that she was expecting and braced for an attack. Better to strike when she went on the offensive and her attention was split. Trying to rush a prepared witch was one of the fastest ways to achieve a painful death.

"A living corpse. I thought those tales all died out ages ago." The witch was glaring at Frank, not without good reason, as she spit a hearty amount of green liquid onto the floor.

"I come from a land with tales all its own." Frank had produced another of his blades, one in each hand, as he watched the witch for any signs of movement.

She was going slowly, carefully measuring her opponents, aware of the standoff that would end the moment she attacked. "My, my, what a strange lot comes breaking into my home. A corpse, a woman with a fairy curse, some trollop in a red cloak, and…"

Her eyes went wide as she took a good, careful, magical look at Jack for the first time. "Boy…where is your cricket?"

"And that's enough of that I think. Marie, flank!" Jack charged forward, trusting his teammate would be there. His blade left its sheath in a blur, whipping around to take the witch's head from her shoulders. Marie was already half-shifted and barreling down on the witch from the other side. It should have been enough to break their enemy's will; unfortunately, witches were made of sturdier stuff.

With a flick of her hand, the massive stirring branch landed in the witch's fingers. She swung it around as if it had no weight at all, deflecting Jack's blow before twirling it back to sink the other end deep into Marie's gut, somehow pushing her back despite the size difference between them. Now that it wasn't submerged in a cauldron, they could see runes lighting up along the wooden surface, revealing the magic sealed within.

"I thought only wizards used staffs," Jack said. He danced away from a blow aimed at his head, studying the witch carefully as he searched for an opening.

"Times change, as your friend over there proves well." She jabbed at him with one end of her staff, moving faster than the tree branches had by a wide margin. Jack found himself losing ground, getting pushed back toward the wall where he'd be pinned down. Despite this, his endless smile only grew wider. In making the first move and drawing the witch's attention, he'd given the others an opening.

Moments later, Scarlett leapt forward and jammed her sword into the witch's side. Frank was close behind, slicing into her back again, doing as much damage as he could to her spine. The witch let out a howl of pain and spun around them, keeping an eye on Jack all the while. Sadly, for her, that split her attention in too many directions and she didn't notice the fully transformed Marie get back to her feet. Marie pounced without hesitation, driving the witch to the ground as she tried to chew the head from her shoulders, hat and all.

To her credit, this witch wasn't done yet. Staff still in hand, she let out a few whispered words and tapped the edge of it onto the floor. Instantly, the entire building began to shake violently, throwing everyone off their feet as well as everything not nailed down to the floor. Bottles full of potions and ingredients shattered, creating a stinking miasma that forced everyone to hold their breath. In the confusion, the witch slipped out from Marie's grasp, barreling toward the door.

She made it just past the threshold and paused to look back at them, still shaking as the house seemed to be breaking apart at the foundation. "I'll get you all for this. If it takes me a hundred years you, and your children, and your children's children will pay for—"

No one heard the rest of her speech, as a massive wolf appeared for a split second in the doorway, tackling the witch to the ground. While they couldn't see exactly what happened next, there was a very audible *crunch* followed by the building suddenly coming to a peaceful halt. Together, the four bolted out the door, slamming it shut behind them before any of the fumes could escape. There was no telling what those would do if released, especially in a forest already coated with the witch's magic.

Scarlett grinned as she saw the scene before them. "By the way, *that* is why my wolf gets a share of the gold." Near the cabin, sitting as if he expected a treat, was Peter. And next to his paws was the roughly chewed-off head of the witch. Not a clean kill, true, but people probably wouldn't complain about a messy head. They'd just be glad to have their friends and family back. The ones that were still alive, anyway.

"Do you smell smoke?" Marie asked. She glanced back to find that emerald flames had appeared at the edges of the house, and everyone quickly skirted away as the whole cabin began to burn in earnest. Whether it was caused by all the broken potions or aided by them, the flames made quick work of the home, the whole thing turning into an inferno in mere moments.

"Dammit all to the lowest kingdoms." For the first time that day, Jack looked as though he were in pain. His face pinched and his smile took on a sad, almost ironic taint. "Her gold was in the chimney, remember? We just lit up our own payday."

"Maybe some will survive," Frank said. "Precious metals still have value, even if melted out of coin shape."

The chimney in question began to wobble, slowly tumbling into the burning cabin. The flames got brighter and hotter, burning so greatly that everyone had to take a few steps back. Above them, they noticed for the first time that the people of the village were crawling out of their branch cages, the magic binding them now undone.

"Great. All of this for nothing." Jack slumped to the ground and glanced up to the people freeing themselves, weeping with joy and relief at their second chance at life. "Absolutely nothing."

"Well now, looks like we arrived a little late to this party." From the edge of the forest, two new figures stepped into view. They were clearly related, siblings if not fraternal twins, both wearing leather armor with blades on their hips. "Jack, did you bungle things again?"

Slowly, like a phoenix from the ashes, Jack rose to his feet, grin blazing as he turned to new intruders. "Hans. Greta. What an unexpected pleasure to see you both."

"Same to you, Jack," Greta replied. With a quick motion she drew her sword, pointing it in his direction. "We always love it when you save us some trouble. Now then, why don't you toss over the witch's head and whatever gold you took from the cabin like a good boy? If you're quick about it, we won't even stab any of your friends this time."

Jack's smile was so big it threatened to split his face; the grin was well past merely dancing with madness. "My, that is some fancy equipment you've got there. And are those coin pouches as well? Quite full ones at that. Frank, what's the morality of taking from someone who has stolen from you in the past?"

"A justified reallocation of assets," Frank replied. His hands were already on his daggers, quite aware of where this was going. "Especially if they are trying to steal from you once more."

"I thought so. Marie and Scarlett, you take Greta, Frank and I will handle Hans." Jack's eyes darted to Peter, who was watching the whole situation unfold with a bloody lip curled up, bearing its teeth. "Peter, buddy, all you have to do to get your cut is not let anyone run away."

"Five against two? That's not much of a fair fight." Hans was starting to backpedal, pulling out both his swords even as he scanned for a route of escape.

"You're the ones who just tried to rob us. This is self-defense at the worst, justice at the best. Besides, no fight is truly fair." Jack drew his sword for the second time that day, the gleaming blade looking almost green as it reflected the light of the burning cabin. "You're either strong enough to survive, or you're not. The rest is just excuses and whining."

* * *

Splitting the gold from Hans and Greta's equipment in five different portions meant no one got a lot of pay for the day's work, but they did all have the satisfaction of a job well done. Not to mention the satisfaction of leaving those jerks stripped to their skivvies and tied up in the forest. They would probably survive, if they were lucky, though Jack hoped they would think twice before trying to rob someone again, *especially* if that someone was him.

The town held a grand celebration over the witch's defeat, cheering all who were returned to them while quietly mourning the ones who were lost. Neither the Bastard Champions nor Scarlett took part in the festivities much; the former were busy hunting for clues about their mystery rider while Scarlett went into the woods to talk with her wolf. By the morning, when most of the town's folk had drunk themselves into a heavy sleep, four figures were at the stables, saddling their horses. Off in the woods, just barely out of sight, one could, if they looked carefully, spot a large wolf waiting.

"Where are you off to now?" Scarlett asked, hefting herself into her saddle with smooth grace. "More witches to kill?"

"I hope not, the pay for this one was awful." Jack mounted his own horse with ease, keeping a watchful eye on Frank in case his steed decided this was a morning it would be problematic. "We didn't find any sightings of our target here, so we might have lost him, or the people might have been too lost in witch-fever to notice one more stranger in town. We'll keep heading north to see if we can find any more leads. If we don't then we'll come back south in case we missed our man somewhere."

"Be careful if you're heading north," Scarlett warned. "There are rumors that the Blue Fairy made an appearance in the town of Collodi, and I know how well you get along with fairies."

Jack's whole body stiffened, and Marie let out an involuntary growl. "The Blue Fairy? You're sure about that?" he asked.

"No, it's only a rumor as far as I know. Still, better to swing wide just in case, don't you think?" Scarlett looked at the trio, noting with curiosity that they looked more interested than scared. "Or maybe not."

Frank finally got atop his horse, and Marie followed suit. "We've got business to attend to with her," Frank explained. "If she's been in Collodi, that's our next stop."

"Be careful then. Fairies are dangerous enough, but the ones with names of color are on a level all their own. I rather liked you both; it would be a shame to hear you'd passed on," Scarlett said.

"What about Jack?" Marie asked.

"Less of a shame, although I'm not worried about it. Nothing seems to kill Jack, even when it really ought to." She turned to her old training partner and, perhaps, friend, before setting off. "By the way, what was that about a cricket? I've never seen someone goad you into striking like that before."

"She didn't mean an actual cricket. It's nothing but a long story that none of us has time for." Jack rode over and stuck out his hand, which Scarlett took in a firm grasp. "Ride well, fight fast, and live long."

"To you as well. And may our paths cross again further down the road."

With that, they parted, Scarlett giving a brief wave to the others before riding south out of town. Moments later, they heard a brief howl that they took to be a farewell from Peter. With nothing else to do, they pointed their own mounts north and began to ride.

"Any idea of what we're in for?" Marie asked.

"No telling for sure. If the Blue Fairy came through a town then anything might be left in her wake." Jack had a distant expression in his eyes, his vision clouded with far more than the simple road ahead of them. "We might find a town made of glass and light, or a smoking hole where a city used to be. That's why we're going after the Blue Fairy in the first place. Because all of them are powerful, but she's the most unpredictable. If we're lucky, that personality trait might just break in our favor. Or it could get us all killed."

"The usual parameters for a job then." They might have been imagining it, but Frank looked as though he was hiding a smirk along with that comment.

The Tale of the Stolen Delinquents

Monster. That was the only name they ever gave him. Even now, years later, it seemed almost nightly that Frank would dream of that first stormy evening, or some mentally constructed version filling in all the gaps he couldn't remember quite right. To be fair, he had only just come to life moments prior, and his brain wasn't yet as fully developed as it would become. Some details still stood out though. The stink of roasting flesh, the sound of thunder booming overhead, and the sight of his father looking down at him. So much pride shined in those crazed, brilliant eyes. Father looked at him, beaming, watching as his creation pulled against the restraints.

"It's alive. Alive! We've done it, Igor. We've created life."

"Nay, sir, I fear what we've created is naught but a monster." The hunchback didn't share Father's enthusiasm. He never had, not really. In time, Frank would realize that he'd only played along because it was his job, not because he'd truly believed they would succeed.

"A monster?" Father tilted back his head and laughed, cackled really, neck twisted at an inhuman angle. This part, Frank was almost certain to be imagination over memory. His father had never been prone to such displays of mirth, even in his maddest of moments. "Perhaps you're right. We've created a monster to tear down the false ideology of those who insist that life is more than an amalgam of scientific reactions. Our man here will be a monster to those who laughed at my ideas or tried to stone me for blasphemy. Yes, Igor, we have indeed created a monster."

Father leaned down, examining him more closely. "A monster who is already in need of replacement parts. Seems the lightning overwhelmed and popped his right eye. We'll have to get him a new one as soon as possible. I can't very well have my boy greeting the world not looking his best. I've got such grand plans for him."

Delicately, Father pressed his lips to Frank's forehead, kissing his creation as if it truly was his own son. "So many plans for my wonderful monster."

* * *

"It was hard at first. People thought I was a monster." The young boy sitting before them looked perfectly mundane, from his rosy cheeks to the small scrapes on his knees that any lad would get from playing in the streets. There was no hint that he'd ever once been anything different, no outward sign of where he came from. But they'd asked all over town and gotten countless corroborating testimonies. There was no denying the truth of the situation: either the boy in front of them had once been a puppet, or the entire town was bewitched into believing he had been. From the Bastard Champions' perspective, there was little difference between the two scenarios. Both pointed to the kind of power that only someone like the Blue Fairy could wield.

Gepetto, still eyeing them suspiciously, returned from the kitchen with tea poured in mismatched cups. He served one to each of them, blanching slightly when he caught sight of Frank's hand, yet continuing to offer the cup all the same. It was a small gesture of respect, but one that didn't go unnoticed.

Pinocchio accepted his own cup of tea with a grateful nod. "Over time, I started getting used to it. But I never stopped wanting to be a real boy. The Blue Fairy told me I'd have to work hard for it, and wow was she ever right. We got there though. Me and dad, together, we got there." Pinocchio reached out and took his father's hand, the simple act of kindness visibly filling the old man with joy. The bond between these two was powerful, forged in tribulation and tested through adversity. Frank felt a twinge of envy for this child who, at such a young age, had already gained so many of the things Frank wanted for himself.

"That's what we came to talk with you about." Jack took a polite sip of tea before setting it aside; he was never one to waste time on proper drinks. Anything less than ale or coffee was water, and if that was the case he preferred the real deal. "My friends and I have been looking for the Blue Fairy for a long time. We have some…issues of our own, the sorts of problems only one of the five fairies of the colors can solve."

"I know." Pinocchio squeezed Gepetto's hand, the two of them both looking a tad more nervous. Something was off, and the trio all felt it.

Jack took his time responding, leaning forward slightly and working to ensure his tone was amiable. "I beg your pardon? Could you please explain what that means?"

"She told me you'd be coming," Pinocchio replied. "Before she left, the Blue Fairy said that a man, woman, and person in a hooded robe would come visit me, asking about her. She even left me a message to pass on to them."

There was a lot to unpack in that statement, not the least of which was that the Blue Fairy knew they were after her. It was always a risk, hunting someone with so much power. Between her connections and a place in the center of the Narrative's will, the odds of getting discovered were always against them. To know for sure that she was aware of them changed things, though. Had they been led here? A trail of breadcrumbs left in their path to make sure they stayed close on her heels? And if so, what did she want? She might have some complex plan in store, or she might just be messing with them for fun. That was the trouble with the Blue Fairy; her unpredictable nature could cut for or against those who dealt with her.

While the revelation gave them all a moment of pause, Jack soon recovered. "We are eager to hear her words. It has been a long journey, and this is a welcome surprise."

Pinocchio opened his mouth, but Gepetto cleared his throat loudly. The former puppet looked at his father uncertainly, then nodded slowly. "Right. I almost forgot, I'm supposed to test you first."

"Test us?" Marie's brow creased, her annoyance slipping through. It was hard to blame her; this was the closest they'd ever been only to find another hurdle before them. "What does that mean?"

"She said that the ones her message was for were brave, smart, and fearless. That I shouldn't give her words to just any who came asking, because as rumor spread many would come to me seeking her. So I was supposed to think of a test for the real people to prove themselves with. She…insisted."

It was there, only for an instant, but unmistakable: a flash of fear in Pinocchio's eyes. He knew that just by saying her name this much, the Blue Fairy was aware of the conversation, probably listening in. Much as he was grateful to her, perhaps even loved her for what she'd given him, part of Pinocchio was human enough to understand the terror of dealing with beings of such power. It complicated matters greatly, because there was no amount of careful words or convincing that would overcome such a fear. If they wanted that message, they'd have to pass the test.

"Very well then, if we must prove ourselves then we shall do just that," Jack said. "Pray tell, what trial have you chosen for us? Are we to find a tree magical enough to bear you a sibling, or perhaps you wish us to return with a sack of gold for you and your father?"

"No. I don't need any siblings, and we have more than enough as we are now." Pinocchio paused, squeezing his father's hand once more for strength. "Before I became a real boy, I had a friend named Chadwick. We were taken to a place called The Land of Toys, where children play all day long and never work. It seems like a good place, but it's not. Eventually the children there all turn into donkeys, and the owner sells them off. I found my friend Chadwick at his end, worked to death in his short time as a donkey. I know…I know that you can't find and save all of the children who have been turned, but I can't stop thinking about them. Dreaming about them. While I couldn't save Chadwick, I don't want anyone else to suffer his fate. Your trial is to find The Land of Toys and shut it down for good. If there are any children there, please save them, too. Do that, and I will pass along the Blue Fairy's message."

A long, weary sigh escaped Jack's lips as his gaze darted briefly to Frank. There was no wiggle room on this. Even if the boy hadn't asked for something so selfless, Frank probably wouldn't budge on the demand anyway, not with innocents in the mix. Jack was keenly aware of how Frank felt about children in peril, and now that they knew someone was kidnapping and cursing them it was an issue they were going to have to deal with either way. At least their reward would help them on their hunt; that was a bright spot to focus on.

"That sounds truly terrible. Why don't you tell us all about this Land of Toys and we'll see what we can do about it. The location and owner would be an excellent place to start."

* * *

"It's not taking. Why isn't it taking?" Igor pulled the eye out of its socket and tossed it into a bin, slipping a piece of cloth over the opening.

For Frank, the dreams of the early days were always fragmented, but this part stood out. It was a strange experience, having his flesh operated on even as he was aware of everything happening. They were trying to replace his lightning-damaged right eye again. Four eyes had been placed into his head already, connected to the nerves, yet failed to bring him any sight. Overhead, his father had opened his skull and was examining his brain.

"I think what we have here is an issue of degradation." Father poked something in the monster's skull and his left leg kicked slightly, narrowly missing Igor's arm. "The lightning and our procedure were able to breathe life into these pieces of flesh, however not all of them were able to withstand it. The eye was one example, and I can see pieces of the brain that have atrophied as well. Our monster is working with basic motor function and not much more. The new pieces we're stealing from graves have the same issue: degradation. Too much time and rot have worn them down."

"Then what shall we do? Perhaps we can take off its head, repurpose the good parts, and try again?" Igor shifted slightly closer to an axe leaning against the wall, and the creature felt his lip curl involuntarily. The hunchback never liked him, never trusted him, and always seemed to be at the ready to scrap the project as a whole. Dimly, somewhere in his primitive mind, the monster had begun to understand that, eventually, one of them would have to go so the other could stay at Father's side.

Hopping down from the stool he'd been perched atop, Father walked over to the front, into his creation's line of sight. Dark, clotted blood coated his gloved hands as he examined his monster with a critical eye. "Don't be silly, Igor. I would never so callously toss aside a life I helped bring into this world. No, this is a simple fix, really. If the issue is one of degradation then we simply need fresher parts."

He moved closer, looking in the lone eye that still functioned. "And for the brain, perhaps we should use something younger, with bits more able to cope with the trauma of suddenly being relocated out of their original skull. If we only replace the pieces that are failing, I think the system as a whole will be able to absorb the shock of new components. Even if it fails, we'll get valuable data. But if it succeeds…I imagine my boy here will be capable of great and wondrous things."

* * *

Not surprisingly, an enterprise built around tricking, kidnapping, and then cursing children wasn't one that operated openly. Pinocchio, despite having spent months there, couldn't recall anything more about The Land of Toys other than it was on a pier, surrounded by water, and even that he only knew because he swam off during his escape. More useful than the description of the place was how he'd managed to get there: by getting a ride from a mysterious fellow who went by the name Coachman. As leads went, it wasn't much, and it had taken all of Jack's willpower not to point out that maybe the fact that their driver used a blatant code name should have tipped Pinocchio off that all wasn't right. There was no point in shaming a child for naivety though, so they took the meager lead and did the best they could with it.

There had been, briefly, discussion of trying to pass one of them off as a child. The idea fell apart in moments, as the only way to pull it off would be through magical means, all of which would be ludicrously expensive if they could even locate such an option. Instead, it was decided that their best bet would be to try to find the mysterious carriage, then trail it until it arrived at The Land of Toys. That, of course, led them to the dilemma of how to find a carriage that only stopped to pick up wayward children.

Here, however, Jack proved to be an invaluable resource. For some reason, which both Frank and Marie could easily guess, Jack seemed to have an intimate knowledge of the sorts of things young troublemakers would get up to.

They kept watch on sweet shops, especially ones where the owners were known to have poor eyesight or slow reflexes, as well as any area with lots of things that could be easily smashed. It was at one such location, the site of a cottage whose construction had been abandoned halfway through, that they got lucky. Not only were there at least a dozen children hanging around, occasionally breaking what little was left whole, but Jack even caught sight of a few comparing baubles they'd stolen from the townsfolk. If ever there was a crop ripe for the picking, this would be it.

Together, they began to watch the site, noting that the children showed up around when they should go to school and stayed until they'd be expected home. There was, of course, the strong possibility that they might never see the Coachman. They had no idea how often he came through to recruit more children. Despite the odds being against them, they did all have hope it would work. Rescuing kidnapped children was an errand to which the Narrative might very well lend its support, which greatly increased their chances of having the right timing. It was decided that they'd give a week to this method, and if that failed then they'd simply try to hunt down The Land of Toys another way. Giving up wasn't an option, not with a message from the Blue Fairy on the line, it was just a matter of how they'd find a way to succeed.

Luck, or perhaps the Narrative, was with them. On day six of their watch, a dark coach pulled up just as evening was beginning to settle across the land, an hour at most before the children would be expected home from a day of school and play. The trio watched as the driver hailed the children, freely tossing out toys and trinkets.

"What's he saying?" Jack whispered. While he was more consistently aware of noises around him, none of them could match Marie's hearing.

"He's far away, it's hard to make out." She craned her neck forward, verging on the edge of slipping into the Coachman's view. "It sounds like he's promising to take them somewhere with endless toys and playing. If this isn't our man, we should probably stop him anyway. There's no chance this ends well for those children."

"Looks as though they like whatever he's selling," Frank noted. His stomach churned as he watched the children climb into the carriage, poor innocent souls being led to their doom. Frank's right eye grew cloudy, but he blinked away the tears. Much as he felt for them, if Frank went charging in now he'd only be condemning more children to be cursed and sold. He would help these children, all of them. It just required being a little patient first.

Once the last child was inside, the Coachman shut the door, showing a darkly gleeful smile to what he thought was the empty evening. One quick snap of his reins and the donkeys pulling his cart rushed forward, pulling these innocents off to their doom.

"Marie, you've got their scents, right?" Jack asked. They'd spent the better part of their nights finding items that the children had left behind, making sure Marie could familiarize herself with as many of their odors as possible.

"I still smell them, so I don't think the carriage is enchanted to hide their scents. We should stay close for a while until I'm sure." She rose from her perch, heading down the path to where they'd stashed their horses. It would be close, but if they hurried they'd be able to trail the Coachman to Collodi's main road out of town. Once they knew for sure Marie could follow the children's smell, it would be safe to fall back.

"They just went right with him, didn't they?" Jack pushed himself up to follow Marie. "I'll admit I swallowed some dumb stories as a child, but I can't imagine even I would have gotten into a stranger's carriage like that."

"They're children." Frank moved as quickly as the others, if not more so, mounting his horse so speedily that it nearly tried to toss him off. "Children are inexperienced and naïve. They inherently trust people. Even when they really, *really* shouldn't."

* * *

Make a friend. It seemed such a simple task, yet back then Frank barely had enough cognitive function to understand the simplest instructions that Father gave him. He didn't grasp the true reason behind the task, just as he didn't understand what friendship actually was, or why the task was assigned to him, rather than Igor or Father. To be fair, he didn't yet know what crimes were, or trials, so he certainly couldn't fathom anything as complex as the need for an alibi.

Wandering the forest for several hours, he came across many potential friends. Squirrels, birds, wolves, and all manner of creature populated the area. Dimly, he recognized them from the multitude of books Father made him read, trying in vain to expand his mental horizons. None of them would work, however, both because they all fled at the sight of him, and because Father had given him very specific instructions for his new friend. They had to be human. They had to be young. They had to come play at the castle, even if they were hesitant to do so. They would be scared of him, everything was, but Father assured him that once they were back at the castle and there was time to explain the situation properly, he would have a friend. He didn't know what that would entail, and it didn't matter. Father had made a demand of him, and Father was the giver of life. As his monster, it was a privilege to carry out even the slightest of Father's whims.

The sound of splashing caught his attention, and he lumbered through the trees until he came to a stream. In the middle of it, gasping for air, was a female human child. His muscles moved on their own, plunging into the flowing water without hesitation. Swimming was new, an experience he'd only read about, but some part of his mind recognized the motions and fell into a rhythm. Slow though he was, he was also strong, and in moments he'd shoved his way through the water to reach the girl's side. With one arm, he scooped her up and carried her to the shore as she coughed and clung to him for dear life. They reached the other side without incident, and he deposited her carefully onto the soft grass of the bank.

"You…safe?" Forming words was a struggle. He could process them, both the audible and written type, yet creating his own took significantly more effort. The thick rasp of his voice drew the girl's attention, and for the first time she got a good look at her savior. As her eyes met his, he braced for the shiver of revulsion that would run through her. It happened every time someone looked at him too closely; even Father couldn't completely mask his disgust at the sight. Yet when this small girl turned her piercing blue eyes upon him, there was no fear or repulsion. Her face shone with joy as she tottered forward and wrapped her arms around his torso as best she could manage.

"I'm safe. Thank you, mister. You saved me."

He didn't know what a hug was. Father's scientific texts had never mentioned such a curious gesture and there certainly weren't any to be had in the castle. Yet the moment he received one, he knew they were special. Something flickered in his heart, a sensation of joy. Although he hadn't given any thought to saving this girl, all of it had been reactionary, he still found himself impossibly glad that he'd done it. Saving people, helping them, it felt good. He wanted to do more.

"You…lost?" They were in the middle of the forest, and he hadn't passed a single house in some while, so the answer seemed obvious.

She released her grip on his chest and looked around, seemingly aware of her surroundings for the first time. Those bright blue eyes filled with fear at the unfamiliar setting, and he began to regret his words that had caused this child pain. "I think so. I was playing on the bridge even though Mama said not to. I fell, and the water was fast, and I swam until my arms got tired but I kept moving and…I don't know where I am." Sniffles filled the air as she grew frantic, her familiar world gone and replaced by one she didn't know in the slightest.

"No cry. I take…you home. Father…help…new friend." Father would see the girl back to her family; he knew the local area well. And this would complete his task in the process. He would be able to help the girl as well as make Father happy. This was a great stroke of luck indeed.

"You live close?" The girl was still scanning the area, searching for a house.

"Far. Can…carry." He pointed past the tree line, to the hillside where the manor was half visible against the night sky. "Home."

Her eyes widened, but she nodded. "I trust you. Let's go before it gets too late. I don't want Mama to worry." Slowly, she reached out and took hold of his hand, her tiny fingers barely getting around a few of his own. "My name is Shelley. What's yours?"

"No name. Just…monster."

Her giggling was unexpected, and she craned her neck to look up at him. "That's silly. You're not a monster. You're nice. You saved me."

There were many moments in his life that Frank dreamed of and woke up stifling screams. But this memory was one of the few from which he would wake to find himself weeping. Or weeping as well as was possible when one had only a lone eye that cried.

* * *

Whether it was bravado, stupidity, or a simple lack of resources for the task, it turned out the carriage had not been enchanted to seal the scents of the children it had taken. And really, from a logistical standpoint it made a certain amount of sense. These were delinquent children, so it would be some time before anyone noticed they were actually missing and not just off having some unsanctioned adventure. By the time somebody realized the problem, it would be far too late to try to trail a few rogue smells across kingdom roads. Even Marie had trouble doing it, and they were following barely a mile behind the carriage, sometimes further when it hit long, uninterrupted stretches of land where they might be spotted. Blocking the children's scents would be very expensive and had low chances of paying off. It was the sort of thing only someone like Jack would do, and Jack was mad as a hatter. That was, in fact, part of what made him so dangerously effective.

At last, they saw the pier Pinocchio had described come into view. It was certainly a massive structure, more akin to a floating town than a simple place for boats to dock. Brightly colored tents dotted the landscape, and even from a long distance they could catch a few snippets of calliope music drifting on the wind. However, all of that existed on a giant platform at the end of the pier. To get there, a rider had to cross nearly a half-mile of narrow wooden planks with multiple gates stationed at regular intervals. As they watched, the Coachman's carriage was halted at each one, its driver talking to the guards who then swung open their respective gates and allowed the procession to move forward.

"They really don't want strangers getting in," Marie noted.

"That, and they probably also don't want the children getting out," Jack added. "Once a few of them see friends turn into donkeys, I'm sure they make a break for it. This explains why Pinocchio took the seaward route rather than escaping onto land. Maybe we should do the same. Swim over, climb up from the rear and catch them off guard."

"We can't." Frank's left eye was focused on the waves crashing beneath the pier. It had excellent vision, and that was certainly useful, but it had also belonged to a predator. That meant it was an eye meant for seeing potential prey, as well as other predators, and there was ample danger to make out below. "This pier stopped being used as one for a reason. There are sharp rocks and reefs that would crash any boat we used, and the whole area is teeming with sharks and other sea monsters. The only reason Pinocchio was able to swim through there is because he was made of wood. Anything with flesh is going to start a feeding frenzy."

"Hmm." Jack took the news well, merely shifting his gaze slightly as he assessed the area. "I suppose that means we can't just burn it all down either, not without killing the children. I was hoping we could make enough chaos to give them a chance to break for the water. So we can't go around the back, and the front is heavily fortified. This message had better be worth the trouble."

"It doesn't matter if it's a dirty limerick. The Blue Fairy left it for *us*, so we need to hear it." Despite her flippant words, Frank noticed a shine of yellow in Marie's eyes. She was angry, about their situation and about what was being done to these innocents. If she did make it inside, Frank imagined many of the workers there would have just enough time to regret the choices that brought them there, albeit barely.

Jack chuckled at the idea of getting little more than a limerick for all their trouble, yet his eyes never left the pier as he mulled over their situation. "No one this careful is going to believe it if we stroll up and pretend to be in the market for donkeys. If we waited and ambushed the Coachman when he leaves again we could try to force him to get us in, but if he tipped off even one guard the whole thing would be sunk. Anything we could do to make the staff panic puts the children at risk, and I don't think Pinocchio is old enough to understand collateral damage. There's also the danger that if anyone there realizes they're under attack they might kill all the children to be rid of the evidence. Hmm. This is a good one."

"I have a thought." Frank wasn't sure where Jack planned to land on this one, but he wanted to make sure they took a path that emphasized stealth above all else. "Remember when we were trying to recover stolen artifacts from that miser king's vault? It was in the deepest dungeon of a castle on a mountain top, guarded on all sides by a veritable army. What did you say to me?"

The grin on Jack's face threatened to split his head as he recalled the moment. "If you can't go around or through, try under and over. That enchanted pickaxe cost us a fair chunk of gold, but it was worth it to break into the vault without having to deal with so much as a single guard. I think I see what you're driving at."

"Good. Then you know we need to take a rest. The only way we can do this is at night, and we'll need our strength at its peak. One slip-up, and any of us could be dead." Frank wasn't usually one to push for riskier plans, but his friends knew what they were doing. They'd each chosen this life, and the risks that came with it. One couldn't say the same about the children on that pier, innocents who'd been lured to their doom by a seemingly friendly face.

* * *

It took the creature some time to understand what had happened. To be fair, even with his newly improved brain he was still little more than a child. So he didn't question it when Father assured him that Shelley had gotten home safe, or wonder at the fact that he wasn't permitted to go see her. It made sense, he'd witnessed how Father and Igor reacted to his appearance, and they had *made* him. The people in the village might very well break into a panic at the barest sight of him, and he didn't want to cause trouble for Shelley. He did wish that she would visit, but he trusted Father's assurances that she would come on the next holiday, when she and her family would have time to make the trip.

Besides, he was busier than he had been before. With a brain that operated at full capacity, he'd discovered a thirst for knowledge. Every book Father owned, and there were quite a few of them in the library, had been read multiple times, even though he could recall them almost perfectly after the first perusal. When Father couldn't get more fast enough, the two of them would have lessons. Father was a brilliant man, and he knew more about the human body than anyone else in the world, or at least anyone else that his creation had met, even if that number was admittedly limited. Sometimes they would get out the cadavers that hadn't been fresh enough to use for parts and practice medical procedures, a vocation that both Father and his creation were adept at. Before long, he could look at the stitched-together pieces of his own body and see them for what they were: a tapestry of flesh artfully woven by the hands of a master. Yet the more he learned, the more he couldn't stop thinking that there was room for improvement, small alterations here and there that would permit him to operate more efficiently.

It was this curiosity that ultimately led to the undoing of their idyllic home life. While they had lessons with the cast-off corpse parts, Father had forbidden him from going to the basement where the good bits were stored. The explanation given was that the environment down there was delicate, and a few minor mistakes could wipe out their entire stock of backup pieces. It was a good reason, one that put his safety in jeopardy if he ignored it, but he was still childlike in his naivety, and mischievous exploration went hand-in-hand. By the time he understood where such impulses were coming from, it would be too late.

One evening, when Father and Igor were drinking and playing cards, he snuck down to the basement. There was a thick padlock on the door, however he'd read more than enough on blacksmithing and metallurgy to find its weak points. A single smooth blow at just the right angle was enough to snap off the lock, revealing the cold room within. He wandered inside carefully, taking Father's warnings to heart, and began to inspect the materials available. There would be no disguising the break-in, but if he could prove his theories to Father then all would be forgiven. Father was a man of science; he would understand the breaking of rules to see boundaries expanded. It was the sort of thinking that had led him to create life in the first place.

Most of what was down there was ill-suited to the purposes in mind, fingers and toes that looked at the point of turning, if not past it. But as he rounded a corner, new options came into view. They were small, too small to be useful for extremities; however the freshness was worlds above everything else in here. As he perused, a trickle of fear and doubt crept into his mind. These pieces…they were *too* small. Too small, and a touch too familiar. With every new bit that came into view, his stomach grew tighter. Part of him screamed that he should run, apologize for breaking the lock, and never come back here. Yet more of him, a part buried deep within his skull, urged him forward, demanded that he see what his Father had done.

By the time he found the jar, he almost knew already, but the sight was still enough to bring him up short. The head was preserved well in whatever liquid Father had put inside. It might have been dropped in yesterday by the looks of it, yet he knew better. Because he knew when his last surgery was, the one that gave him his new, far improved pieces of brain, as well as a replacement right eye. The eye that still dwelled in his socket, a perfect match for the brilliant blue one staring back at him from the depths of the jar. There was shock in the expression looking at him. Shock, betrayal, and terror. She'd thought she was being led to safety. He'd thought the same. But they had both been wrong, and she'd paid the price for it.

A droplet fell from his face, splashing to the cold ground softly. Reaching up to his cheek, he realized the stolen right eye was crying. It was odd; he understood the mechanics of tears yet he'd never experienced them for himself. Then again, perhaps he'd simply never had reason to. Looking around, he took in the body parts with a new perspective. How many had been taken from corpses fresh in the ground, and how many were stolen from those still using them? His eyes continued downward to the tapestry of his own body. So many pieces. So many stolen parts. This was the price of his life, the cost that Father had paid to bring him into the world.

And it was too high.

There was no telling how long he stood in that freezer. The cold didn't bother him; it would take true freezing to accomplish that. He just stared at the jar, and the contents within, trying to comprehend what he should do. This was wrong. *Father* was wrong. They weren't creating life at all. They were stealing it, moving it from one being to another. His very existence was a sin, although he couldn't imagine any god that would allow a creature like him to exist in the first place. He should end this here, tonight, and restore the natural order.

Sounds came from outside the room, stirring him from his reverie. Father and Igor must have finished their game and come looking for him. When the evening began, he'd had such high hopes of greeting them with a cheerful surprise and a successful experiment. It seemed a lifetime ago, and in a way, it had been. Only that life wasn't his. But their arrival reminded him of an important fact he'd nearly forgotten: they would try again. Father was nothing if not driven, and now that he knew it was possible nothing would stand in his way.

More parts would be assembled, more lives lost. They might even start with what they had on hand.

That thought was enough to force his body into action. Shelley had already lost enough for the mistake of trusting him. He wouldn't see her raised as a monster. No one else, ever again, would know the pain of this existence. Turning, he walked briskly out of the room, emerging just as Father and Igor finished descending the stairs.

For a moment, they stared at him and he looked back at them. Something had changed, and Father could sense it. Carefully reaching behind him, he shut the door to the storage room. The dead didn't need to be disturbed by what came next.

"I'm sure you have questions," Father said. "And I will be glad to answer them. I'd hoped to spare you from the messiness of life for a while longer, to keep your education pure and theoretical, but you now know there is a cost for scientific advancement."

"You killed that girl. You used me as your pawn and had me bring her to her own execution."

"She fell into a stream and was swept out of sight before anyone could jump in," Father explained. "So far as the world knew, she was already dead. And she would have been, if you hadn't saved her. Isn't it only fair that she helped to save you, too?"

There was no remorse in Father's words, no guilt at what he'd done. For the first time since his creation, he could see Father's true character laid bare. The man cared for nothing. Not people, not decency, only for science. Perhaps in time he would have become like that as well, but Father had made an error in choosing the new pieces of brain. These still carried the tinge of life and goodness that had existed before. Some part of Shelley still lived on in his mind, telling him that this was wrong. And knowing that made what he had to do all the worse, because it would mean forever tainting the one spark of humanity inside him.

"He's not listening," Igor called. The hunchback was searching for his axe, realizing too late that it was propped up against the wall near the storage room. "He's nothing but a monster with bloodlust in his eyes."

Igor was a toady and a fearful shit, but when he was right, he was right. Carefully, the monster of the manor stepped forward, wrapping a dead man's hand around the shaft of the axe and lifting it easily into the air.

"*You* dare call me monster? You, whose handiwork I've just witnessed?" Looking down, he could see the terror in Father and Igor, see the way they truly viewed him. The axe in his hand trembled ever so slightly. "Perhaps you're right. I am a monster. But I'm far from the only one here. We are all monsters, the whole lot of us. And so it is only fitting that we meet a properly monstrous end."

* * *

Making their way to the pier was the riskiest part, as it was when they'd be the most easily spotted. Only the cover of a cloudy night and dark cloaks allowed them to make it without raising an alarm. Careful as these kidnappers were, they hadn't counted on the possibility that someone would climb along the underside of the pier, dangling above the waters that teemed with gnashing teeth and empty bellies. It was a fair possibility to dismiss, since what sort of fools would have both the physical strength and the lack of self-preservation to ever try such an infiltration tactic? Well, the Bastard Champions, as it turned out.

Frank had the easiest time of them all. His limbs didn't properly produce lactic acid, so fatigue took far longer to accumulate in his muscles. While his stamina wasn't endless, it was near enough to be a meaningless distinction in most discussions. Marie had allowed her body to shift slightly, enough to turn her nails to claws and cause her muscles to swell substantially. Holding that half-form was no simple task—when they'd first met her she'd never have been able to even imagine such a feat, let alone execute it—but as they quietly clawed their way along the pier's underside she held her form steady. That was a good thing, too, since the rope around her waist and tethered to Jack was their leader's only lifeline if his own grip failed him. Jack was the only one among them without any magical enhancement, so he was the most at risk for tumbling into the water below. Luckily, as Jack had brought up then refused to expand upon when Frank raised the concern, he had a *lot* of experience climbing.

Nonetheless, by the time they finally passed the last gate and arrived at the spot where the wooden area expanded to accommodate an entire theme park, even Jack's well-trained muscles were beginning to shake. They wasted no time, moving to the nearest edge and hoisting themselves up behind a tent that played host to a shooting gallery. Thanks to the late hour, the Land of Toys was largely silent, as even the most rambunctious of children still needed sleep.

Hunkered down behind the tent, they all took a moment to rest and compose themselves. Not a word was whispered among them; all the necessary details of the plan had been worked out before the sun had set. Marie was going to track the children's scent to wherever they were being held and then lead or terrify them all to freedom. As the most physically imposing of the group, she stood the best chance of dealing with any guards or security she might encounter, and a few well-placed roars would get the most defiant of brats sprinting away from her as fast as their legs would carry them. Jack and Frank had another job, however. Pinocchio had been clear, he didn't just want to save the other children, he wanted to be sure this never happened again. Young as he was, he probably had no idea what he was really requesting, but the task was still given. Every captor here would have to die to ensure the scheme wasn't resurrected elsewhere. Frank's powder would have made the job easier, but they hadn't found time to buy supplies to make more of it, so they would have to do things the hard way.

Once everyone was ready, they all exchanged brief nods and made their way off in their own directions. Finding the children might be a difficult task, but locating the owners of this establishment was no trouble at all. Like most tyrants, the adults valued comfort and decadence, which manifested in a large, lovely mansion plopped down in the middle of the pier. A pair of guards stood outside the front door, keeping a cursory watch as they visibly struggled to stay awake.

Frank's first blade caught his target in the eye, sinking deep into the brain and killing him instantly. The second guard began to turn as he noticed his companion wobble, just in time to catch a blade to the throat. He struggled to cry out as blood poured forth, but Frank had aimed for more than just the jugular. With severed vocal chords it would have taken a miracle for him to wheeze loudly enough to draw attention, and there was no miracle coming for this man. Only Jack, with a blade of his own, to finish the job.

That done, they dragged the bodies out of sight and quietly slipped inside the mansion. If they were quick and quiet, they might be able to dispatch most of their targets before Marie's chaos fully bloomed. The quick worried Frank more than the quiet, for few knew better than he just how silently Jack could move when the need possessed him.

* * *

Fire burned all through the mansion, claiming every scrap of Father's research. When it was done, when the morning came, there would be nothing left. No notes or journals to stir curiosity in new minds, no experiments to cause a commotion, no machines to recreate. He'd smashed everything he could, burned every document there was, and now he was letting the flames finish the job. Only once in his night of destruction had he left the manor, one trip outside to dig a small unmarked grave and offer up a prayer to a god he was already sure wasn't there. But he could see why humans did these things; it was a ritual that gave comfort to the living, if he could even be described as such. With everything finished, he walked into the study on the top floor, filled with the books he'd so enjoyed. This was the closest thing he had to a room, or a place of peace, so it only seemed fitting he'd meet his end here. Father's final experiment, his greatest and most terrible work, would burn with the rest of the manor.

Lying on a nearby table were the few personal effects he'd bothered to keep. The axe, with which this monstrous nightmare had been put to an end, a few of his favorite books, and Father's black equipment bag that he'd used to both patch and teach his creation. A few items of comfort to go with him as he departed this world. He didn't know how one was supposed to die; this just seemed as good a method as any.

"You know, when the soothsayer told me a corpse unlike any other awaited me across the Endless Sea, I have to say this was not what I'd expected."

He whirled around to find a man standing nearby, casually examining the bloody axe as smoke began trickling into the room. Noticing the movement, the stranger gave a cheerful wave of greeting. "Evening, sir, or perhaps we're nearly to morning. My name is Jack, and it is a genuine pleasure to meet you. I have to say, I've been watching all of this for the last couple of weeks and I am truly impressed with what the doctor managed to create in you. One of a kind, you know?"

"Who… How…" His mind faltered under the sudden shock and strangeness of the situation. It was all winding down, he was at peace with the ending, and now suddenly this Jack fellow had disturbed everything. Worse, he just admitted to having seen all that transpired over the last few weeks. That meant he knew what Father had created, and perhaps even bits of how it was done. No one was permitted to live in this world with that knowledge. Much as he wanted to be done with the killing, it seemed the task wasn't over yet.

Lunging forward, he expected to wrap his hands easily around Jack's neck and grind it to powder. Instead, his fingers closed only on air as Jack moved nimbly out of the way. An instant later Jack delivered a swift kick to his knee, sending him tumbling down hard to the floor.

"Careful there, your creator might have educated your mind to the ends of the world but he obviously didn't teach you much about using your body. Sorry to say, but I'm afraid I won't die nearly as easily as those two. Or that girl."

Rage burned in his chest as he hefted himself up, swinging wildly for Jack, who dodged the strikes as if he already knew where they'd be. Jack repaid the attack by smacking him across the skull with the flat of the axe, though he had no idea when Jack had picked it up.

"That's what this is all about, right? Your creator tricked you and you led that girl to her death, so now you're trying to atone by dying." Jack was suddenly overhead, axe in hand, and in a flash Jack stooped down while pressing blade against his foe's throat. "Fire is a bad way to go, trust me on that. Since you've decided to piss on that girl's memory and take a coward's way out, why not go all the way? I'll chop your head clean off and spare you the pain of burning. It's what a fearful fool on this path deserves."

Who was this madman? Why was he fighting an undead abomination in a room filling with more and more smoke? And what right did he have to belittle the choices of atonement made by someone else? "I am a *monster*. What else can I do but die to make right my sins?"

The slap was quick and fierce, though it hurt little. Jack's hand moved so fast it was a blur; the only proof it had twitched was the slight stinging on the pale cheek above the axe blade. "I don't care much for that word. Never have. You want to be a monster, then prove it by dying here. But know this: no one made you one. You chose to be a monster right here and now by leaving only blood as your legacy. If you're truly sorry for what you've done, if you really want to atone for that girl's death, then a peaceful end isn't the way to prove it. Stand up. Stand up, grab your things, and go make amends by actually *doing* something. You've got strength and smarts the likes of which most men will never know. Do you really think there's nothing, no one, no child, out there who those gifts couldn't help save?"

Just like that, Jack was up and the axe was back on the table. Slowly, the creature pulled himself up from the floor, watching Jack hesitantly the whole while. "I am hideous. Dead parts stitched together. No one will ever allow me to do good. I'll be feared and hunted everywhere I go. There is no one who can see me as more than a monster."

"Really? Do I look like I see a monster?"

It should have been a nonsense question, yet he realized for the first time that Jack was right. In all the madness of the last few minutes there had been many strange moments, but not once had Jack looked at him with the flicker of fear or disgust that always lingered in Father's and Igor's eyes.

"Am I to take you as an example? You broke into a burning manor to harass a beast woven from the flesh of the dead. You are clearly insane."

“Very much so,” Jack agreed. “But that doesn’t make me wrong. Not much time left, you know. Soon this place will go up in flames. Are you going with it, or would you like to come with me? I can take you somewhere new, across the Endless Sea, where people are a little more accustomed to the unusual. The path won’t be easy, there’s danger at every turn where I go and few who join me survive. There will be people along that road, though, ones who invariably need help. I’ll even make you a pledge that if those people are children, I’ll make sure we lend them any aid possible. And if you join me, you will never be alone. I take very little seriously in this world, but loyalty is a rare exception. Walk out with me tonight and until the end I will stay at your side.”

“You can’t possibly make such an extravagant promise to a thing like me, especially one you’ve only just met.”

“It’s my life, my freedom, and I can do with it as I damn well please,” Jack rebutted. “Now what are you going to do with yours?”

The air had turned acrid, smoke was pouring through the crack in the doorway, and soon there would be no chance for escape. Death, only moments ago, had felt so inevitable. It seemed the sole way out, the only thing he could do to make amends. Yet this Jack, mad as he was, raised a good point. What good did he do by dying? What wrong was he righting? Shelley was gone, and would be forever. The only parts of her that lived on were inside his skull. Should he burn those, wipe her clean from the world, or put her sacrifice to use? He remembered how it felt to see her look upon him after pulling her from the stream. What it was like to know that, just for a few moments, he was better than a mere monster.

Moving steadily, finally sure of himself, he picked up Father’s bag of supplies and put it over his shoulder. If they were leaving the manor, he’d need ways to repair himself when injuries arose, and depending on where Jack was leading him supplies might not be easy to come by. He turned to face this intruder who’d upended his life, surprised to find a smile of his own was growing to match the one on Jack’s face.

“One more thing,” Jack said. “You need a name. Monsters might go nameless, but scoundrels don’t.”

A name. Such a simple thing, yet it had been denied him. It was tempting to pick something ancient or fitting, like Prometheus, but such grandeur felt wrong. Looking down at the bag, he saw Father’s surname on a metal tag woven into the leather. Reaching down, his mighty fingers snapped off half of the plate and let it tumble to the ground where it would burn with the rest of Father’s legacy. Only the first part of the name remained, the piece that he would claim as his own.

"Frank should be a fine name."

"You sure you don't want something else? Something without all the memories attached?" Jack asked.

Frank shook his head. "No. I want to remember what I am, where I came from, and what happens to those who let ambition override humanity. My name is a good reminder to myself of what I'm atoning for, lest I ever grow lax and forget."

"Well then, Frank, I'm glad to meet you. Now let's hurry out this window, because I'd hate for our new friendship to be cut off by burning to death." With that, Jack raced to the window and tumbled out, catching himself on the lip of the ledge and scaling down quickly.

For a brief moment, Frank watched him go, wondering just what sort of man he'd cast his lot with. If things got too dire, he could always cut out on Jack, although he wasn't quite sure he would. There were few people in the world who could look at a thing like Frank without blanching, and he rather wanted to see what sort of mad adventures this odd man led him to.

* * *

In the end, Jack and Frank managed to kill most of the mansion's occupants before the screams from outside began to wake them. The last few were half-awake as the pair stormed into their rooms and cut their throats, not that it did more than make their final moments more terrifying. The last of the occupants was in the largest room on the top floor, and neither Jack nor Frank were surprised to find the Coachman himself awaiting them as they broke through the door. He held a sword in his thick hand, though not with the grip of one accustomed to using it.

"Who are you? Why have you come here?"

"Is that sincere?" Jack asked, his own rapier already out of its sheath. "You're stealing children and cursing them as an enterprise and you're surprised someone came to stop you?"

"I have protection!" The Coachman's gaze wobbled between the two of them. "The Hemlock Witches Guild keeps the knights and princes off my trail in exchange for discounted sacrifices. If you kill me, you will incur their wrath."

Jack and Frank exchanged a brief glance before the former tilted his head. "This will make the fifth act we've committed to make a group of witches swear revenge on us, right?"

"Sixth," Frank corrected.

"Right, sixth, I always forget the walking house." Jack turned back to the Coachman. "Anyway, as you can see we're not afraid of witches, and if you can't tell by the fact that we snuck in rather than charge the front gates, we're certainly no heroic knights either."

"Then…then you must work for gold!" The Coachman was backing up, visibly growing more desperate. "I have gold. I have heaps of gold. Let me go, and I can take you to a cave where I've hidden at least ten thousand pieces of it."

Jack's throat made a sound like two squirrels fighting in a wine barrel as he processed that number. "Did you say ten *thousand* gold pieces?"

"Yes! All of it yours if you let me live!"

The offer hung in the air for a long, tense moment, before Jack let out a weary sigh. "Damn you, Frank. And damn me for my promises." In a blink Jack leapt across the gap between them, neatly planting his blade in the Coachman's throat before he could muster even a halfhearted defense.

"I love gold very much," Jack explained as the Coachman fell to the ground, blood and life pouring out of him. "And I value all it can do highly. Yet sadly, for you and my wallet, I hold my friendships in *slightly* higher esteem."

It was a nice moment, one that was somewhat compromised by the sudden smell that hit Frank's nostrils. "Do you smell smoke?"

Jack tilted his head and gave a sniff. "Why, yes I do. Looks like Marie has moved onto the second part of the plan."

They wasted no more time after that, both bolting for the door and down the steps. If she'd already set fire to the pier then it meant it was time for them to go. Fire didn't care who was right or wrong, who was just or who was evil. Fire burned everything indiscriminately, and if they weren't gone when it arrived then it would claim them too.

* * *

By the time the sun rose on the remains of The Land of Toys, there was little left to see. The fire had claimed nearly everything, and what it didn't take had fallen into the depths where it was snapped up by waiting jaws. Thankfully, no children were part of that count, as Marie had evacuated them all before setting the blaze. She'd also smashed through the gates and terrified the guards half to death, or all the way to death in the cases of those who tried to stop her, clearing a path for Frank and Jack to escape. It had taken some nimble work, but they'd eventually made it. Of course, only now did they realize that they had to transport all these children back to Collodi, which would demand several more days of their time.

"I swear, if we were getting paid in normal gold I would tack on extra fees for this," Jack grumbled. They were putting the smallest, and therefore slowest, children on the horses and walking with the rest of them. With luck, some idiot bandits would try to ambush them and they'd be able to get more horses along the way.

"Good luck negotiating with the Blue Fairy," Marie chuckled. "And the kid doesn't have any gold to offer in the first place."

The two of them bickered as Frank hung back, carefully watching over the children to ensure none wandered off. Whatever troublesome natures they had, each was too terrified to make problems. Sometimes, one of them would look over to him, only for a moment, before quickly turning away. It was an expression he was used to seeing after so many years, though it still stung to this day. Their fear didn't matter, though. If they told the others of the monster with the scarred flesh who pulled them from a land of fun and toys that was fine, too. All that mattered was that they were safe. He would never be able to truly make amends for the life he'd had a hand in ending, but moments like this gave him hope that if there truly was a life beyond this one, Shelley could be at peace.

"Come on Frank, time to hit the road," Jack yelled. "We've got a long few days ahead of us, and then who knows what kind of information the Blue Fairy left with Pinocchio. Let's just hope it's not a curse that turns us into birds or some nonsense."

Although he gave no verbal reply, Frank made his way slightly closer to the group as they started off, keeping a healthy enough distance to not worry the children while still keeping them all carefully in sight. The convoy began to move, and just as he had every day since that fateful evening in the burning manor, Frank followed Jack on to the next adventure.

The Tale of the Enslaved Elves

Jack was in a mood. That wasn't to say his ever-present smile had vanished, but it had taken on a slight twist near the corners of his mouth that Marie and Frank had both learned to recognize as a sour sentiment taking hold over him. Although he'd worked hard to hide it, the dark cloud had settled over him since they'd returned to Pinocchio and received the Blue Fairy's message, if one could even call her scant smattering of words by such a term. It had barely been a sentence, let alone a real indication of what she wanted, but it technically qualified as a lead, which made it all the stranger that Jack was in lessened spirits.

My path will take me through the lands of Summerly.

That was all the Blue Fairy left behind, the small smattering of words that told them little more than the next place they might find a clue to follow her. Summerly, as it turned out, was a town even further north. From what Marie had gathered talking to people in Collodi, it was a small hamlet of relatively minor importance to its kingdom. Truth be told, their journey was taking them further north than she was entirely comfortable with. While Summerly wasn't quite within the borders of her own kingdom, it was closer than Marie might have preferred. The nearer they drew to her homelands, the greater the chances of being recognized. A cloak and a haircut would only conceal so much.

They were still a good ways from Summerly, drawing near the thriving merchant town of Sagan, when a rustling in the trees caused Marie's ears to prick up. She let out a short spurt of a whistle, quick enough to be mistaken for a bird's song, to alert Jack and Frank. Both men slowed their horses, with Frank turning his dragon's eye to the trees and searching. After several long moments, he held up a hand with his palm open, silently telling Marie and Jack no attack seemed to be coming. That could always change but, for now, they were to play things peacefully.

Seconds later a small form came tumbling out of the branches, somersaulting end over end until it was snatched from the air by Marie's quick fingers. She held the creature at a distance, taking a careful measure of it, ready to hurl it away if it bit or scratched her. She'd been expecting an animal of some sort, perhaps an enchanted squirrel or a gopher cursed with confusion. Instead, she found herself looking at the diminutive form of a tinker elf. They were notorious through the lands for their skill at crafting items both mundane and magical, although she was surprised that one had allowed itself to be seen so easily. Her only experience with viewing a tinker elf up close was when Jack had taken her to one of their shops to get her enchanted shapeshifting clothing. It hadn't been cheap, but where magic was involved, quality was worth the price, even if Jack had fought tooth and nail to keep it as low as he could.

"Found you! Found you I did! Told the others I would and now I have!" The tinker elf, a male one judging by the shape of his hat, was cheerfully swinging about in Marie's hand, words coming out as a strange mix between singing and shouting. He was staring at her with such resplendent, unashamed joy that Marie grew a touch uncomfortable. Gently, she set him down in the palm of her other hand as Jack and Frank moved in closer.

"Well met, good sir elf," she said, falling back on formality since she didn't know how they preferred to be greeted. "My name is Marie, and the gentlemen with me are Frank and Jack. Tell me, is there a reason you sought us out this fine day?"

"Names, right, names. Always forget humans and your need for the things." The tinker elf paced around her hand, looking at his surrounding with sweeping gazes. "Very well, call me…Leaf. No, sorry, that's silly name. Acorn will do. Yes, Acorn sounds far more majestic."

Marie chanced a look at Jack, uncertain if this was normal behavior for a tinker elf, but he merely met her curiosity with a shrug. She hadn't heard Jack use names when they bought her clothing; then again, he'd mainly been focused on haggling about gold. With few other options at her disposal, she decided to simply go with it.

"As you wish, Acorn. Now that proper introductions are past, allow me to ask if there is some task you would like to hire us to perform?"

"Hire you? Why do that, when you already have debt to pay?" Hunkering down to a squat on Marie's hand, a position that briefly alarmed her until she saw his intent, Acorn took the sleeve of her tunic in his hands and delicately rubbed the fabric. "Yes, yes, I can feel it in here. These wares were sold with debt to tinker elves, one that's not yet settled. By magic of the bargain, I hereby invoke debt. Should you refuse, your enchantments will wither as punishment for welshing."

"A debt? Acorn, I fear you must be mistaken. We bought these wares outright years ago. We paid in gold…" Marie's words fell off as her mind drifted back to that day. It had been at the very beginning, when she first met Jack and Frank, before she knew just how close of an eye to keep on Jack where a bottom line was involved. The bargaining for the clothes had entailed an awful lot of clustered whispering, now that she thought about it.

Her head turned to Jack, who had already prepared by putting a somewhat shamed expression onto his face, and even a tinge of regret into his smile. "It's possible I may have agreed to a few options on the deal that lowered the overall cost. The biggest of which was a debt to the tinker elves, which any of them could call in if they were in need."

"Why would you do that? We'd already agreed that I was going to pay you back out of my share of the jobs, which I did. It wasn't even your gold."

Jack looked to her, then Frank, and back before letting out a short sigh. "Partly it was because I can't resist a good bargain, but mostly I wasn't sure you'd stick around long enough to make good on the debt. Frank and I have had other traveling companions through the years; few of them lasted more than a couple of weeks before quitting or being retired. So I figured if you skipped out on the debt, this would be your problem to handle."

"And what do you call it now?" Marie asked.

"*Our* problem to handle," Frank interjected, moving slightly closer. As he did, Acorn took notice of the pale man in the robe and took several steps back across Marie's palm, nearly toppling over the edge. "Acorn, this task you have for us, will it clear the debt on Marie's clothing?"

"Y-y-yes. She has strong debt, but we has BIG task, so it will balance. You help Acorn and his friends, no more debt on clothes. I swear it upon the bargain of the craft." At Acorn's words, a small ripple of light ran along Marie's outfit. If she'd had any doubt whether he was bluffing or not, that pretty much put it to bed. Acorn had them over a barrel, because Marie would be damned if she was going back to tearing up her outfit at every change and having to hunt for new clothes.

"Very well then, I think we can make this arrangement work." Marie lifted Acorn slightly higher, so she could more easily look him in the eyes. "Tell me, Acorn, what is it that you would like from us?"

For the first time since his sudden arrival, Acorn grew a touch shy. In that moment, she knew he was going to ask for something difficult, a task that would probably be worth much more than a debt on a few items of enchanted clothing. Even with that insight, she still underestimated just how big of a request Acorn had in mind.

"I need you to free us. All of my friends and family, the enslaved tinker elves of Sagan."

"How many is that?" Jack asked, clearly wary of the deal they were getting themselves into.

Acorn lowered his head, breaking eye contact. "Hundreds, if not more. We are almost entire crafting force of town."

To her surprise, Marie noticed that Jack didn't seem nearly as annoyed by the news as she'd been braced for. If anything, he looked a tad more chipper than before Acorn's arrival. Since they weren't being paid for the job, there was only one possibility: it meant more time until they reached Summerly. The revelation made Marie all the more curious, but it was a feeling she'd have to wait to explore. For now, there was a job to do.

"Acorn," Jack said, leaning down to meet his eyes. "Why don't you go ahead and start at the beginning."

* * *

It certainly wasn't a tale as old as time, but it was at least as old as capitalism. The whole thing started, as was often the case, with a good deed gone awry. Some tinker elves had taken pity on a poor shoemaker fallen on rough times. They snuck into his home at night, turning his scraps of leather into beautiful shoes that sold for far more than his own wares ever could. With the new capital, he bought more leather, turning out more shoes, until his shop was renowned in villages all around for the quality of his fine footwear. Considering their job to be done, the tinker elves took their leave, believing that now the shoemaker would be able to subsist on his own.

That had not been the way things went, however. With no elves to keep making the high-quality goods, the shoemaker's reputation soon fell, with people calling him a cheat and a charlatan. How dare he charge so much for shoddily made goods? Within a year, he was worse off than before. The only difference was that now the shoemaker knew a way out. Unbeknownst to the tinker elves, he'd stayed up nights watching them work, and was well aware of who had been the architect of his good fortune. With his income in peril once more, the shoemaker dove into lore and research, until he eventually learned enough to trap and ensnare another batch of tinker elves. These he bound, damning them to his will. Their children were born into his service, as were any more elves he managed to snatch up through the years. Soon, his reputation was grand once more, but it wasn't enough. The shoemaker began to sell other crafters on the marvels of tinker elf labor, turning his surplus of workers into a business all its own. Within a decade, all of Sagan's wares were elf-made, and it was known as a jewel of a place where one could purchase the highest quality of any goods.

There was silence as Acorn finished recounting his terrible tale. That quiet was quickly broken by Frank, who had backed off slightly in order to keep Acorn comfortable. "One element of this tale confuses me, Acorn. If you're bound to this shoemaker, as you say, then how were you able to escape and wander the forest to come find us?"

"No. No escape." Acorn lifted his arm and pulled back a sleeve the color of summer grass. There, on his forearm, was a small glowing circle winding all the way around. "Many elves captured, all with different purposes. Mine is not to craft, but to lure. Lure more of my kin into traps, to be bound and taken like all the others. I wander these woods in search of more elves, always hoping not to find any. I cannot tell them truth; mouth won't make words. You're not elves, though. Magic not stop me from telling you."

"Interesting. I'm surprised your captor didn't stop you from telling anyone, not just elves," Marie noted.

"The shoemaker probably didn't think it was worth the effort." Jack was examining the circle around Acorn's forearm carefully, which was no easy feat given its tiny size. "Tinker elves tend to stay out of sight by nature unless they're cutting a deal, and even then it's only for brief intervals. Not to mention, who would Acorn have told? Do you think the average traveler has the means to do anything about this, or that wandering knights are going to upset an entire town's economy for the sake of some elves? Even we might have brushed off this little fellow if he wasn't holding your enchantments ransom."

They were valid points, although Marie wasn't quite sure she wanted to accept Jack's pessimistic outlook. "I'm sure someone would have helped."

"Humans do not always have the best record of working against their own interests for the greater good, and even in a situation like this it could be argued that the value of trade and prestige brought to Sagan and its kingdom outweighs the suffering of a few elves," Frank said. "The argument would be wrong, but I'm sure it could be used for self-delusion."

"People are selfish," Jack agreed. "And I count myself well within that number, which means I have no intent of seeing the gold I spent rendered useless by letting Marie's enchanted clothes turn mundane."

"Actually *I* spent it, since I paid you back. With interest."

Jack waved her off. "Details. Silly details. It still came from my pockets. So then, Acorn, what do you need us to do? Sneak in and kill this shoemaker of yours?"

Acorn blanched visibly at the suggestion, shaking his head so furiously that his hat threatened to be knocked askew. "No! No no no! No blood. We don't kill."

"Technically, we'd be doing the killing," Jack pointed out.

"No. If Acorn asks you to kill, Acorn has taken part in the killing." He stamped a foot on Marie's palm to drive the point home. "We just want to be free. Killing won't do that. Shoemaker has magic contract; he makes us sign it to escape the traps. We all resist at first, but eventually hunger and fear win. When he dies, contract goes to son, and then next son, and so on. Has much gold now, and many sons. Only way to free elves is to destroy contract."

Leaning back, Jack swooned theatrically and held a hand to his forehead. "Let me guess, the contract is under lock and key in some well-protected dungeon, and you and your kin are magically bound not to help us to reach it."

Tiny as they were, Acorn's eyes widened considerably. "You right! You magic? Wizard?"

"Just a man who's done enough of these jobs to have a general idea what they entail. So we sneak in, destroy the contract, and then that's it, you're free?"

Acorn nodded vigorously. "Yes. Yes, we be free and run and never look back. Your debt paid. Shoemaker on his own."

"No killing, a clean objective, and plain stakes. This is actually easier than I was expecting," Jack said.

Both Marie and Frank winced slightly. They didn't know if it was the Narrative or just the way of the world, but those words were almost never followed by anything good.

* * *

"This one is on me. I'll own that." Jack's words were of little comfort as they stood in the street, staring at the massive compound that was the shoemaker's estate. Apparently he'd learned quite a few lessons from that first encounter with the tinker elves, the first of which was not to underestimate the need for good security. Private guards were stationed at regular intervals, with more making patrols in squads. The high walls around the perimeter were sheer, clearly meant to be unclimbable. Rather than trusting in that alone, though, sharp blades ran along the top of the wall just in case anyone did make it up. Every entrance to the estate was gated, guarded, and locked up tight. Presumably there would be even more security inside to bypass, and then they'd have to search the whole giant mansion to find the elves' contract. It was not quite the easy job they'd been hoping for.

"I hate to be the one to say it, but…brute force?" Marie asked.

"Against that many?" Frank rubbed his chin, the only part of his face visible from under the hood of his robes. "It's technically possible, though we'd have to set up a lot of distractions to make it seem as if we have a much larger force than we do. If we went in without a plan we'd be slaughtered."

"Sneaking in might be possible. I could get over those walls without too much trouble, then take out the guards at a gate," Jack suggested.

"Again, possible, but we don't know how long we might need to search the mansion, and the moment those guards are found the entire estate will come alive to hunt us down."

"You have any ideas, Frank, or you just want to spit on ours?" Jack asked.

The reply was slow coming as Frank turned, examining the area around the mansion. Sagan was a thriving city, and it had the fine touches to prove it. Stone-paved streets, torch stations to light the roads at regular intervals, and grand, sweeping buildings. Directly across from the giant estate looked to be a store paired with a museum. It was a tall structure with spires that stretched high into the air, catching the attention of anyone who passed by. Based on the signs around it, this was the site of the shoemaker's original store, only now it had been built up to accommodate the increased demand. On top of selling luxurious shoes and filling orders for custom-enchanted goods, it also had a wing dedicated to telling the tale of a struggling shoemaker who had, through hard work and determination, helped mold Sagan into the thriving hub it had become.

It was a nice story, though one that wasn't quite so charming once a person knew the real secret of the shoemaker's success. Frank wasn't taking note of the signs advertising what lay within, however. Instead, his head was tilting back as he noted the height of the various towers and decorative spires. Jack followed his eyes, smile dimming as he realized what Frank had in mind. "You want to go over?"

"Worked when we had to get past the wall of thorns."

"The wall of thorns didn't have guards stationed all over the place," Jack reminded him.

"So we use dark cloth, wait for a cloudy night, and land on the roof. If we're lucky, security will be a little lighter once we're actually inside. If not…well, we are going to have to fight whoever is in there anyway; at least this saves us the trouble of battling our way in."

While Marie hadn't been with them for the wall of thorns job, she'd heard the story enough to know what they were talking about. "Even if we did slip in that way, there's still the matter of getting out. Our shoemaker isn't going to be thrilled that his whole town's industry has suddenly vanished."

"True, we need an escape plan," Frank agreed. "Since we'll need a day or so for me to fashion the canvas for our entry anyway, if you two fetch me ingredients I can make more powder as well. Blasting our way out wouldn't be ideal by any means, but it would probably produce enough confusion for us to slip past. Let's reserve that as a backup plan, though. I'd like to have a chat with Acorn, because I think there might be a more natural distraction we can utilize to make our escape."

"So that's the plan then? Break in, hope there are no guards, and then have a few flimsy ideas for how to bust our way out?" Jack paused, taking his time to think it over. "Not bad, given what we're working with. Maybe we should take a few extra days though, really research what's going on here and form a well-thought-out strategy."

Marie and Frank both stared at Jack in shock. The mere idea of Jack spending unneeded time on a job where he wasn't being paid by the hour was ludicrous; doing it when he wasn't being paid at all was enough to make them wonder if he'd been bewitched when they weren't looking. There was only one conclusion to reach: Jack *dearly* didn't want to keep heading to their next destination.

"Perhaps we may, if our task demands it," Frank finally replied. "But we don't know how long the Blue Fairy's next clue will be in Summerly, or if she herself is waiting for us. Best not to dally any more than strictly necessary. I'll head back to talk with Acorn. I have an idea for our exit he might be able to help with. While I do that, you two rent a room for me to work in. I'm sure you know how important privacy is during my crafting."

With a sweep of his robe, Frank turned from the mansion and began walking away. Marie followed, and a few minutes later Jack did as well. Even as he moved, there was an unusual heaviness to his steps. Marie wasn't sure what was going on with him, but she hoped it wouldn't continue. Dangerous as these jobs could be, they were far more perilous if one member of the team wasn't in top condition.

* * *

By the time sunset arrived, the group had already secured lodging and gotten the materials for Frank to begin work on the cloak. But the supplies for his powder proved a slightly more cumbersome task. Not because of availability; in the merchant town of Sagan one could find nearly anything. No, the holdup in this case was Jack. He insisted on butting in during the haggling, going past the point of good taste, often souring deals on the verge of closing, and slowing the process of getting each component to a crawl. Ultimately, Marie forced herself into the conversations, taking over for Jack and pushing the deals through. They were still short a few bits by the day's end, but with the shops shuttering there was nothing to do except wait until the morning.

Since Frank needed privacy and quiet to work in, Marie and Jack dropped off the supplies and then made their way to a local tavern. They'd been on the road nearly nonstop for a while now, and an evening with a few drinks felt well overdue. After the first few ales, Jack's mood seemed to dissipate slightly, his ever-present smile taking on a charming gleam rather the mild irritation that had plagued it all day.

It was a lively night in the tavern, with people playing games of chance, arm-wrestling, and generally making a ruckus. There was a time when this sort of environment would have been so stressful that Marie might have shifted at the slightest glare in her direction, yet now she felt perfectly at home. The realization filled her with a pang of homesickness for her old life, and a much larger sense of worry. If she ever did return, would she be able to slip back into that world and her role so easily? The Marie who had left was very different from the one who would be returning.

"This place reminds me of the bar we met you in," Jack said after taking a long draw from his tankard. "Same energy, similar decor, even people raring for a fight in the corner." He nodded to the edge of the room, where several men were having a discussion that had begun to involve ample yelling and flexing. "Funny how the Narrative works. If a few brawling idiots hadn't accidentally slammed into you, Frank and I would have left that night with no idea whom we'd almost met. You ever wonder where we'd be if that evening had gone differently?"

"You must be deeper in the drink than I noticed if you've already grown nostalgic and philosophical." Marie took a sip of her own, mulling over the question. "You two would probably be doing about the same things, I expect. Taking jobs, making gold, generally getting by. Me…it's hard to say. Perhaps I would have found someone else to help me learn to control my beast, but there's just as good of a chance that a wandering knight would have met me during a fit and done away with me. It's really anyone's guess, but that evening set me on a very particular path."

With a flourish, Jack lifted his tankard and drained it down to nothing before dropping it back to the table. "That it did. All because we both happened to walk into a tavern on that particular night, on the same one where rowdy bruisers couldn't contain their violent tendencies. It's interesting how a seemingly insignificant choice can have such lasting repercussions on the rest of your life."

"I have a hunch we're not talking about just me," Marie said. "Are you finally going to tell me why you've been in poor spirits since you heard the word 'Summerly'?"

Jack looked at her for several moments, mouth opening and closing briefly, before he gave a soft shake of his head. "No, I don't quite think I'm up for that tonight. But you're right; I haven't been conducting myself properly. I'll try to get a hold on that."

"Whatever is waiting for us there, it can't be that bad. I know you're not the best man, and I've still followed you this far. Frank, I imagine, has seen even more than me, and I don't think he'll ever leave you behind. So whatever is in Summerly, whatever you're dreading, know that we'll still be your team."

"I appreciate that, I do. But I have...other concerns. And that's enough talk about it for tonight." Jack rose from his seat with the unnatural grace that never seemed to falter, even after having a few ales. "Now if you'll excuse me, I'm going to get us another round. I may even stumble past those arguing gentlemen. If we're lucky, one of them will take a swing and I can snatch their purses in the chaos. The only thing better than a cold ale is a cold ale bought with someone else's coin."

With that, Jack wandered over to where the brawl was forming like clouds on the horizon, smiling as he plunged headfirst into trouble.

* * *

True to his word, the next day Jack was back in usual form, helping Marie locate and purchase the last of Frank's powder ingredients for a fair price. They decided to buy more than they expected to need, both because racing out of a heavily guarded mansion was a bad time to suddenly run short, and because the ingredients weren't always easy to locate. Thrifty as Jack was, even he saw the benefit in stockpiling just in case.

While Frank worked, Jack and Marie spent the rest of the day studying the mansion and the shoemaker's shop, watching the guard patrols, searching for any weaknesses in the defenses. There weren't many to find; the shoemaker clearly didn't spare gold in regards to security. The only thing that ran in their favor was that employing such a large staff meant the shoemaker couldn't afford to be as picky as he might have wanted. The true talents of the land went on to be knights for the kingdom, or adventuring heroes, or turned to the side of villainy and worked for an evil queen or a scheming witch. What remained was the sort of muscle available for guard work, and while they could no doubt put the correct side of a sword into an enemy, the squads on patrol were likely not as alert or prepared as troops with real combat experience.

It wasn't much, and if things got violent those low-skilled brutes could still probably overpower Jack, Marie, and Frank with sheer numbers, but it did give them a flicker of hope that they might be able to sneak past after all. An alert squad would know to check every angle of approach, even the sky, but the lunks they watched barely looked past the end of their own noses. There was always the possibility that someone might turn their eyes skyward on a whim, of course. All this meant was that they had a chance to sneak in.

The shop/museum proved to be a far less intimidating target. The security was thick around the shop itself, especially where gold was changing hands, but the museum had little more than a few token guards minding the place. It was a font of history, and an ego-driven temple to the town's "hero", but there was little inside worth taking. Even the few guards present slunk off at the end of the day when the doors were locked up. Slipping inside would be simple, so long as they avoided the shop areas. That was the trouble with men like the shoemaker: they only fortified the things *they* considered to be valuable, rather than bracing at every point an enemy might use.

All in all, it was a fruitful afternoon of investigation. As the sun began to set once more, it was barely visible through the thick layer of clouds moving in. If the weather held, they'd be looking at a night devoid of stars or moon to betray their entrance. Whether it was the Narrative, the Blue Fairy, or mere fortune at work was impossible to say. The only thing that mattered was that their opportunity had arrived, and they were going to seize it.

* * *

Helpful as the clouds were, Marie could have done without the wind. It didn't hinder them in the first part of the infiltration—picking the museum's lock and easily sneaking past the guards—nor was it an issue as they made their way up the tallest tower. But once they reached the top, they had to emerge into the night and begin scaling one of the decorative spires. They'd all donned dark clothes to camouflage themselves, however the longer they climbed the greater their chances of being spotted, and the wind tearing at their limbs and faces certainly didn't help speed things along.

Mercifully, by the time they reached the top of the spire no cries or alarms had sounded below. Quickly, Frank hooked the shaped sheets of canvas he'd prepared to joints on their shoulders and backs they'd donned before the climb. The joints were crude, rough bits of metal bound with leather, but Frank assured them they would hold.

"Remember, once we take off from here, there's no stopping until we make it to the roof. If any of us misses the target, try to break in from the ground and find the others inside; we can't risk coming back for anyone. Oh, and Marie, remember that these are made to hold the weight of a standard human body. If you transform and the leather joints somehow don't snap away, you'll still be coming down *very* fast. So, if possible, don't transform."

"Drat, you really killed my whole evening's plans there." Marie checked the joints and the canvas once more. She couldn't quite help wondering how this simple device was supposed to work, but she trusted Frank. While the lands he came from had different kinds of magic than theirs, she'd seen how effective it could be many times over. If he said this would get them there, she had faith it would. Hopefully.

"Truth be told, this is one of my favorite things Frank can make," Jack whispered. "I've been hoping we'd have another job that needed them for the pure fun of it."

"Just don't have so much fun you forget where you're going. Don't think I've forgotten that you nearly went into that thorn wall because you were having such a grand time playing around in the air." Frank finished fastening the final piece of canvas onto his own back and surveyed the other two. "Everyone ready?"

"And then some," Jack replied.

"I'm prepared to go whenever you give the word." Marie liked to keep things somewhat professional during these parts of the job. It felt like a necessary contrast to the kind of work she'd be doing for the rest of the night.

"Then remember to jump as far from the spire as possible. If the canvas catches, you aren't going anywhere." Frank took a few steps back, clearly readying himself for a running leap, a move that Jack and Marie both mirrored.

Together, the three of them ran as one unit, bolting toward the edge of the spire and hurling themselves off with all their might. For a brief moment,

Marie felt her stomach drop as the ground came rushing toward her. She could hear her blood pounding through her ears, and every instinct she had was screaming to transform in hopes that she'd be tough enough to survive the fall. With all the mental willpower she possessed, Marie pushed the beast away from her mind, refusing to give it control. Yet with each instant that passed, the monster in her grew louder, the demands more insistent, roaring that she would die without its power.

And then she felt the sudden jerk along her body as Frank's canvas sheet snapped open, slowing her fall substantially. She could barely see the other two floating along as well, drifting through the night air as they passed easily over the mansion's wall. Tilting the joints on her shoulder as Frank had taught her, she directed her movement slightly to the left, putting her on a straight course with the mansion's roof. The wind that she'd been cursing turned into an ally, moving them at a brisk pace over the heads of the patrolling guards. Marie allowed herself to look around on pretense of scanning to see if they were spotted, although, in truth, part of her was simply admiring the view.

Jack was right, this was a splendid experience. She might have liked to try it when the risk of capture or death wasn't hanging over their heads, but even with those in play there was still something marvelous and thrilling about flying through the sky. It was hard not to get lost in the sensation, which was, unfortunately, exactly what she did.

It wasn't until she was over the roof that Marie realized she hadn't lost enough altitude. Jack and Frank were both turning in tight circles to lower themselves slowly onto the roof, while she was floating high in the sky. Marie was going to overshoot their target. Not by a lot, but by enough.

Thinking fast, Marie mentally reached for the monster she'd inherited in her blood. Most of the panic was gone now, replaced by the wonder at her flight, but she had more than enough fear at the idea of overshooting to draw out some of her curse. As best she could manage, Marie allowed her body to grow slowly. The leather strapped around her made strained noises as it was stretched, barely holding together. Her increase in weight had the desired effect, though, sinking her at a faster rate. Just when it looked as if she'd land with room to spare, a rogue gust of wind pushed her slightly. Scrambling, Marie felt her hands turn to claws as she leaned down and reached for the edge of the roof. Her claws sank in at the last second, and she pulled herself back before the wind could carry her all the way over the edge. Landing as softly as she could manage, Marie focused on turning back to human form, trying to lessen her size so she wouldn't stomp around the roof and alert everyone below. After a few seconds, her body was more or less back to normal, though her enchanted clothing was peeking out from the holes ripped in her dark robe by the shift.

Allowing herself a few moments to catch her breath, Marie rose to her feet and began to unfasten the battered leather joints from her back and shoulders. Nearby, Frank and Jack were both finishing up the task. Once it was done, they piled the canvas and joints back into a bag slung over Frank's back.

They'd successfully made it onto the roof without being spotted. Now all that remained was to search a massive mansion for a heavily guarded contract before an alarm could be raised. Soaring through the sky didn't seem quite so difficult by comparison.

* * *

Getting in proved easy. There was so much attention focused on protecting the ground level that no one seemed to consider the possibility of invaders entering through the roof. After Jack picked a lock leading down to the top floor of the mansion, they encountered only a single guard in the first hallway. Frank knocked him out quickly, taking care not to do lasting damage. While the team often found themselves in situations that demanded killing, when the chance to avoid needless murder arose they tried to make a point of taking it. They stripped the guard of his keys and weapons, then set about searching their surroundings.

Although they'd been braced to fight their way down, past each floor and into the basement dungeon, it didn't take long for them to realize that they'd miscalculated. Turning down a few hallways, they soon found themselves looking at a massive metal door protected by no fewer than ten guards. It was only fortune and Jack's quick reflexes that allowed them to duck back out of sight before being spotted.

The three exchanged confused glances. Surely this had to be a decoy. Then, Marie thumped herself gently on the forehead as realization finally hit. Pulling the others in, she whispered as loudly as she dared.

"This whole place is built assuming someone will come in from the ground, so why would they store the contract in a dungeon that's easy to get to from the first floor? The shoemaker went with the 'tallest tower' approach."

Both men nodded in agreement. Sticking a valuable object in the highest room of the tallest tower was indeed a classic strategy, although more often used with prisoners. If that was the case, then they'd already reached their target. On the other hand, if this *was* a decoy, they were going to have to reveal themselves much sooner than planned and fight their way down. Plus, it would only be a matter of time before reinforcements arrived.

"Marie, you and I will charge. Frank, blow the stairs so their companions can't come help."

Digging into his bag, Frank produced a small pouch with a wick poking out the top, as well as a handheld tool he'd designed for smashing flint and steel together. For her part, Marie allowed the beast that was already barely contained to make its way out, the hallway quickly growing cramped as her body expanded. Jack merely drew his sword and gave it a swing to test his range in the enclosed space.

There was nothing else that needed saying, so they didn't waste the words. Instead, Marie waited until Jack and Frank were directly behind her, making certain she'd shield them from any bolts or arrows, then hunkered down into a crouch. She felt a gentle tap on each of her feet, signaling that the men were ready. That was her cue, and she didn't dawdle. Letting out the beast brought along its temper, bloodlust, and desire to cause destruction. All she needed was something to channel those instincts toward, something like a squad of guards at the end of the hall.

Marie kicked off so hard that boards snapped under her heavy, clawed feet, tearing around the corner on all fours to get as much speed as possible. When she made the turn, she could see the confusion and terror suddenly fall upon the guards like a collapsing sky. They'd been relaxing, having a chat, sure that if trouble came they would have ample time to prepare themselves. Now, without warning, a massive creature had appeared before them and was charging fast. A few managed to keep their heads, grabbing the crossbows slung across their hips and trying to take aim in spite of their shaking hands. Marie was ready for this, roaring at the top of her lungs to surprise and disorient them. It didn't buy her much time, perhaps a few more seconds, but it was enough to let her get within claw's reach of the first guard and that was all she needed.

Her initial attack didn't even try to scratch the guard, instead she merely smacked him away, into and over the railing of the nearby stairs, sending him tumbling out to fall through the several stories of open air to the ground floor below. A crossbow bolt slammed into her shoulder, barely piercing her thick hide enough to stick in the flesh. She repaid the attacker by slamming him into the metal door so hard that she could hear bones crack. Gentle tactics might be preferable when they had the time, but in a real battle there was rarely a chance for such niceties.

From the corner of her eye, she could make out Jack whipping around, his thin blade moving too quickly for her eyes to track. Not every blow left a corpse behind, but the strikes severed tendons and muscles. That made the cleanup all the easier for Marie, who was careful to bring down the guards before they could recover. It was such frantic, fast-paced work that she lost track of Frank, which made the sudden explosion of his powder such a shock. She jerked in surprise, accidentally tossing another guard over the railing with what was meant to be a simple punch. Below, the middle of the stairway was in smoldering ruins. It could be crossed, if one was determined and an *incredible* jumper, but not easily. Hopefully, the obstacle would buy them enough time.

All at once, Marie realized there were no more targets to strike. The guards were all either dead, down, or tossed out of the fight, leaving the trio a clear path to the door. Not wasting a moment, Jack dropped to his knees to examine the lock, set of picks already in hand. No sooner had his hand grasped the lock than he dropped it, though, cursing under his breath.

"Enchanted. Guess we should have expected that." He began looking over the downed guards, nudging them slightly to see their possessions. "Might be too much to hope that one of these idiots would be trusted with a magical key."

"We don't need it," While Jack was working on the lock, Frank had slipped around to his side. "The lock is the only part that's enchanted, not the door. If Marie can smash though this section of the wall, I should be able to pop the hinges off in under a minute."

From below, they could hear commands being yelled forcefully along with the stamping of feet. Many, *many* feet. If that force made it past the ruined staircase, they were going to have to retreat. Without the element of surprise, there was little chance an attack like this would work a second time.

Marie didn't waste seconds they couldn't spare, driving her claws into the wall around the door, tearing away at the wood and bits of metal that were reinforcing it. Frank yanked out tools from his bag and swiftly banged on the hinges with expert precision.

The first one was off by the time they heard guards running directly below them. Frank popped the second hinge just as the first group of guards tried racing up the final part of the stairs, only to find a huge section conspicuously missing. Quickly, Marie swung around, tucking her head and putting her back between the guards and Frank. He couldn't afford distractions, not when they were so close. Crossbow bolts slammed into her back, most failing to pierce her hide but a few sticking painfully deep. She made no noise though. Frank was already doing his best; he didn't need her pain for motivation.

Finally, the last hinge popped off and Frank roughly shoved the door forward. It was barely enough for him to slip by, yet he did all the same, with Jack following quickly behind. Marie was the last one in, violently wrenching the door out so she could shove her massive frame through. A few rogue bolts slammed into the steel door as she darted past, blows she was glad to have missed. Her back already hurt like hell, and pulling out those bolts wasn't going to be much fun.

Past the door, they found themselves in a lovely white chamber, filled with flickering candles and trimmed with gold along the ceiling. There, in the center of the room, was a large cage over a marble podium. Resting atop the podium was a golden piece of parchment, rolled tightly and sealed with an emblem that quite resembled a shoe. They already suspected this cage was enchanted as well; it was clear from the slight glow gleaming in its polished surface. Thankfully, this much they'd expected.

"Frank, you may want to hurry." Jack was peering out through the hole in the wall that had once been a door. "I think there were more stairs leading up here, because it sounds like the guards are on our floor."

"Moving as quickly as I can." Frank had produced another pouch with a wick, and was measuring it against the gaps in the cage's bars. Reaching the parchment was impossible; it was too far away even if the gaps had been large enough for a hand to slip past. But Acorn hadn't hired them merely to take the parchment. He wanted it destroyed, and that was a much simpler task to accomplish. Frank poured some of the powder from the sack into another bag, shrinking the size of the first pouch. He gave it a test shove and found it able to pass through a gap in the bars, then motioned for Marie. "If you don't mind, I'll need a boost."

Keenly aware of the sound of approaching guards, Marie leapt over, picking up Frank by the waist and holding him directly over the top of the cage. Frank angled the pouch carefully, moving slowly even as he held his flint and steel device near the wick. One spark, and the wick was burning. With a few minor adjustments, Frank let go of the pouch, which fell cleanly through the bars and landed with a satisfying *plop* onto the podium, directly next to the parchment.

Marie didn't bother to set Frank down. She ran to the corner of the room still holding him by the waist. When the explosion came moments later, she'd pulled him in close and once more put her back between Frank and danger. The few marble shards that were sent flying missed her, though a couple did leave dents in a nearby wall. Turning around, she found the cage looking largely untouched despite the fractured podium and burning remains of the parchment within. That was the trouble with going for ambiance over functionality; a sturdy lock-box with the same enchantment would have provided a far greater challenge.

The guards were nearly there; footsteps seemed to be thundering all around them. Then, Marie realized she could hear another sound, louder than the guards'. Cheering, crying, shouts of joy, these noises were rising up from all through the mansion. Throughout the town, actually. All of the captured tinker elves were suddenly discovering that their bonds were cut. The contract was destroyed, and with it their servitude.

A slight pop drew her attention as Acorn appeared in front of Frank, far less wary than he had been at their first meeting. "Did it! You did it!" Acorn waved his arm around, showing the absence of the golden circle. "Elves free! Thank you, scary man. Thank you!"

"Of course. We always uphold our bargains," Frank replied. "Speaking of, I believe you and I have another." From his robe, Frank produced a single gold coin, which he tossed to Acorn. "Payment upon request, as agreed. I assume our terms are still amenable?"

"Far less than we'd normally charge for such a task. Far less." Acorn held the piece of gold in his small hands briefly before it vanished from sight. "But pleasure, oh such pleasure, we shall take, that makes up for the cost." Like the gold before, Acorn vanished.

Marie could still hear him though, he and the other tinker elves laughing and cheering mirthfully from out in the halls. As their joy came, so too did myriad sounds from the guards. Cries of confusion and shock, along with the sound of rivets being torn out, strings being snapped, and seams getting ripped. By the time she managed to look out the door, quite a sight was waiting for her.

To a man, the guards' equipment had been completely broken apart. Armor, weapons, even all but the most essential of clothing had been scattered to pieces along the ground. The charging warriors were suddenly stripped near naked, a revelation made all the more terrifying as Jack, Frank, and Marie stepped out from the chamber, weapons perfectly intact.

A few brave souls raised their fists and put on looks of grim determination, but Frank stepped forward before they could do anything truly foolish. “Gentlemen, as you have just seen, the tinker elves are now free. On top of that, they are going to tear this entire mansion apart just as they have your gear. You currently have two options: stay, fight us, and die, or run for all you’re worth before the building comes down.”

At Frank’s words, the roof began to groan, and several walls let out snapping cracks that in no way boded well for the structural integrity of the mansion. Between getting stripped of their weapons, seeing three armed opponents, and the sounds of snapping wood, the guards all decided that their pay wasn’t nearly enough for this level of risk. The first one broke into a run, back down the hall toward whatever set of stairs they’d taken up, and that was all it took for the rest to follow.

Marie didn’t give chase. Instead she tucked Frank under one arm and Jack beneath the other, then took a ferocious leap across the wrecked section of stairs. She cleared it easily, slamming hard into the wall on the other side and leaving a sizable dent in the wood. They didn’t pause to admire her handiwork; instead, she set her friends down and together the three raced as fast as they could down the remaining floors.

Occasionally, they would see more guards, also surrounded by broken equipment, though none bothered to challenge them. Dust rained from the ceilings and cracks were crawling up the walls; it was plain for anyone to see that escape was the top priority of those who wished to live.

They soon reached the bottom floor, where Marie was surprised to notice that the tinker elves had even taken apart the equipment on the corpses she’d knocked over the railing. Credit to them, they were nothing if not thorough. Together, the trio joined the exodus of guards running for their lives, bolting through the front entrance into the lovely cloudless night they’d left behind.

What awaited them was so surprising that Marie almost slowed for a moment. The wall around the mansion, much like the guards’ equipment, had been taken apart at impossible speeds. What was more striking, however, was the shoe shop/museum they’d climbed less than an hour ago. That building was not in pieces; instead it had been engulfed in flames. The whole structure was burning fiercely, lighting up the night like a fiery beacon.

“Was that part of the bargain?” Jack asked.

Frank shook his head. “No. I think that’s a message from the tinker elves to the town that captured them. Perhaps we should keep running until we hit the forest. Something tells me they may have more messages to send.”

Marie wasn't going to dispute that, especially when she needed a quiet place to have the crossbow bolts yanked out of her before she turned back to her human form. Jack silently agreed as well, as all three of them picked up the pace, racing to be clear of town before anyone was entirely sure what had happened.

It was, in truth, their preferred method of leaving a city.

* * *

By the time the sun rose, Marie was back in human form. Frank had pulled the bolts out as carefully as he could, though they still hurt like hell on the way out. Thankfully, her beast form healed quickly; within an hour she was well enough to be normal Marie once more. While they'd been tempted to ride away as quickly as possible, Frank informed them that he and Acorn had a meeting scheduled at dawn. Given the sounds and fires they were hearing from back in Sagan, it seemed wise to make sure they parted with the tinker elves on good terms.

Just as the sky was lighting up with sunshine, Acorn appeared, tumbling down from a tree once more before catching himself on a long branch. "Is done. Is done. No more cages. No more tinker elves held. All free. All free, thanks to you." He dipped his head in a deep, formal bow, which Marie and Frank both returned.

"We owed a debt, and we always pay our debts," Jack said. "To be clear, though, this settles the matter on Marie's clothing?"

"Yes! Many times yes! You paid debt to tinker elves and more. When you come back, you ask for Acorn. I make sure you get goods at friend price."

"Get goods? Acorn, it sounded like you wrecked the whole town last night. Are there even any merchants left?" Marie asked.

Acorn shook his head. "None! Drove them out we did. No blood, no blood, just took apart everything we made, and many things we didn't. But we like town, and we like gold, so we keep making. Only now, we work for us." He was beaming with joy at the revelation, grinning so widely he could have been mistaken for a cousin of Jack's.

"You'll forgive me for bringing up a sore memory, but I feel I should ask: what about the shoemaker? He knows how to trap and bind you; it's entirely possible he might come back to reclaim his town," Frank said.

The grin on Acorn's face faded slightly, and he broke off eye contact. "Shoemaker is danger, yes, but no threat. Can't bind or trap without materials, and he get none. We not break *everything* in town. Jail and cells still strong. No blood. We not killers. But fair is fair. We made him many shoes. Now he makes the same number for us."

A slight chuckle arose from Jack. "Fitting. The shoemaker is trapped making shoes. I like it. You've got a fun side, Acorn. If you ever want to go on a journey, I'm sure we could find uses for someone of your talents."

"Thank you! Will think over later. For now, tinker elves need me. Acorn has been elected mayor." Acorn tapped his chest proudly. "Maybe talk when you come back. For now though, you go. Much work to do, and tinker elves not all want to see humans yet. Safer to leave."

"We were planning to do just that," Marie assured him.

"Then I leave too. Much work. Much work to do. Ride safe, and come back soon. Just not too soon." Acorn leapt up from his branch, back into the leaves, and vanished from sight.

Since the discussion seemed to be over, everyone went about mounting onto their horses and preparing for the day's ride. They were just about to set out when Jack cast a lingering glance back toward Sagan.

"This might be one of the only towns that gave us a happy goodbye and invited us back, and it's a town we more or less destroyed. Does that mean we should wreck more places if we want to be welcomed upon our return?"

"An interesting proposal, though one I'm not eager to test," Frank replied. "If you'd like to try it with Summerly, perhaps we can see if there are any subjugated elves to free there."

Jack kept looking back to Sagan for a few moments, then finally turned toward the road ahead. "No, not Summerly. We'll find plenty of strange things there, but we won't find tinker elves."

"Going to give us any more than that?" Marie asked.

"Wasn't planning on it." Jack met her eyes and flashed that endless damn smile, thankfully without the sour tinge they'd seen on it before stopping in Sagan. "At this point, I'm resolved to what's coming next. Still, no reason to ruin the fun of a perfectly good surprise."

The Tale of What Was Left Behind

Neither Marie nor Frank was quite prepared for what awaited them as they rode into Summerly. Marie's best wager was that it was a town Jack had previously swindled, where the mere sight of him would cause alarms to sound and citizens to gather as they tried to hang him in the street. The only problem with such a theory was that they'd already been in towns where that happened, and Jack had never been bothered by the idea of visiting any of them the way Summerly had unnerved him. Frank, on the other hand, was playing a different kind of odds. He suspected that Jack had accidentally spawned a family here during one of his trysts, and was eager to stay away from any potential offspring.

Ultimately, neither was proven right, though Frank was technically closer to the mark, even if it seemed the victory would go to Marie at first.

As they began riding past farms, and then small cottages, Marie saw the people of Summerly out and about. Many were farmers, toiling hard in the fields, yet she noticed that the children were being allowed to play rather than help with the work. Summerly must be a prosperous place or a lax one, if children weren't needed to help their parents in the fields. It was at these farms that she and Frank received their first clue, as the people started waving as they saw Jack ride in, some even racing over from the fields to their homes and raising a ruckus to alert those inside. More people poured out, but not to try to tear Jack from his horse. No, they were…waving to him. A few even seemed to be cheering.

For his part, Jack merely smiled and waved back, even as he seemed to sink deeper into his saddle. Curious as the incident was, what made it all the stranger was how many times Marie watched it play out again and again. Every farm they passed, every cottage they rode by, people were clamoring to see and greet Jack. As they drew nearer to the town proper, word had apparently spread, as citizens were waiting along the road to joyfully cheer Jack's arrival.

"This is peculiar." Frank had a real talent for understatement sometimes. Marie had seen a lot of reactions to Jack, but celebration was a new one. Even when they were helping clients, those people tended to be more afraid of the devil they'd made a deal with than thankful for the aid. Yet there was no terror in this group, no fearful glances being exchanged, only wild enthusiastic happiness at seeing Jack ride into town. It was a mystery, albeit a short-lived one.

"Agreed. I feel as if I'm back in a parade procession, there's so much waving and cheering," Marie said.

"Oh, yes, the people are behaving strangely for certain. But I was referring to that." Frank pointed toward what looked to be the town square. Marie squinted hard, yet all she could see was a lump of yellow metal in the middle. "You should be able to make it out soon."

In fact, it took another several minutes of slow riding before Marie could see what was in the town square. If not for Frank's warning that it was stranger than the people, she very well may have tumbled from her steed at the sight. For there was a gold-painted statue showing a younger, slightly more serious-looking Jack, as he stood atop the belly of what she assumed was a not-to-scale giant. It shouldn't have been so surprising; they both knew he'd had adventures before meeting Frank. Yet the idea of Jack making a good enough impression on people that they would build a statue of him seemed as mad as Jack himself.

"I think I understand now." Marie rode a touch closer to Jack, so she could keep her voice low around the crowd. "You came through here when you were younger, not quite so…*you*…and saved these people from a giant, right?"

"More or less," Jack replied.

From the crowd on the street, a burly man muscled his way forward, pushing himself dangerously close to the path of the horses and clapping Jack on the leg. "You bastard! You couldn't be bothered to send word ahead? Your mother is going to be right pissed that we didn't have time to make you a proper welcome feast."

Marie started coughing in shock, while Frank made a strange series of noises in his throat that she felt relatively certain humans weren't supposed to be capable of. Deep down they both knew that Jack had come from the coupling of a man and a woman, but it was hard not to imagine him dropping fully formed into the world, a grin on his lips and blood on his blades. Marie's shock turned to annoyance as she glared at Jack.

"More or less?"

"Less *was* an option," Jack pointed out. "And you weren't that far off. The only part you got wrong was about me passing through Summerly, and even that's open to interpretation. If you look at the first part of my life the way I do, as one long stopover, then I was indeed merely passing through."

"Jack's hometown." Frank was whispering under his breath, and it didn't seem entirely intentional. "So much to learn. So much to understand. We should start checking the local supply of water to see if there's any mercury or curses in it."

"Or we could find the Blue Fairy's next message and be on our way." Jack turned back to the man by the horse and leaned down, slapping him gently on the shoulder. "Benjamin, would you do me a grace and run ahead to tell my mother, as well as her caretaker, that I've arrived and I'm bringing guests?"

"There's little chance word hasn't reached her cottage by now," Benjamin told him.

"All the same, I would appreciate if you made sure they were properly prepared."

Benjamin looked up at Jack for a moment before giving a sharp nod. "Of course. Anything for you and your friends." The burly gentleman began muscling his way back through the crowd, which soon parted, and then he broke into a brisk jog as he headed through the town.

Although he certainly hadn't meant to, Jack's interaction had apparently opened the floodgates, as the townsfolk nearby surged forward to greet him, shake his hand, and occasionally hold a child or baby for him to meet. Marie and Frank allowed themselves to be pushed out, leading their horses carefully through the crowd and into the town square.

It was here that Marie again noticed the wealth of Summerly. While it was certainly no great kingdom's city, there were more niceties here than rightfully should be. They'd been through many a farming village like this one; usually the buildings were thatched just to the point of working and the roads were so torn a wagon risked a wheel with every journey. Here, however, everything was well-kept. There were no ostentatious or out-of-place elements like magical street lanterns. What gave away the prosperity was the simple lack of concern reflected in the faces of the people who lived here. They weren't worried, their children could play, they could take a day off from the fields to greet a returning town hero; none of these would be the case in a less stable town.

"If you're wondering whether or not Jack has been sending money here, I'm uncertain." It was the first thing Frank had said since they'd left Jack with the crowd, and it confirmed Marie's own suspicions quite well. "I know he'll occasionally stash some or have it magically transported away, but where it goes is beyond my knowledge. Jack keeps his secrets well, even from those he trusts."

"This entire morning has proven that." Marie looked again at the statue of Jack and the beaten giant. Whoever had made it did a fine job; the work was of a high quality. Yet they hadn't quite managed to capture Jack's face properly. He looked triumphant, and happy, both of which were fine feelings after conquering a giant, but the sculptor had failed to etch the hunger in his eyes, the gleam of adventure on the horizon. Jack was never as content as his statue, not so far as she or Frank could tell. Proud, happy, celebratory, all of these things and more, just not content. Part of Jack was always looking to the road ahead, wondering what the next job would have in store. "Do you think we'll get any clues as to what makes Jack…Jack?"

"Do these people seem as if they have the slightest idea what sort of man they're cheerfully greeting?"

The crowd around Jack had swollen, and someone had thrust a baby in his arms. He was grinning as always, beaming really, yet Marie knew him well enough to trace the annoyed twists at the ends of his lips that betrayed how little joy he was getting.

"No. Not at all. But perhaps he was different before. Perhaps being here will give us some insight into who Jack was before all the adventure."

"Perhaps," Frank echoed. "Although I have my doubts. I have traveled with Jack for many a year, and I have seen him do many a strange thing. But change, change does not come naturally to Jack. I can't help but wonder if the Jack they celebrate ever existed in the first place, or if he struck out on his own to no longer hide who he truly was."

* * *

It took more than an hour for the crowd to disperse. Eventually, someone made their way over to offer Marie and Frank refreshments, which they both accepted. This was the kind of day that would go smoother with a drink. Finally, Benjamin came riding into town on a dark mare and forced apart the crowd, insisting it was time for Jack to see his mother. The crowd was surprisingly respectful, clearing out so that Jack, Benjamin, and Jack's friends could head off.

More people waved to them from the road on their short ride, but the numbers thinned out as they grew further from town. The road led them upward, over a series of increasingly tall hills, until they crested one and found themselves staring at a large building that wasn't quite an estate, yet wasn't as far from one as they might have expected. It was a tall white stone building with what appeared to be a hovel of a shed in the back, sitting atop one of the lower hills so that only the top portion peeked over. While that no doubt limited the views, it also made the place harder to spot unless one knew what to look for. Several people were working the grounds, all of them greeting Jack and Benjamin on sight. Summerly was so friendly that Marie found it off-putting, especially after so many years riding with Jack. True, she might have been greeted with fanfare if she returned home, but part of her wondered if it would have the level of sincerity these people were showing to Jack.

Once the horses were put away in the spacious barn, they entered the house and found the inside even nicer than the exterior. Again, it was not overt luxury, merely that every piece of the home looked either new or well cared for. There was wealth here, along with a desire not to display too much of it. Frank and Marie's inspection of the home's interior was short-lived, though, as they were almost instantly distracted by a woman with dark, graying hair darting forward and wrapping Jack in an impressive hug. She squeezed him tightly, and to their surprise Jack wrapped an arm around and hugged her back. It wasn't that Jack never showed physical affection, more that he tended only to use it as one of many charming tools when bedding a barmaid.

"No warning? Not even a letter telling me you were bringing guests?" The woman pulled back, looking Jack in the eye. "I know you were raised better than that."

Jack hung his head, not quite daring to break eye contact. "Sorry, Mother. Our trip has been rather harrying. I only found out recently that we would be passing through here."

"Passing through? Nonsense, I'll hear none of that. Unless the kingdom is burning down around us I'm sure you can make time for a few days to visit and catch up. It's been a long time since you were last here." Finally breaking away from her son, the woman turned to Frank and Marie with an assessing gaze that was oddly familiar, until they realized how many times they'd seen the same expression on Jack's face.

"You two must be his friends. My name is Flora; it's a pleasure to meet you both. I do hope my son hasn't made too much trouble for you." She took a hand from both of them and squeezed. Both braced for her realization that Frank's was too cold, too pale, and too scarred to be natural, but it didn't come. Flora merely stood there, waiting for her greeting to be returned.

"The pleasure is ours," Marie said at last. "Please call me Marie."

"And I'm known as Frank."

"Marie and Frank, no surnames?" Flora asked. "Or are you like my boy, leaving his name behind, as if the Spriggins clan weren't good enough for him?"

While Marie was trying to figure out how to hide howling laughter at the revelation of Jack's surname, Frank seized control of the situation. "In our line of work, surnames pose a liability. If the allies of the wicked people we stop were to know the names of our families, then they could strike at them. So we forsake the pride of our surnames, in order to protect the others who wear them."

"I see. So you're the charming one of the group." Flora released their hands and patted Frank on the shoulder before looking to Marie. "I take it that means you're my son's lover? Or perhaps wife? It's certainly been long enough for him to have taken one."

Whatever mirth Marie felt at the uncovering of Jack's name evaporated instantly as she began to scour her mind for a way to tactfully explain to this mother all the reasons Jack would never make a suitable mate for her, if anyone. Ultimately, she decided to forgo the explanation and hope Flora accepted the truth at face value.

"No, madam, Jack and I are merely colleagues who work together, just like he and Frank."

"Ah, I see." Flora leaned in and whispered conspiratorially. "So you're in love with him but have yet to win his heart. Don't worry dear, he's a stubborn lad but eventually he can be brought around. Although it wouldn't hurt you to don a proper dress and perhaps put in some effort with your hair."

Marie was lost for how to respond, and thankfully another voice interrupted the awkward discussion before things could progress further. This voice was lighter than any of the others, with a musical quality even though it wasn't singing outright. At just the sound of it, Marie felt some of her tension ease, as though she'd just slid into a warm bath.

"Jack Spriggins. From across lands and seas and kingdoms unknown, you return to us at last. What an honor we have been bestowed with." The voice's owner entered the room, held by Benjamin. It was a harp speaking, golden and lovely with the carving of a woman on one side. Her metal eyes took in all of them, lingering on Frank and Marie particularly, before settling on Jack himself. "And you brought vagrants, what a thoughtful present."

"Be kind, Goldie. These are my friends you insult, and I've grown no more patient of that than I was when I left." Jack's grin was wider now, and for the first time since they'd arrived some of the usual ruffian was poking through the happy facade.

The harp looked at them once more, then managed a half bow. "My apologies. When I saw you both, I assumed you were bandits who'd waylaid Jack and forced him to lead you here so you could rob us. Clearly I was mistaken, and I meant no ill intent."

While it was technically an apology, both Frank and Marie noted that Goldie had managed to insult them more during it. This was Jack's home, though, so rather than making an issue of it they both nodded acceptance.

"Goldie, my mother seems a bit flustered at the suddenness of my arrival. Perhaps you should take her into the parlor and play for her before dinner." Jack suggested. "My *friends* and I haven't come to Summerly by accident. We're on the trail of someone we think might have passed through here, and I'd like to go speak with the townsfolk more before evening."

"Well, that sounds like a glorious waste of time," Goldie replied. "But before you go off accepting the accolades of the town for your great deed, perhaps you could be bothered to go out to the site of The Fall. Something strange has been on the wind from that direction for the last few weeks. Something…magical."

Frank and Marie exchanged a brief glance; this certainly seemed like the sort of breadcrumb the Blue Fairy would leave on their trail. Near enough to Jack's home that he wouldn't miss it, yet insubstantial enough that the risk of others finding whatever she'd left behind was minimal. As they contemplated the idea, Benjamin began to walk both Flora and Goldie out to the other room. The harp craned its neck to yell one last parting greeting before she was gone.

"And even if it turns out to be nothing, you should still go. Paying your respects is the least you can bother with after what you did."

Then she was gone, leaving the trio alone for the first time in hours. Jack stared at the doorway for several seconds before shaking his head. "That harp is rude and petty, but she's not a liar. We should head that way now, before the sun starts to set. I don't want to find anything the Blue Fairy may have left after dark."

"What is this 'site of The Fall'?" Marie asked.

Jack hesitated, a rare action for him, before responding. "Trust me; you'll know it when you see it."

* * *

The ride was brief, though solitary. No more houses or farms awaited them. Gone were the smiling crowds and cheerful waves. From the moment they left Jack's house, there was nothing but more empty hills, all covered with the same soft grass that coated the land like a rug. It was strange, at first, since despite the inclines this land looked perfectly suitable for farming. Then they crested a small series of hills and Jack's words were proven true: they did indeed know that they'd arrived at the site. And both Marie and Frank understood instantly why these lands were deserted. Villagers were, as a whole, a superstitious lot. They spit in their shoes to ward off rain, spun around three times if a crop wasn't growing, and spoke only in whispers when passing near a graveyard. So of course they wouldn't set up farms or homes in this area.

It would mean a lifetime of whispers.

While the dirt piled atop the massive mound had grown grass—albeit a yellower, less lush variety than what surrounded them—it was still unmistakable as anything other than a grave. Assuming one could call it a grave when the land around had been dug up to toss onto a corpse rather than to lower the dead into the ground. It was an understandable compromise; the size of the hole needed for such a ceremony would have taken weeks to dig. Even the fact that the giant was properly covered spoke to a monumental task.

Jack rode slowly, his smile taking on a distant, wistful quality. As they made their way around the mound, toward what could only be assumed was its front, he turned his eyes up to the fluffy white clouds dotting the sky. "These lands used to be barren. Just hard dirt with a few spots that barely managed to grow even a single sack of potatoes. The villagers make a big deal out of the bag of gold I came back with, and Goldie, and the goose more than anything, but it was actually the beanstalk that did the most good. When I chopped it down, it released some manner of seeds or spores into the air, and the stalk was so tall they spread for miles. The new grass took root and revitalized the soil. Within a year, you could throw away an apple and come back to find a tree sprouting from the seeds. No surprise, really; the beanstalk was magical after all."

"Beanstalk…giant… I've heard this tale." Giants were not entirely uncommon across the magical kingdoms; however, there were only so many that were also tethered to skyward stalks. Marie had heard of such a foe on their journey, though the details had apparently been lost in the gossip process. "You're the boy who climbed a beanstalk, lured down the evil giant that was terrorizing his people, and then chopped it out from under him so that he fell to his death."

"Is that how it goes these days?" Jack looked to the sky once more. "I am that boy, yes, in that I killed the giant we're walking past. But he wasn't terrorizing us; we didn't even know he was up there. I'll spare you the long version; suffice it to say I came into possession of some magical beans, planted them, and the beanstalk grew into the clouds. Of course I climbed it, you both know me well enough by now to assume that, and when I arrived I found a castle large enough for a giant, which was a good fit for the one already living there. I snuck in, saw some gold, and being both poor and me, I took it. Then I went back for more and found Goldie. She asked to be taken down too, wanting to see the world below the clouds, and even instructed me on where to find a goose that laid golden eggs and a…well, the goose was enough to sell me on it. I took them both, but the goose made a racket and the giant gave chase. When I hit the ground, he climbed after me, so I took an axe and chopped the magical beanstalk down. As you can see, the fall was a bit much even for a giant."

"That makes you sound more like a thief and a killer than the hero of a town," Frank noted. It wasn't exactly a kind response, but it was honest, and Frank often took the latter route over the former.

"I was," Jack agreed. "Any way you look at it, I was the villain in that tale. Yet because of my selfish actions, I was able to reinvigorate my village. The goose eggs were sold off and the funds used for necessities like town repairs and food until the land started growing once more. We also bred the goose as much as possible. Its children didn't consistently give the same huge, golden eggs, but they'll lay a gold egg in about every ten. Enough to pad our coffers, just in case. You're still right, Frank; this was theft and murder, outright. But it also was the day I realized that sometimes doing bad things can lead to good ends."

If the Bastard Champions had bothered with a motto, that likely would have been the best choice. All of them had done things that, perhaps while not outright evil, certainly danced along the edges more closely than any moral person should. Neither Marie nor Frank felt qualified to judge Jack for what he'd done to this giant, especially knowing he was merely a poor farm boy when it happened. It didn't redeem him or exonerate him, but then again Jack had never seemed to care about either of those concepts. He was what he was, he did what he did, and the Narrative was welcome to stop him, if it could manage.

Silence fell as they continued their ride, making their way around the huge hill that was the giant's corpse until Jack motioned for them to slow. Dismounting, they walked near the edge of the mound, where several stones could be seen sticking up from the ground.

"Robbing and killing him was bad enough. It felt like I at least owed him a proper burial." Jack pointed to the first headstone, where a short inscription was clearly visible.

"Here lies Fee-Fi, a giant." Frank lifted an eyebrow as he read, and turned to Jack. "Fee-fi?"

"I didn't know his name, neither did Goldie, and the goose couldn't talk. So I went with something he said a few times. If the scarcity of words didn't give it away, I was working with limited information."

Marie had wandered over to the next headstone, this one much smaller. "Here lies Hortense, a good friend and a savior of Summerly. Who was Hortense?"

"The goose," Jack replied. "Geese can live for a while, but Hortense was already an adult when I stole her, so she eventually passed away. No one wanted to eat a creature that had given us so much, and the town decided to bury her out here with her original owner. I think they might have been trying to appease the giant's spirit by returning one of his possessions."

Frank ran his hand along the goose's headstone, his left eye examining it carefully. "I can understand the sentimentality, but why the name?"

That question earned him a shrug from Jack. "We let my mother name the goose. She can be...peculiar, at times."

After their first meeting with Flora, neither Frank nor Marie was going to contradict Jack. Instead, they continued examining the area, searching for a clue the Blue Fairy might have left behind. There was nothing on the headstones, but when Frank turned his attention to the goose's grave he noticed something with his dragon eye.

"Strange. There's movement here." Pale hands pressed on the top of the grave, touching the grass without disturbing it. "Something is forming, rising, from within the soil."

"She wouldn't...raise the goose, would she?" Marie asked. "I didn't think fairies could work magic on the dead; only witches and wizards can."

"It's imprudent to assume someone as powerful as the Blue Fairy has any domain that is out of her grasp, but I don't think the magic at work is as deep as the corpse." Frank was barely inches from the ground now, in danger of taking a blade of grass to the iris. "What I can see is close, and it's growing upward, not down."

A breeze whipped across the grasslands, causing the blades to ripple in an emerald wave. Jack hunkered down next to Frank, resting a gentle hand on Hortense's headstone. "How long until it forms?"

"Not very," Frank said. "Given the rate of movement and the time of day, plus what we know about fairies and theatrics, I'd wager we'll see whatever this is by sunset. Fairies love dusk and dawn."

"Magic coming from an area I'd know, near enough for Goldie to notice it, and tucked away in a spot only someone like Frank could see. I'm getting a little uncomfortable with how well the Blue Fairy seems to know us and what we can do."

"We knew the risks when we started chasing her," Marie reminded him. "At least so far she hasn't left a trap for us, although if she were going to, this is the perfect time. We're out here alone, no cover, no plan, only our wits and skills to keep us alive if she tries something."

"Good point." Jack's smile brightened as he leaned back and took a seat in the grass. "I was starting to get bored, but this does bring up the potential for some fun. Very well, I suppose we've got no other choice. We wait for sunset and go from there."

In the hour that followed, they got comfortable and spent time distracting themselves from the ticking clock that was the setting sun. Jack polished his blades, Frank read, and Marie paced about sniffing the air to make sure an ambush wasn't approaching. It was a rare moment of forced quiet, and while none of them would have elected to have it, they all appreciated the downtime.

Finally, as the sun was half-obscured by the horizon, movement came from Hortense's grave. The dirt rippled, and from among the soil something new began to grow. It was crisp green, with a soft glow, as it stretched up from the grass until it was two feet high. Then a red tip appeared, expanding rapidly until it was clear what they were seeing. A rose was blooming, tall and soft and bright as blood. Marie let out a barely muffled gasp, but said nothing. The rose was still changing, shifting, as it reached full maturity. A petal fell, vanishing into light when it hit the ground, then another, and another. Within a minute the rose was down to its final petal, and when that too broke away the stem withered instantly, turning back to the dirt from which it had come. The petal drifted down slowly, wafting on the breeze until it hit the ground and vanished in a final flash of red.

"If that was some sort of death threat, it may very well be the third most lovely one I've ever received," Jack said, breaking the spell of silence they'd cast upon themselves.

Frank shook his head. "I'm not sure if it was a threat at all. It seemed more like a message, though as to what it was meant to convey I confess I'm at a loss."

"It was a message." Marie's voice was thick, her eyes blazing yellow as she visibly worked to push away her inner beast. "Directions, in a way. The Blue

Fairy is telling us that we need to head further north, to Villeneuve. Or, as it's commonly called, the Kingdom of the Roses."

"Where do I know that name from?" Realization hit moments after, and Jack looked back at Marie. "Right…that's your kingdom, isn't it?" She gave merely a nod in reply, perhaps because her tongue was in a state of shift, or because she simply didn't have words to offer.

While Jack hunkered down to see if there were any tangible signs left behind in the soil, Frank walked over and put a careful hand on Marie's shoulder. "If you're not ready, we needn't go. There are other leads to follow, other fairies to chase, other jobs to take. With more time and effort, it's possible that we could manage to meet her on our terms, rather than hers."

It was tempting, oh so very tempting, to let Frank talk her into turning away from the path before them. He was right; there wasn't technically any rush to follow her. They had things well in control at the moment. Marie could nod, and they would ride off to another town with more jobs to take. More adventures to be had. More time to learn, grow, and prepare for how to deal with the Blue Fairy. They could go back to the way things were, the fun and frantic pace of their lives with little more to worry about than how they'd survive the next task. All she had to do was nod.

"No." Marie spat the word, forcing her tongue back into action. "Look at how these messages were sent, Frank. We end up on a job that just *happens* to have a lead to the Blue Fairy, following the trail of a rider I'm not sure ever even existed until we're far enough north to reach her bread crumbs. The first one was left with a creature brought to life and turned human, which involved saving children in need. The second is in Jack's literal backyard, tied to a piece of his past, and it's sending us to *my* kingdom. She knows us. She knows what we want, what we care about, and what we wouldn't want to lose. These are more than messages; they're *warnings*. Everything we love, she knows about. Do you really imagine that to be a coincidence?"

There was no reply from Frank, but as Jack stood he chimed in. "Marie is right. We either go to Villeneuve, or we ready ourselves for consequences. Fairies have pulled innocent people into their schemes before, and no one ever knows what the Blue Fairy is going to do from one moment to the next. We started this, we were the ones hunting her, and she may not have cared for that. Either way, it's on us to finish this. The Bastard Champions never back down from a job, especially one that we've given ourselves."

"Very well," Frank said. "In the morning then?"

Marie and Jack both agreed. This was the sort of journey that demanded rest before undertaking. Together, the three walked back to their horses, then mounted up and rode for Jack's house.

* * *

"But you just got here!" Flora's eyes flashed as she dropped her ladle into the pot where she'd been cooking a thick stew. Jack's news that he would be leaving in the morning had not gone over well, to say the least. While Benjamin had seemed saddened, Jack's mother went in another direction, turning to anger like a spin of her heel. "Surely there can't be anything so pressing that you need to go already. Stay a week, catch up with everyone, spend some time with your mother. There's no telling how many years I have left, you know."

"Mother, I told you when we arrived I was just passing through. We're on a trail right now, and every day we lose here means it grows colder." It didn't escape Marie's or Frank's notice that Jack's explanation had neatly darted over whether or not he actually *wanted* to stay. "I'm sorry, but we have to ride on in the morning."

Flora stared at her son, then turned to the stew pot on the stove. "So be it." With a single strike, she knocked the pot to the ground, sending brown liquid and chunks of partly cooked meat spreading across the floor. "I wanted to make a meal for my son and his friends, not travelers treating my home as a way station. Feed yourselves, vagrants."

Jack looked at the slop that was sloshing onto his boots and let out a tired sigh. "Goldie, if you don't mind."

"Of course." The harp's melody started up without warning, sharp and brisk and lovely all at once. As it played, everyone save for Frank felt themselves grow more at ease, tension falling out of them as the strains filled the air. Flora was affected strongest of all, the rage in her face shifting to confusion as she looked at the mess around them.

"Oh dear, what happened?" Flora spoke as though she hadn't just sent the stew to the floor.

"An accident, Mother, just an accident." Gingerly, Jack took her by the shoulder and led her over to where Goldie and Benjamin sat. "I'll clean it up, and we'll go fetch dinner from the market. Why don't you let Goldie play for you until then?"

Flora's eyes fluttered, her expression oddly serene. "That does sound lovely, but I don't want to be rude to our guests."

"We'll all visit over dinner," Jack assured her. "Until then, you just relax."

Rising from the table, Benjamin hefted up the harp as it continued to play, leading Flora out of the kitchen. Once they were gone, Jack grabbed a rag from a nearby cupboard and set about trying to wipe up an entire pot's worth of stew. After a few seconds, Frank made his way over to the cupboard and removed more rags, offering one to Marie.

"Thanks, but you two needn't bother. I can handle this," Jack said, smile unwavering. "It's my fault. I knew the news might upset her and I didn't properly ready myself."

"At least let me run to the market for dinner," Marie suggested. "We *will* need to eat."

After a brief consideration, Jack nodded his agreement. Marie didn't give him a chance to change his mind, heading out the door before he started insisting that he do that as well. For his part, Frank did what he often did when Jack said things he didn't care for: Frank ignored the words entirely. He stooped down, dipping a rag into the brown mess and herding it back toward the pot.

They worked in silence for several minutes, wringing their rags out into a bucket frequently. The only sound besides the shifting of liquid was the occasional strains of harp music drifting in from across the house.

"It's not her fault." Jack's words came suddenly, yet Frank wasn't surprised. He'd been waiting for some form of conversation to start since the cleanup began. So he said nothing in reply, merely continuing to work and allowing Jack to speak at his own pace. "I mean it. She wasn't always like this. From the tales I've heard, she used to go on adventures, take on tasks of danger and excitement. Apparently some of it runs in the blood."

Jack paused to wring out his rag, casting more brown goop into the bucket. "And then her reach exceeded her grasp. She took on a fairy. Not her first, but this one was smarter or stronger than what she'd faced before. This was one of the five fairies of the colors, although I haven't been able to find out which one. Mother barely escaped, but not without paying a price for her ambition. Her mind was addled, cursed and warped, so that it was hard for her to stay focused or controlled. Brilliant tactic, really. Cut off a hand and the owner can replace it with a hook, remove a foot and a peg leg will still work, but if you scar the mind…there's no salve or replacement for that. Those wounds are eternal."

"Unless another, equally powerful fairy were to reverse it." Deep down, Frank had always wondered about Jack. He was off, clearly, and saw the world in a way that was strange to those around him. Yet he'd never seemed unhappy about his lot in life. If anything, Jack seemed to prefer his own mindset to what everyone else had. Here, seeing this display, Frank finally understood why his friend had been so willing to go along with the search for a powerful fairy. "You were never looking to cure yourself, were you? This has always been about her."

"Why would I want to cure myself? A little inherited madness has provided me with a far more interesting life than I could have ever achieved on my own." Bringing his rag back over, Jack rejoined the cleanup. "Hers is more terrible by far, and it only gets worse with each passing year. When I was young, she could still manage much of the time. Now the only thing that keeps her calm and centered is Goldie's music. Before we had her help… Suffice it to say there's a reason I was so willing to climb a beanstalk and explore an unknown land. Between home life with her and my father's promise of—"

The words cut off sharply, and for the barest of moments Frank could swear he saw Jack's grin falter, nearly vanishing entirely. They locked eyes, both keenly aware that something deeply personal had just slipped out by accident. Whether it was the effects of Goldie's song or the emotions of being home, Jack had mentioned his father for the first time in their entire friendship. Several long seconds slipped by, during which Frank wondered if Jack was about to flee or earnestly try to kill him, before Jack let out a short, sputtering laugh.

"Damn this place. And damn its effects on me. The sooner we're on the road, the better I'll feel. The damage is done though, and I suppose if it had to happen I'd rather you be the one to know. May as well see it through." Jack leaned in closer to Frank, his tone dropping below a whisper. "I'll tell you a secret, Frank, one I've never shared with another soul living or dead. I've always claimed that I got those beans by trading our cow away to a wandering merchant who told me they were magic. That's a lie. Even as a boy, I was never quite that foolish. The truth is that was just a cover story concocted by the man who actually gave me those beans. You see, on the road that day I met my father."

Frank had always assumed Jack's father had passed, since he never spoke of the man. This was stranger, yet somehow more fitting for the odd man that was Jack Spriggins.

"He told me that the beans were magic, and that they would lead me to riches untold. More than that, my father said they would lead me to my true inheritance. That giant was a collector of magical relics, as you may have guessed from the harp and the goose. He had another piece in his collection though, a relic that had once belonged to my father. Finding that was the real reason I climbed that beanstalk. Everything else was just a lovely bonus. And I think that's all I'd like to say on the matter tonight."

"Such is certainly your right," Frank concurred. "I won't pretend I'm not curious; however, we have lasted this long by respecting one another's boundaries. If you'll permit me a lone question though: that peculiar talent you have, is the relic part of it?"

"The biggest part," Jack confirmed. "Which is why I speak of it so rarely. The better a magic is understood, the easier it is to undo."

Tempting as it was to press on, Frank truly did respect Jack's privacy. It didn't ultimately matter what lay in his past, or what strange relics he'd owned over the years. Jack was one of only two people in the world Frank could trust without hesitation, and that was a far more relevant fact than any tidbits from the past.

Marie returned just as they were finishing wiping down the floor, clutching enough food to feed their number several times over. Evidently the shop keepers had refused to send a friend of Jack's back with anything less than a feast. Together, they all sat down at the table, joined soon by Benjamin, a soothed Flora, and a still softly strumming Goldie. It was a nicer meal than any had expected at the start of the evening, and one they allowed themselves to relish deeply.

* * *

The Bastard Champions rose well before sunrise. This was not a day for cheers and waving. They had a task set before them once again and haste was their ally. Although it would be impossible to slip past so many farms unnoticed, the hope was that they would at least be able to avoid turning their exit into another parade. Breakfast was a quick, quiet affair composed of leftovers from the night prior. Once they'd eaten, Marie and Frank headed out to saddle the horses, leaving Jack alone in his childhood home.

Jack stepped out from the main building, walking around to the small hovel that Marie and Frank had mistaken for a shed. In truth, this was the shack where Jack and his mother had lived before the beanstalk. She had been struggling to keep it together, and he was a mere boy who didn't yet understand the world or his place in it. When he'd financed the new house, with all its luxury and comforts, there had been a temptation to rip this place down. Burn it, and all the dark memories that lived here, into ash. Yet Jack, never one for sentimentality, had resisted the urge. He wanted this shack to endure, for days like these when he passed through. It was an important piece of where he came from, and what he wanted for himself.

Stepping in, Jack brushed off a dusty stool and took a seat. A deep breath of the musty air filled his lungs as he let himself be transported to days long since lost. It wasn't the poverty that was the worst of it, although that certainly hadn't made things better. Nor was it his mother's fraying grip on the world. No, what Jack hated most about this place and the time tied to it was the uncertainty. He hadn't known what to do to help her, or himself, or their situation as a whole. Jack had been lost, aimless, fractured in a way he could recognize yet wasn't able to articulate. As he sat, alone in that dark dusty pittance of a home, Jack did something he'd have never allowed to happen in public.

Jack stopped smiling.

There had been nothing to grin about here. Only desperation, fear, and tenuous strands of hope that snapped the minute he tried to grab them. The world he'd lived in then, the person he'd been, they were things he never wanted to go back to. But if you ran without looking back, it was easy to forget what you were running from. That was why Jack kept this building, why he stepped into it during every visit. Whenever fear or worry tried to rear their heads, Jack needed to cast his mind back to this hovel, to remember where those sorts of feelings led. Pain, mutilation, even true death were better options to him than ever going back to feeling this way.

Slowly, he rose from his stool and walked to the window, staring out in the direction of the giant's grave. So long ago, yet he could still remember that day. The pain of the beanstalk on his hands after hours of climbing, the beating of his heart as the giant searched for him, the sweat of his brow as he frantically chopped the beanstalk with all he had. In many ways, it was an awful experience. However, for Jack it would always be a positive moment in his life. That was the day he stopped being uncertain. Stopped being afraid. That was the day he finally understood what he was, and gained a glimmer of what he was meant for.

That was the day that Jack had found his smile. And as he stood at the window it crept across his face once more, taking its rightful position as guardian and keeper of all of Jack's secrets, be they bits of kindness or dark, terrible urges. Grin fixed in place once more, he walked out of the shack from the past and headed into the lovely home. Moving quietly, Jack made his way into his mother's room, where Goldie rested in the corner, soft sounds humming from her strings.

"She's resting," Goldie whispered.

"Good. I wasn't quite in the mood for a long goodbye." Jack stepped closer to his mother's bed, leaned down, and planted a single kiss atop her forehead. "Thank you, Goldie, for staying with her."

"You saved me from the giant. Waiting out the span of a single mortal life is a debt I can pay, even if I'd rather be out seeing the world. But you could come visit more often. She misses you. The entire town misses you."

"No, they don't." Jack moved away from his mother, back toward the door. "They miss a memory. A shadow. An idea of a man who never truly existed. If I stayed here, if they saw what I really am, it would tarnish that memory. I prefer that they, that she, at least have one version of me they can think upon pleasantly. I can't imagine she has many happy memories left."

"They slip slowly thanks to my song, yet they are still slipping," Goldie confirmed.

"Then let's not replace happy illusions with wicked truths. Watch over her for me, Goldie. Her, and the rest of Summerly. There are few towns like this in the lands, and I should know, I've been all over them. Places like this are special. They need to be protected, and nurtured. Kept safe from the darker truths of the world. From things like me."

He was out the door before she had a chance to reply, closing it soundlessly behind him. Jack lingered there for a moment, listening to the gentle sounds of the harp strings.

Before walking out the front door, Jack took a pouch of gold from his belt and set it on the kitchen table. Benjamin would be up soon, and the man deserved a bonus for all the work he did taking care of the place. With that done, Jack finally walked out the front door toward the stables, where Marie and Frank would be waiting for him.

Reconnecting with the past was well and good, but Jack's eyes naturally inclined toward the future. And on that horizon, he hoped there was still much adventure to see.

The Tale of the Silver-Tongued King

There were many ways to infiltrate a castle. One of Jack's favorites was dressing as a humble servant and slipping in with a crowd of actual workers. There was something delicious about using the nobles' tendency to not see the faces of their servants against them. Frank, on the other hand, liked to tuck himself into a barrel ostensibly filled with mead or supplies and allow others to haul him inside, a more achievable goal given his difficulty at blending in. Sometimes the entrances weren't quite as peaceful, involving lots of fighting or floating over a wall of thorns. But for all the strange methods they'd used to enter castles over their career, Marie had proposed one that was totally new for this occasion. It was a gambit so mad even Jack would have turned it down, were he not all too aware of Marie's true nature.

As the morning sun rose over the castle that sat in the heart of Villeneuve, three figures rode right up to the front gate. It was too early for merchants or deliveries to be calling upon the nobles, so the guards were already waiting as they drew closer. These were tense, serious men who, one could tell at a glance, were comfortable with drawing blood. Their armor was clean and polished, each displaying the kingdom's crest on his chest plate: a single red rose. Before the three riders were fully upon the gate, a loud voice rang out from the oldest of the guards.

"Halt, strangers! You are approaching the king's castle, and no trespassers are permitted past this point. Show us your hands so that we see you do not have bows or daggers to strike with, and then you may state your business."

Although there was some chuckling from one of the figures, the one with a visible grin on his face, all three complied. It was noted by a few of the guards that the rider further back was wearing dark leather gloves that ran down onto his forearms, into the robe that obscured most of his skin, but since those gloves weren't wrapped around a weapon it seemed of little consequence. Satisfied, the guard in charge motioned for them to approach closer.

"Your compliance is noted and appreciated. Now, quickly and concisely, state your business. There is much going on at the castle, and I warn you that we have little tolerance for wasting time. What brings you here?"

They were close enough now, time for Marie's plan to be put into action. Slowly reaching up, she took the sides of her hood and pulled it down, revealing her face for the first time since they'd ridden into these lands. Keeping her hidden hadn't been an easy task, yet it was one they all understood to be necessary. Had she been exposed, their approach would have been far more difficult. Throngs of screaming and cheering peasants didn't do much to aid speedy travel.

"What brings me to the castle? I wish to have a good meal and spend the night in my own bed. I have returned from my diplomatic training across the kingdoms, and would like to properly greet my parents."

There was a moment of dumbfounded silence as the guards all stared at her, lasting only until the head guard began to smack those nearest to him. Taking the hint quickly, they fell to their knees in succession, until all were kneeling with bowed heads before her. Only then did the guard speak once more. "Forgive me, princess. We knew you were approaching, but did not expect you to come in such humble attire. Had we realized it was you, we would have never spoken in such a manner."

"Rise, my guards. I will not chide you for treating suspicious characters appropriately. This garb was a necessity so that I could make my way home undisturbed." Marie paused for a moment as the guards got back to their feet, taking in what had been said. "Tell me, how did you know I was approaching? I sent no word ahead lest it be intercepted."

"I know not from whence the information came," the guard replied. "Only that a handful of days ago I was told to keep an eye out for the return of our princess, and that she might have strange men in tow with her." His eyes looked at Jack and Frank for the first time since Marie's hood had been pulled back. "Are they causing you any trouble, my princess?"

A flicker of a smirk flashed across Marie's face before vanishing. "Nothing of the sort. These men are mercenaries I found in my travels, swords for hire who ensured I stayed safe."

"I see." The guard bowed deeply, first to Frank, then to Jack. "We of Villeneuve thank you both deeply for your service in keeping our princess well. Your task is done; we of the royal guard will see her on from here."

"No." Marie nodded to both of them. "There are still accounts to settle, and I am uncertain whether this will be a short return or a permanent stay. I was sent away to learn, and if the king decides my education is not yet complete then it is my duty to travel once more. These men will stay with me until such time as I am sure they are no longer needed. Any who have issue with that may bring their problems to me directly."

There was a bit of shuffling among the guards; obviously this idea wasn't a popular one but they knew better than to question the judgment of a royal. After a few moments, the head guard glared the others into quiet submission before turning to Marie. "Very well, Your Highness. Would you permit me at least to lead you and your mercenaries past these gates and over the moat? I fear the king will be cross if you enter his lands without the oversight of a single royal guard."

"Saddle up quickly, we shall wait for you on the other side of the gate." Marie didn't pause for any more talk; she began riding forward at once. The guards sprinted into action, furiously shoving the gate open lest she be forced to break her horse's stride. Jack and Frank followed closely, stopping only when she did after the gate was past.

"The idea of you needing protection is pretty humorous," Jack remarked in the brief moment they had to themselves. "As is calling what we've been doing 'diplomatic training'."

"No one in the kingdom knows of my ailment, so when my father allowed me to head off in search of a cure we couldn't very well tell them the true purpose of the journey. So far as they know, I've been going around the kingdoms, learning about their cultures and forging alliances."

Watching the guard hurriedly mount up, Frank leaned in slightly. "Technically, one *could* say that's what you've been doing. You just haven't forged very many alliances, and even fewer would qualify as the sort that a kingdom could openly acknowledge."

Those were the last words anyone got out before the guard rode over. At his approach, Frank and Jack resumed the roles of simple mercenaries to the princess, riding along quietly behind her as they drew near to the massive castle looming in the distance.

* * *

"My girl." The words were barely out of the king's mouth before he'd bounded across the courtyard, easily lifting Marie up in his arms and swinging her about in a fierce hug. It was a good thing they'd dismounted before entering the garden, one that was positively bursting with roses, or the king might very well have knocked her horse over in an effort to get to his daughter.

The king and queen had both been waiting for them in the garden of roses. Clearly the guards had sent word ahead somehow, and they'd scarcely gotten in before the king ran forward. He was a big man, strong and wide in the shoulders, looking more like someone who worked for a living than a king. The queen walked over more carefully, her yellow-gold dress hovering just a few inches above the ground. One glance made it plain where Marie had gotten her looks. The queen was a vision of loveliness even as her eyes watered and her face grew red, the emotion overtaking her.

"I've missed you, Father." Marie was squeezing the king back, and as he finally set her down Marie immediately stepped over to the queen. "You too, Mother. I have seen so much since I departed, and learned a great deal, but every night when I close my eyes I've dreamed of being back here with the both of you."

"We felt incomplete with you away, my dear. As though a part of our very hearts had been taken on the journey as well. Words fail to capture the joy I feel at your safe return." The queen's voice was softer than the king's, an easy task to accomplish given his apparent natural volume, yet there was something powerful about it that compelled one to lean in and listen.

Stepping back from her mother, Marie gestured to the duo behind, standing a distance from the guard who'd led them here. "Guard, as you can see we have safely arrived. Thank you, but the gate demands your attention." She waited until the guard had bowed and was well out of earshot before continuing. "On the subject of my safety, I would like you both to meet the mercenaries who have helped me a great deal over the last few years. They are strange men, I'll be the first to admit, yet they have been steadfast and loyal at every turn. This is Jack and Frank."

Frank bowed as his name was spoken, while Jack merely gave a polite wave. Turning around, Marie faced her friends. "And you two, allow me to introduce you to my parents, the rulers of Villeneuve, King Adam Beaumont and Queen Belle Beaumont."

"Anyone who has aided my daughter is welcome in my castle." While King Adam stood and boomed, Queen Belle took a more direct approach, stepping forward to shake the men's hands. Jack's she took without issue, but when she reached Frank the queen paused, making note of the gloves. Leaning down slightly, she peered inside the dark hood of his robe. Frank tried to pull away, but she put a comforting hand on his shoulder. "Be at ease. I have seen much, and I do not frighten easily. You need have no shame here. I would like to properly look upon the man whom my daughter trusts."

Reaching up, she gently lifted the robe's hood upward, allowing a full peek at the scarred face inside. Frank and Queen Belle locked eyes for several seconds before she let the hood drift downward once more. "You have clearly endured much, good sir. There are some of our older staff more familiar with those in unusual situations, the same ones who cared for my husband once. I will ensure they are the ones to serve you during your stay, in the hopes that it will make things more comfortable."

"Thank you very much." Frank stopped, then remembered who he was talking to and stammered out a quick addition. "I mean, thank you, Your Highness."

"Please, no formalities. I was common-born and I've never been comfortable with the need to add such obligations onto simple conversation. I may have to tolerate it in court, but from my daughter and her aides I won't hear of such a thing." Queen Belle released Frank and made her way back over to her husband, who was still beaming.

Now that introductions were over, Marie was finally able to cut to the heart of the matter. "I'm not actually sure how long we'll be here. While I have made great strides in learning to control the curse I inherited from Father, I have yet to find a proper cure. We thought we were chasing the Blue Fairy when we realized she was, in fact, leaving us clues to follow, the last of which pointed in the direction of Villeneuve. I'm not certain if she is here or this is another waypoint, but I couldn't chance leaving our kingdom at her mercy."

King Adam, who had been cheery since they first caught sight of him, seemed as if he might very well explode from joy. Loud, peeling tears of laughter roared from his mouth as he slapped his knee. The man was far from king-like, which led Jack and Frank both to the conclusion that they rather liked him. When his laughter finally subsided, he looked at Marie with a smile that could rival Jack's.

"My wonderful daughter, we know the Blue Fairy led you here. We know because she sent word that you would be coming. There is much to discuss, but what you need to know most is that the neighboring kingdom of Nivelle has finally opened up to the idea of peace talks. No more constant skirmishes on the border or disrupting trade lines. For the first time in centuries, our two kingdoms can be allies rather than enemies. And, as a token of good will, they sent a gift to show their sincere intentions." King Adam stepped forward and wrapped Marie in another hug. This time there was no swinging, however. This embrace was solemn and heartfelt.

"They've offered you a cure, darling. One conjured by the Blue Fairy herself. Finally, the terror I passed onto you can be over. You can be human at long last."

“That’s…amazing. Too good to be true.” Marie pulled back from the king, giving a brief glance to Jack. Once, she might have been willing to accept such fortune, but years traveling with scoundrels had shown her that such things didn’t simply happen. There was always a price, always some cost, and the most dangerous ones were those that went unseen until it was too late. “I mean that sincerely, Father. That sounds too good to be believed. Nivelle has simply decided to stop their aggression, and they come forward to show it with something that just happens to fix my condition, a condition they shouldn’t even know about in the first place? There must be a catch hidden in their overtures.”

“It isn’t hidden.” Queen Belle stepped to her husband’s side, laying a dainty hand on his massive biceps. “The old king passed while you were gone, and after some battle over succession his second son, Godric, took the throne. He did so by aligning with the Blue Fairy, though no one is quite sure what he offered to secure her aid. Godric has a new vision for our kingdoms, one not tied up in petty aggression. He seeks to unite our lands, to tie us together with unbreakable bonds so that the old grudges can finally be put forever to rest.”

It was the tinge of sadness in her mother’s eyes that gave away the truth, more so even than her words. Marie took a shaky step back from her parents as understanding of the full situation settled in. Deep down, she had always known such a thing was possible, and while they would never force it upon her they didn’t have to. Since childhood, Marie had learned what it meant to be royalty, the duty she owed to the people who relied on her. That duty could take many forms; sometimes it meant war, while other occasions would call for surrender or diplomacy. And, sometimes, it meant sacrifice, doing what was necessary for the kingdom regardless of what a royal might want for themselves.

“Godric wishes to tether our kingdoms together, to bond them in a way that cannot be undone.” Marie’s voice was softer than usual, yet just like her mother’s it demanded those around hang on every word. “This gift that he offers, this cure to my condition. Tell me, does it perchance happen to be in the form of a wedding ring?”

The joy in King Adam’s face was dimming as he noticed Marie’s reaction, yet he didn’t look away from her as he responded. “It is. Godric has proposed to marry you, with hopes to eventually sire an heir and wed our kingdoms together in blood, ending the constant conflict once and for all. I had thought you’d be overjoyed at the chance to finally be rid of your curse, but if this is not what you want—”

“I am the princess of Villeneuve. What I want is what’s best for my people. If you believe that this will give them peace and greater prosperity, then it is what must be done.” Marie hesitated for a glimmer of a moment. “Assuming he tells the truth, of course. Perhaps you’d be so kind as to lead us to him. Before we plan the wedding, we should confirm that this cure of his actually works.”

“That is a…prudent suggestion.” King Adam looked from his daughter to the two silent men behind her. When Marie had left Villeneuve, she still had the naive nature of the young and innocent. It seemed that in her time away she had learned to doubt. It was a necessary trait for any ruler to have, yet his heart was still pained to see such a change. “Come, we sent word to Godric of your impending return. We can go to him and test this magic while your friends settle into our guest chambers.”

“They stay with me.” Marie’s voice turned unexpectedly firm for a flash, subduing significantly when she spoke again. “My apologies, Father. What I meant to say was that until we know for certain Godric is being honest with his intentions, I would prefer to keep them with me. They have useful talents and are quite resourceful in a pinch. And I know without question that if anything should go awry, they’ll cover my back.”

The king’s gaze fell upon the two men once more. One who was covered nearly completely, and one with a dangerous grin. They were oddities, no doubt, yet Marie herself was far from normal. Perhaps in finding more of her kind, she had finally discovered a kinship that she’d lacked while in the castle. Either way, it was heartening to see that she was still capable of trusting, even if she gifted that trust to curious choices. Some of her innocence might linger on after all.

“Very well,” King Adam said. “Follow me; we will take you to the wing where Godric has been staying while we awaited your return.”

* * *

Gleaming silver armor trimmed in gold, blond hair that stopped short of the shoulder so it could be contained in a helmet, piercing eyes that drew one in from across the room; one couldn’t say that Godric, new king of Nivelle, didn’t look the part. At a single glance, he stood out, even surrounded by the dozen other knights at his side. He smiled constantly, not the slice through the face like Jack’s grin but something earnest and cheerful, the sort of expression that set others at ease. From the moment they’d entered his chambers, the man had been a picture of politeness, even sending his knights from the room so they could discuss Marie’s condition in secret. He was from every angle a knight and prince-turned-king who would have looked more at home driving off wicked dragons than presiding over court.

Jack didn't trust him. The trouble was, he was having trouble pointing to exactly the reason why. Normally, he could see through people in a heartbeat. Whatever parts of his brain were off, whatever pieces of his mother's curse he'd inherited, it came with a clarity that few others seemed to possess. That talent was why he'd known there was more to Frank than a mindless creation, and Marie was more complex than she'd seemed during her first tavern brawl. Godric, however, was a conundrum. No matter how Jack looked at him, the king of Nivelle didn't seem to be lying or putting on a show, yet some part of Jack's mind whispered that this wasn't true. By the time introductions were finished, he and Frank given only a passing mention, Jack had begun to suspect that perhaps the issue was not with Godric, but with himself. Was it possible that he simply didn't want this whole thing to be true, because it meant saying farewell to one of his friends? The idea of self-delusion seemed ludicrous, it was something Jack thought he lacked the capacity for, but as more time passed and no evidence of trickery appeared, he had to entertain the idea that it was possible. Especially once the ring came out.

"How lovely." Queen Belle spoke from over her daughter's shoulder, with her husband standing on the other side. Marie and Godric were seated, while Frank and Jack lingered near the back of the room. This discussion, this place, it wasn't for them. They didn't belong in the happy moments leading to resolution, and their looming presence would only make the whole thing feel off.

The ring was lovely indeed, a brilliant blue gem set in white gold that seemed to cast a slight glow regardless of how the light hit it. It matched well with the necklace clinging tightly around Godric's neck, resting just above his armor. He held the ring out to Marie, presenting it without demand, so she could examine it closely.

"As I was told by the Blue Fairy, this has the power to grant your heart's dearest wish. So if it were donned by someone who wished for power, they would grow strong and tough. By one who sought knowledge, then wisdom would flow forth. You can see why it is such a dangerous object, no doubt. Thus, I can think no one in all the kingdoms better suited to wear it than you, princess. On the hand of a woman who only seeks to have her humanity fully restored, the ring serves its greatest purpose: undoing a wrong caused by the fairies."

"That's all there is to it? I just put it on and—*poof*—no more beast?" Marie, intentionally or not, reached out toward the ring. She didn't quite take it yet, though it didn't seem to be too far off. "After everything I've been through, all the searching, this seems so…easy."

"I wouldn't quite say 'easy'. For most, they would have to struggle with themselves, making sure there was nothing else they secretly wanted more. Only one with a heart as pure as yours could turn the task into a simple one." Godric extended the ring a little closer, bringing it nearer to Marie's fingers. The implication was clear: it was hers to take if she so chose. "And of course there are the other obligations. I do hope you'll forgive the fact that I have to tether such a gift with so many strings, but as a ruler I must do what it best for my people. That means securing a lasting peace with Villeneuve, even if I must use this ring as part of the bargain."

Marie was barely looking at Godric now, her eyes lost in the ring. It was strange to watch. Jack was positive she knew better than this. He'd watched her shrewdly haggle and negotiate for hours on end without so much as a misspoken word. Today, she couldn't seem to focus past the ring. Even with what it offered, that didn't make sense. Something was off; he just wished he could put his finger on it.

"We are all bound by the same duty; I understand your predicament well. While a kind gesture, you couldn't very well hand over an item of such power without gaining something for your kingdom in return. Given all the things you might have used it to acquire, peace is among the noblest of pursuits. It would do Villeneuve well to have an ally at our side, rather than an enemy. What you offer does seem to be best for both kingdoms. There are, of course, many details to work out."

From behind, King Adam coughed lightly. "Godric has been here for a handful of weeks, and we have had much time to negotiate. The details have been handled; the treaties are ready to be signed. Even the wedding is set and can be held in as little as a day or so. We only held off so that you could make your own choice. I swore to you that I would never force you into marriage, and I mean to honor that vow. If you decline, then we will forge a new deal—a weaker one, true, but one that doesn't require a wedding to seal the arrangement. This is your life, and none but you can decide what to do with it."

It occurred to Jack that if he had lived under a king like this, he might not have detested royalty quite so much in his youth. King Adam's kindness was an unexpected blessing, as it gave Marie a natural out. Obviously she wasn't going to agree to marry someone she just met, in a wedding that would be days away, all for a trinket from a fairy she didn't even know she could trust.

"You're not quite right, Father." Marie moved her hand forward, taking the ring from Godric's grasp. "From birth, I have known that my life is not truly my own. It belongs to the people, to be used and lived so that I might fulfill the trust they have placed in us to watch over them. This arrangement allows me to do that in ways I never dreamed. I can secure us a new ally, take the fear of war from their minds, and finally become the princess they deserve rather than one hiding a dark secret. For myself and my people, Godric of Nivelle, I accept your proposal."

With a quick motion, she slipped on the magical ring. The blue stone in the center brightened briefly, and the band of white gold tightened around her finger. Marie's eyes fluttered shut, and when they opened again something had changed. There was a peace in those eyes neither Jack nor Frank had ever witnessed. For the first time, Marie was fully relaxed, not devoting part of herself to keeping the unseen beast at bay. A content sigh slipped from her lips, strange and out of place from the Marie Jack had known, but perhaps befitting this new incarnation.

"I feel…normal. Perfectly mundane. It's not there anymore. No urges, no instincts, even my senses feel muted. The beast is finally gone."

To the surprise of most in the room, King Adam let out a choked sound of someone clearly fighting back tears and turned partly away, only staying close enough to rest a hand on Marie's shoulder. "You have no idea how long I've waited for this day, when my sins would finally stop haunting you. Godric, from the bottom of my heart as king, and as father, I thank you for what you've given my daughter."

"As a knight, it is my duty and pleasure to right the wrongs of the world. Saving a lovely princess is what we do, and I take great pleasure in knowing this task will also aid many of our citizens in the process." Godric rose from his chair for the first time, looking more at the king and queen than Marie. "With the princess agreed to the marriage, it seems we have much to do. Shall we begin the preparations for the wedding, so that this joyous news can be shared across the land?"

The king and queen both nodded, as did Marie, who stood up as well. "The word of impending peace will be a wave of joy that washes across this kingdom. Let us start it as soon as possible." Her eyes slid to the far wall, where Jack and Frank still waited quietly, and for an instant something danced in Marie's eyes. Not the flash of yellow they were so accustomed to seeing, rather a moment of wavering, uncertainty. Had she forgotten that they were there? Living remnants of her old life haunting the room. "As for my mercenaries, I think they would have little interest in the tedium of such work. Let us take them to guest chambers where they can have a nice rest. They've certainly earned it."

Jack was about to throw that idea into the moat that encircled the castle by asking what in the kingdoms Marie was thinking, but a steadying hand from Frank paused his tongue. While not one easily given to silence, he trusted his companions. If Frank wanted to speak, then Jack would defer until he better understood the situation.

"That sounds lovely," Frank told her. "Happy as we are to see your journey at an end, I'm sure you have much to attend to that will be easier without us underfoot. Please, anywhere you have will be fine; we are by no means accustomed to luxury."

"Well, then, we have only a few days to get you accustomed," King Adam replied, finally having quelled his budding tears. "The men who brought my daughter back to me will stay in the chambers we reserve for visiting royalty and diplomats, and I'll hear no more on the subject. Come, we can show you to your rooms and then meet with the royal messengers. There is news to spread!"

In a flash, Jack exchanged a brief glance with Frank, who gave the barest shake of his head. Whatever was going on, Frank hadn't been taken in either, but he didn't think this was the place to talk about it. Biting his tongue, nearly literally, Jack remained silent and followed where he was led.

* * *

"It's magic."

These were the first words Frank said. They didn't come immediately upon being dropped off at their admittedly luxurious accommodations. No, he'd remained silent, and held up a finger so that Jack knew to do the same, for some time after they were left alone. Rather than talk, he'd watched the door, sometimes the walls, with that stolen left eye of his. Only after an unknown level of safety had arrived did he finally deign to speak, and when the moment came Jack could scarcely believe this was the big secret he'd wanted to wait on.

"Of course it's magic. The stone glows, we saw how it worked on Marie, and it was given by a *fairy*. The ring being magic was a rather essential part of the marriage agreement so, yes, I picked up on that."

Frank gave him a strange, almost confused look, before muttering under his breath. "Interesting."

"If you have something to say, come out and say it."

"I'm just surprised," Frank explained. "It seems as if you're not entirely under the spell, yet now it becomes clear that some aspects of it are affecting you after all. Before I say my side of it, tell me your impressions of Godric. Did you think he was being honest?"

It took all Jack had not to grind his smiling teeth at the question. Even thinking back to the meeting made his eyes narrow in frustration. "No…but I can't say why. Nothing he said rang false, it all read as genuine and heartfelt. I've got no reason, no evidence to point to, yet still it feels wrong. Off. Just… I can't explain, and it is turning into quite the bother, so if you have something to add I'd greatly appreciate it."

"I already told you, Jack. It's magic. You mistakenly thought I meant the ring, which I suspect is part of the enchantment. It certainly helps explain why, for all of the talk about Marie's present, not one person in the room bothered to ask Godric what his matching necklace does."

With that statement, Jack felt as if he could breathe properly again. The *necklace*. It was enchanted, fairy work just the same as Marie's new ring. Perhaps it held the same gift, to make a heart's true desire real, or maybe it was designed specifically for one purpose. Whatever the case, now that Frank had drawn Jack's attention to it he could finally focus on the detail that should have stood out from the beginning. Based on what they'd seen and how Jack had felt, the necklace probably laid some kind of charm or compulsion on those to whom Godric spoke, making them trust and follow him. Jack had been a bit curious at just how two kingdoms with such a history could broker peace so easily, but the task became far more manageable if one side was wielding fairy magic. He had a hunch that if they were to take a look at the terms of this peace, they might find that Nivelle was getting a far better deal out of it than Villeneuve.

"You were able to partially resist it, I'm guessing?" Frank asked.

Slowly, Jack nodded, thinking back to the meeting once more. While there was still nothing he could point to that spoke of falsehood, it no longer bothered him. Seeing through the magic of the fey was no small task; only someone like Frank would be able to pull it off completely. Jack was mad, not stupid, which meant he understood his own limitations. "Part of me did, anyway. Just barely at that. A small boon of the addled mind my mother passed on. For those with normal brains, I imagine the enchantment would be irresistible. No wonder Marie agreed to the idea so quickly; her beast does nothing to help resist such compulsions. She's not in her right mind."

"None of them are. And none of them can be, so long as Godric retains his enchanted item. Magic from fairies is potent already, items handcrafted by the Blue Fairy would be almost impossible to overcome without a natural resistance. Godric has wormed his way into the kingdom's heart with an item that will compel others to listen and believe him." Frank paused, glancing over at a nearby wall before continuing. "In a way, Queen Belle was right. He does indeed want to do things differently than his father did. Rather than conquering through force, he will take this kingdom with magic and trickery."

"Under different circumstances I could almost respect that," Jack admitted. "But he made the mistake of trying to swindle a Bastard Champion, and that is a sin for which there is no forgiveness. Marie wouldn't want the cure to come like this, not at her kingdom's expense. We have to find a way to stop him."

Walking over to the window, Frank carefully stuck his head out, examining the stone around the outside. "Let's assume that with no preparation or specialty supplies, sundering the necklace is beyond our current capabilities. And since Godric has come this far, he's doubtful to be foolish enough to take it off for any reason. That leaves us with the most expedient of options being simple assassination. We sneak around the outside of the castle, climb to his chambers, and dispatch him while he sleeps. There's a slight risk we might fall into the moat below, although given your faith in your climbing ability it's a minimal concern. The greater issue is what happens after."

"When people's senses snap back? I'd assume lots of cheering and maybe a parade in our honor."

"Jack, Godric staying in the castle means he could only be meeting with and influencing Villeneuve's royalty, as well as some of the servants, at most. To everyone else from both kingdoms, he will be seen as a new ruler who came here asking for peace and was killed in his bed. Even if the ones he's tricked do realize it was all because of magic, the people of Nivelle will never believe such a tale. The only way Marie and her family will survive this scandal is if they put it all on us. We'll be cast as mercenaries who tricked the princess and snuck our way into the castle just so we could murder Godric. They'll label us as killers and traitors, both of which I know you're fine with, but the crucial part is that Marie can't very well be seen in our company afterward. If we do this, we have to leave her behind."

Much as he wanted to point to the argument's faults and tell Frank how he was wrong, Jack couldn't. As usual, Frank had a knack for seeing the whole picture, and he was spot on. Killing a king was not a small act, even for them. There would be chaos afterward, wild accusations and potential war. Blaming them was the only way out for Villeneuve, and it was the right thing to do. Besides, so far as everyone but Marie knew, they were just a pair of swords-for-sale anyway. Why wouldn't they think that those two strange men had decided to sell those services for assassination?

"I don't like making this sort of decision about Marie's kingdom without her being present, but the very fact that we can't trust her to weigh in proves why Godric must be stopped." Jack walked over to the window, joining Frank and peering out. "Give it a few hours until dark, and then a touch longer so we can be sure he's asleep. We can use that time to prepare for our escape, get the bags and horses ready. When we go, we need to vanish. Let's make this as easy on Marie as we can."

"Do you think she'll forgive us for leaving without a farewell?" Frank asked.

"I think if anyone out there understands why we do these things, it's her. She's one of us, no matter what rings go on her hand. Which is all the more reason why we have to do this. It is what we owe one of our own."

* * *

Scaling the castle wasn't especially difficult. Between the moat below and the sea of guards keeping the unwanted from getting close to the king's home, there was little need to bother smoothing out the stones regularly so that nimble hands wouldn't find purchase.

Working their way around the castle, they finally arrived at the window to Godric's bed chambers. Figuring out where he was staying and how to reach it had taken them a chunk of the day, which was just as well. Neither particularly wanted to be around the new king of Nivelle any more than they had to. It wasn't keeping up appearances that was bothersome; rather, they simply couldn't stand watching the way he took people under his spell. It was irksome, except when he spoke to Marie, which summoned up feelings far more murderous. Seeing one of their own enchanted was enough to make them both draw their blades, but thankfully they had the sense to wait until that anger could do some good.

Jack checked the room and found it dark, with a shape sleeping in the bed. He looked to Frank, who nodded confirmation. One man, in the bed. Guards were probably posted outside the door and all down the hall, but who would bother to watch over a window facing out onto sheer stone? Most of the people in Villeneuve would, actually, once word about this stunt spread. Silent as a leaf falling on grass, Jack pulled himself into the room, with Frank only a few seconds behind. Tempting as it was to wake Godric and make sure he knew why he was dying, the risk was too great. They didn't know what that necklace could do. Frank might be immune to fairy magic, but that didn't mean the room around them was, to say nothing of what might happen if Jack slipped under the spell. No, this was a mission where only results mattered. A few quick slashes before he could wake, and Marie's kingdom would be free.

Choosing a dagger from his belt, Jack noted that Frank had also pulled a crude, larger knife for the job. Together, they plunged their blades in deep, ready to muffle Godric's mouth if he lived long enough to scream. Instead, they found themselves coughing as a green mist exploded outward from the body, filling their lungs and making their eyes water.

"There they are, right on cue." The door outside opened, and in strolled Godric flanked by a pair of silent guards. "I was wondering how long you'd make me wait; I do need to get some sleep tonight."

A trap. How? Jack was blinking through the unbidden tears stinging his eyes, trying to focus. Now that light was pouring in and the covers were partially peeled back, he could see the body of the man they'd stabbed. He was alive, technically speaking, and resembled Godric from the neck up. Below that, however, his skin was taut, swollen, and green. Although he was breathing, the man's eyes were rolled back in his head and he barely moved save to let out a long string of drool.

"One of my brothers who went after the crown. We all had different preferred methods; he was a fan of poison. I made him ingest quite a few of his favorites when I bested him, and the Blue Fairy was kind enough to keep him alive so that he might still be of use to the kingdom. Makes a fine double in the right circumstances, and has quite the effect on those who attack him."

Whatever had sprayed upon Jack and Frank was getting worse; even the undead Frank was visibly having trouble staying on his feet. They had to turn this around, while there was still time. Jack took the dagger still clutched in his hand and lunged for Godric, only to have his blow swept aside by a longsword. Godric blocked the next strike as well, and the next, then kicked Jack in the stomach when Frank tried to join the brawl. He was a gifted combatant; there was no denying that, yet it was their own weakness that was the greater enemy. Between the coughing, watering eyes, and how heavy their limbs felt, it took all they had to move at all. Godric ended the assault by punching Frank in the face, knocking him down next to Jack.

“She told me you two would be coming. Said I had to lay a careful trap. No magic, for some reason, and I had to play into your egos. Make you think you’d succeeded easily because you were so good at what you do. The Blue Fairy knows much about you both. I have to say, after all the build-up, I’m rather let down. I thought you’d be tougher.” Godric took a step toward them, adjusting the grip on his sword. “But I suppose there’s no need to draw out inevitable victory. You two are nothing more than a pair of crooks with inflated senses of self. Did you really think the Narrative would be on your side just because you traveled with a princess? Such a ridiculous notion. I am a king, with the support of the Blue Fairy and an agenda to overthrow a kingdom ruled by monsters. The Narrative was always with me, and always will be.”

He halted, looking between Jack and Frank, sword swaying in his hand. “She did want me to pass on a message, as part of our bargain. Not quite sure why she felt the need to bother, but I know better than to welsh on a deal with a fairy. The Blue Fairy would like you both to know that she does not appreciate being hunted, nor what you three have been doing to her kin. You overreached, and now you will learn the cost.”

In the twitch of a finger, Jack could see Godric make his decision. The sword angled toward Frank, thrusting forward at incredible speed. Summoning every ounce of power he had left, Jack hurled himself forward, putting his body between the sword and Frank. It pierced true, sliding right through Jack’s heart and continuing on into Frank’s body. They stayed there, pinned together, as Jack felt the life draining from him. He looked into Frank’s eyes and gave a wink that no one else could see, before shuddering violently and falling still.

“Look at that, he tried to protect his friend. I suppose there is honor among thieves after all. Useless honor, but honor all the same.” Godric yanked his sword free to examine his handiwork. Despite Jack’s interference, he’d stayed on target, leaving a deep hole in the robed one’s chest. All Jack had really succeeded in doing was to get them both at killed at once, rather than separately. Never one to take things for granted, Godric checked their pulses to be sure, Jack first. That one was dead, no question there. As for the other, Frank they’d called him, his flesh was so cold and pale it seemed he may have been on death’s door already, and he certainly didn’t have a pulse any longer.

“Where shall we take them?” One of the guards spoke; Godric hadn’t bothered learning their names. “It might cause a stir if we drag them through the castle.”

"As always, you make the job harder than it needs to be," Godric told him. "We do as the Blue Fairy instructed: toss them out the window from whence they came. The creatures in the moat will take care of them, and if any bits remain to be found it will seem as though they tried to climb out and fell. Given how they broke in, I doubt the princess will have cause to doubt such a story. Not when I give it, anyway."

The guard approached, then hesitated. "Should we strip their possessions first, sire?"

"No." Godric answered a little more forcefully than was needed, and calmed his tone before speaking again. "The Blue Fairy was quite clear. These two have possessions that are dangerous, and we are not to try to take them. Everything of them dies tonight; no bobbles will remain to betray our secret. Toss them as they are."

The guards did as they were told, lifting each body up to the window and then shoving it outward, where it fell through the air before landing in the moat with a splash. They all stared, making sure the corpses wouldn't float to the top, until they were satisfied that the task was done.

Grabbing a cloth, Godric cleaned his sword and motioned to the small pool of blood on the floor of his chambers. "Have someone clean that up. Hurry up about it, too. I've got a wedding coming up and I need my rest. In mere days I will be addressing my whole kingdom for the first time, and I'd like to make a strong impression."

Jack's eyes opened gently as the water lapped at his feet. With a groan that was more habit than necessity—nothing could *actually* hurt him here—he pushed himself up from the ground and got his bearings. The cave looked much the same as it had last time, and every time since Jack first found the golden coin that led him here. Same rough rocks on the ground, same black waters that surrounded the tiny island within the cave, same golden scale next to a throne of obsidian. And, of course, the same figure who was always here, always waiting. One might have expected him to look similar to Frank, but that was only how people portrayed him. Instead, he appeared to be a simple man, albeit a bit pale, who wore practical trousers and a gray shirt. There was only one thing that had changed since Jack was last here, and that was the books. The small pile next to the throne was always in flux. On some visits they might be all poetry; another occasion could see books of spells, or history. Once, Jack had noted they all had curious titles he was unfamiliar with and that made no sense. How would one ever write a history on the idea of time anyway? It made no sense. He'd been told to disregard that pile, and had been more than happy to do so.

Coughing loudly, an act of politeness over necessity, Jack stepped toward the throne. Its occupant peered over the spine of a tome with dragons on the front and let out a sigh before laying a black ribbon between the pages. "It's been a while."

"We made a new friend some time ago. She's tough, but not quite as resilient as Frank or me, so we've made efforts to work safer. Had a good streak going, too."

"Until the sword in your heart," the man noted. "How was that, in terms of deaths?"

Jack mulled the question over; thinking back to how having steel jammed into his chest had felt. "About a six out of ten, overall. Not nearly as bad as the fire, but still a long way from the peaceful death of a good poisoning."

"Interesting." The man rose from his throne, setting the book down in his place and walking slowly toward the giant scale. "I assume you'll be wanting to go back once more?"

"You know me; I can't stand to leave a job half-finished." The glib expression on Jack's face faltered, as his smile took on a wicked gleam. "Also, someone just killed me. That much, I might forgive, but they tried to take out Frank, too. Not to mention what they're pulling with Marie. No, I'm afraid there are accounts to be settled. Crossing the Bastard Champions comes with a heavy toll, and I'm rather excited to make that chatty cock pay it."

The scales groaned as the pale man laid a hand upon them. Gold began to appear on one side, coin after coin, filling the right pan quickly yet unable to tilt the arms. Something unseen was in the left pan, something matching the weight of every coin perfectly. "On the subject of accounts, you know that every time you come here the price to return only grows higher. Will you be able to afford the trip?"

"Don't you worry about me; I've been working hard and saving up. I think you'll find I've got more than enough wealth stashed about the kingdom to cover my cost." Jack smiled as he watched the coins continue to fill the pan, dozens upon dozens. Once, a lone gold coin had been enough to return home, even if it was a rather special one. Now it took quite a bit more, but that was all right. Jack was a professional scoundrel; hoarding was part of what he did.

At last, the influx of coins halted and the scale remained balanced. Nodding, the pale man patted it gently before looking to Jack. "As one who brought me a sacred coin of the Ferryman, it is your right to purchase passage back to the land of the living. Your body will be made whole once more, and your heart will beat with life. If your body is in peril, however, you may find yourself back here soon."

"Don't worry; I've got a friend taking care of that." Jack stepped closer, holding out his hands. "Although I imagine he's probably a bit torn up as well, so I should really get back and help."

"You are a curious man, Jack Spriggins. Most use this bargain with great care, only coming here on the rarest of occasions. Yet you have come to my home more times than almost any other, second only to your father. If death is what you crave, you need not pay the toll. You can cross on, and be done with the world behind you."

"You've got it mixed up. I crave life, not death, I just don't want to let a little thing like getting drowned or beheaded slow me down. There's too much fun to be had, too many adventures ahead. And, right now, too many people depending on me." Jack lifted his hands higher. "Any books you want me to burn for you this time?"

Reaching out, the pale hands closed around Jack's and the cave began to fade away. "Something cheery would be nice. This place is gaunt enough; I could do with a light-hearted romp."

That was the last thing Jack heard before the loud, shuddering gasp of his lungs filling with air.

* * *

Coughing, Jack twisted over before the water shot from his mouth. He hadn't died by drowning too often, but more than a few people had disposed of his body in water, leaving him well-acquainted with what to expect. When the last of the liquid had been purged from his body, Jack looked to his side, where Frank was waiting patiently.

"How are you feeling?" Jack asked.

"Been better. You managed to knock the sword off course enough to miss my heart, though it was close enough to fool Godric while I slowed my pulse, but I'm still going to need some replacement parts before I'll be fully recovered. Also, a few of those water creatures got some nips in while I was swimming us to safety. All in all, not how I expected the day to end."

"I don't know, it could be worse." Jack spat a few times, trying in vain to get the taste of moat water from his mouth. "Godric thinks we're dead, which gives us the advantage of surprise, and we now know with certainty that he has to be stopped."

"That would make me feel better if we had any idea of how to do that. He's got the backing of the Blue Fairy, a magical necklace that compels people to believe him, and who knows how many other tricks up his sleeve. We, on the other hand, have a few days at most to stop him, one fewer team member than we're used to working with, and no idea how to break his enchanted hold on the royal court."

Frank made some good points. As a rule, they were used to going up against stronger enemies, but they usually had the advantage in terms of planning. Few residents of these lands ever thought beyond what the Narrative stuck in their paths, so if one came at them from an unexpected angle it could take an opponent entirely by surprise. Godric, it seemed, was an exception. He'd planned ahead, laid traps of his own, and forged alliances to bolster his weak points. Defeating him wouldn't be easy, especially without Marie. Any other job and Jack would have likely walked away, unless the payoff was spectacular. But Godric had tried to kill him, which Jack found annoying, and he'd stolen one of their friends away, which Jack found unforgivable.

"Count your blessings, Frank. We've got *some* time to work in, and our supplies were moved out of the castle in preparation for our escape. If we hurry, we can get our gear off the horses before anyone knows it was there at all."

"Do you have a plan?" Frank hauled himself up slowly, the wound in his chest slowing his movements.

"The shadow of one, but it's a start. First, we need to make sure all of the leftover powder from the shoemaker job is safely tucked away. After that, we find some Nivelle soldiers—I'm sure Godric has a few hidden here and there—and we get you some replacement parts. Then, we find a way to deal with that necklace."

Setting a soggy hand on Jack's shoulder for support, Frank's eyes poked out from under his hood. "You've got something that can counteract fairy magic?"

"No," Jack admitted. "But a kingdom this size is bound to have a few witches in it. I'll bet one of them loves gold more than they hate strangers."

Together, the two of them began to trudge away from the moat, leaving the castle lit by the moon behind them. Only Frank's voice could be heard, whispering softly as they vanished into the trees. "Dealing with witches? We really *are* desperate, aren't we?"

* * *

It was hard to believe. No…scratch that, it was impossible to believe, yet Marie found herself compelled by the evidence as she stared at the near-empty room. She'd already gone to the stables and found their equipment missing from the horses, and even the secret compartments in their saddles had been looted. While that alone proved nothing, finding an empty bedchamber did seem to back up Godric's story. No one moved Jack and Frank without them wanting to be moved, at least not without causing the sort of commotion it would be impossible to ignore. So if the room was empty and their gear was gone, the most likely explanation was that Godric was telling the truth. His words rang of unquestionable sincerity, even as part of Marie's mind protested that this made no sense.

"They just…bolted in the night?"

"I wouldn't say just bolted," Godric corrected. He and a pair of his guards were standing in the doorway where they'd been waiting since giving her the news this morning. "They also stole quite a bit of silver, some antiques, and a few of the servants' meager savings. Only after that was done did they flee from the castle, racing away in the night."

When he said it, the story hung together so well. Except…Jack didn't bother stealing anything less than gold, and certainly never from someone as poor as a servant. He liked his targets rich, obscenely so, to get the most from his efforts, if not for moral reasons. Even if his greed had swollen to such levels, Frank would have stopped him. And more than any of that, neither man would take off like this. Not after all they'd been through. They had always known the arrangement was meant to be a temporary one, but they would have told her goodbye. All of these thoughts tried to take hold in Marie's mind, demanding she see through the obvious lie, yet none of them could find purchase. Godric's words smoothed over her concerns, shoving them away to some dark corner of her brain where they could do little more than whisper.

"They were mercenaries, after all. I suppose this was to be expected." Marie couldn't quite keep the tinge of heartbreak from her voice as she accepted her friends' abandonment.

"It is for the best. You and I are starting a new phase of our lives together. Those two were only reminders of a dark chapter in your past, one that is finally drawing to a close. With the power of that ring and the uniting of our kingdoms, you will be a true princess. One day a queen. Your time as a monster is behind you."

Something inside Marie, past her conscious thoughts, in the deepest core of her being, rebelled at that word. No one called them monsters, not to their faces. For a moment, one brief, shining instant, Marie was able to see clearly for the first time since she'd heard Godric speak. She could see the oily smugness in his smile, hear the insincere condescension in his words. For a flash, Marie was free, and her hands tightened into fists as she readied to show him what happened to those who crossed the Bastard Champions. She waited for her righteous fury to summon her inner beast…but nothing came. No shift of the eyes, no swelling of muscles, no sharpening senses. Her curse was truly lifted, the ring on her finger still letting out a soft glow as it kept her trapped in a human body.

"Marie, is something wrong? Be at ease, my future bride. The escape and petty crimes of two mercenaries are not enough to delay our wedding." That voice, that damned *voice*, it poured into her ears and forced her off the small bit of perspective she'd found. In seconds, she couldn't recall what had made her so upset, nor why her hands were formed into fists.

"You're right, of course," Marie said. "Let's focus on happier things. There's a wedding to plan, and I'll tolerate no delays. Our kingdoms are waiting for this joyful moment of peace; we owe it to them to proceed as swiftly as possible."

* * *

Finding Nivelle soldiers was easy, alarmingly so in fact. Word from the castle had gone out and many Nivelle residents were journeying to Villeneuve to witness the joyous occasion. That story wore a bit thin when one considered that many of those coming to watch the wedding were armored, carrying fine weapons, and far closer to the kingdom than they should have been if the news just reached them. No doubt someone with sense would ask Godric about it in the castle, only for their fears to be alleviated with a few enchanted words. Worrying as it was, the surplus of people made it easy to find new parts for Frank. While Jack might have avoided slaying total strangers in other circumstances, it was clear that Nivelle had come here to invade. A little killing was to be expected when one came courting war.

By far the bigger challenge was finding a witch. It seemed Villeneuve kept a tidy order on their kingdom; there were no backwater swamps where people frequently disappeared or whispering forests where the fog never entirely evaporated. King Adam had such locations flushed out or burned down; he had minimal tolerance for wanton magic in his lands. Given what Marie had told them about his life and curse, it was a policy that was hard to argue with, even if it did make their current task more problematic.

Mercifully, after a full day of searching, they picked up on a lead. In a small village not far from the castle was a woman who did minor alchemy, but had allegedly been healing horses beyond what a few herbs and potions should be able to manage. With no other options to chase, Frank and Jack stole some horses from the same soldiers who had unintentionally donated to keep Frank healthy, and set out.

Finding the woman in question wasn't difficult, both because her cottage was off to the side, some ways from the village proper, and because no sooner had they ridden into view of it than Jack recognized the woman in front, working in her yard.

"For a woman named Lily, I see none in your garden." Jack drew his horse to a slow trot, approaching carefully. One never knew what to expect where witches were involved.

She looked over her shoulder, giving the two of them a careful wave. "Was wonderin' when the pair of you would make it out here. Soon as I heard the news about the princess, I had a hunch it'd only be a matter of time."

Frank, whose mind was better suited to equations and numbers than faces, finally recognized the voice of the lady in front of the cottage. "You were one of the women we saved from those kidnappers. That was quite a ride from here; I'm surprised to find you so far north."

"I was only down fetchin' some special ingredients. Came back as soon as I finished my business. Was quite a treat though, I tell you. Not every day a lowly little lass like me gets to meet a princess in disguise."

"You knew?" Frank asked.

"'Course I knew, she's the damn princess of Villeneuve and she didn't even try to change her name. Granted, it's a common one 'round these parts, but a little effort in the southern lands might have been useful."

"Marie can be rather stubborn on certain points of pride; her name is merely one example." In a smooth motion, Jack dismounted his horse and stepped over to Lily. "And while she will do anything for her kingdom, I fear certain people are turning that loyalty to their own means. As I recall, Marie told us you were an apprentice witch. If you'd be willing to take us to your teacher, I think we can make an exceedingly friendly business proposition with her and come to an arrangement."

"I doubt it, unless you've got the power to raise the dead," Lily replied. "Passed a few weeks back, poor thing. I've been fillin' in for her as best I can."

The grin on Jack's face dimmed briefly, before brightening again. "Ah, but as a witch of these lands, surely you know others. Whichever one is the most touched by greed will be our best chance."

His optimism was quashed as Lily shook her head. "I see a few of them at the yearly coven meetin's, but none that are close by or easy to find. I also think I recall gettin' a missive not long back about a few folks matchin' your description being declared official enemies of our organization. Something about burnin' down a pier?"

"I nearly forgot about that, why haven't they already?" Patting his horse, Jack looked over to Frank for any ideas. It felt as though they'd come up against a firm dead end on this plan.

"If I am not being too bold as to ask, how far along in your training are you?" Frank asked. "We have a favor for which we need magic, and I'm afraid time is of the essence."

With a soft grunt of effort, Lily rose from her garden and patted the dirt from her dress. "This favor, would it be tied to the fact that Marie isn't with either of you? I'll tell you now, I won't turn my back on my kingdom for you two. If you're tryin' to mess with her chance for a happily ever after, I'll do my best to curse you where you stand."

"Quite the opposite," Jack assured her. "We can talk more inside, but Marie, in fact all of Villeneuve, is in danger. As a witch, you might be the one person who can help us save the kingdom and its princess."

She looked them both up and down a few times, then nodded to the door. "I make no promises, but the old witch did leave me her tomes and tools. Tell me your story, then I'll decide if I want to help. After that, we figure out if I even can."

It wasn't the ironclad deal with a master witch they'd been hoping for, but Frank and Jack were a team used to dealing with long shots. They'd have bartered with a dragon if it meant the chance to save Marie. Tying off their horses to a nearby post, both men followed Lily into her cottage.

* * *

Being back in the palace was surreal, to say the least. In her time on the road, Marie had allowed herself to forget what it was like to live surrounded by luxury at all hours of the day, as well as what her life was like when she was on a royal schedule. Every moment was planned, down to the barest second. There were meetings to attend, lessons to take, appearances to make, and all of that was without even counting the work for the wedding. She was brought in to consult on table arrangements, color choices, flowers, food, and so many other minor details that felt as if someone else should really be able to handle.

Even as she was being fitted for her gown, Marie couldn't help thinking back to her time with Frank and Jack. Dangerous, violent, and terrifying as it often was, there was also a sense of freedom. No one scheduled her, she was free to come and go as she damn well pleased. There was something else different, too, something she never could have placed until experiencing both lives. The people here who asked for her opinion and orders did so mechanically, seeking her input only because she was the princess. Jack and Frank, on the other hand, had genuinely depended on her. When she spoke, they listened, not out of obligation but because they respected what she had to say. It was the difference in earning a position of leadership and being handed one, a divide she never could have even imagined existed before she left the castle.

The dress was lovely, a crisp white that would be accented by dozens of roses when it was done. Around her, the designers scrambled, taking measurements, placing pins, working with a level of teamwork that both impressed Marie and left her nostalgic for her departed friends. As the gown took shape, she noted that the range of movement in her legs was limited. Without thinking, Marie brought the issue to her designers' attention.

"Can we do something about the way it's clutching my legs? I'll barely be able to walk in this, let alone sprint or dodge."

The room fell silent as they all looked at her in mute shock. Finally, the lead dressmaker stepped forward, head bowed as she spoke. "Your Highness, we will of course do as you command, but why would you need to run on your wedding day?"

That was a perfectly reasonable question, and Marie found to her own surprise that she didn't have an answer. When she thought about the impending day, the way Godric had described it to her, there seemed no cause for such concerns. There would be a lovely ceremony, then an address to all the peasants who would gather in the courtyard to greet the newly married couple, followed by a banquet of celebration. None of that should require the bride to race about or get into any fights. This was just an old habit, a lingering vestige of the life she was leaving behind. There was no rational reason to request such a thing.

Still, something inside her, deep down in the most instinctual part of who she was, persisted that she should be able to move. And Marie trusted that part of herself more than any other. Especially with how she'd been feeling since arriving back home.

"The wedding may run late, forcing me to rush to greet the people on time. Or I could merely take a tumble and have trouble righting myself. I'll feel better knowing I can move freely, and as this is my wedding I hope you'll indulge the request."

Even though she kept her tone as polite as possible the head dressmaker still paled at the mere suggestion that she had disobeyed a princess. What had happened to these people in her absence? Marie's parents were never the types to inspire fear in their subjects; they ruled through respect and loyalty.

"Of course, Your Highness. Anything you ask. I only wanted to know so we might make it perfectly to suit your needs." Without another word, the dressmaker snapped her fingers and everyone else got back to work.

Although Marie was glad for the changes they were making, the reaction worried her. Something was amiss in this castle, but for all her effort she couldn't figure out what it was. Times like this, she dearly wished she had the others to talk to. But they had gone, it seemed, and she didn't imagine she'd ever lay eyes on them again. When Jack and Frank left, they weren't inclined to turn back.

Not even for a farewell to an old friend, apparently.

* * *

"It won't be easy. As I recall, the cost is high." Lily rifled through the massive book, turning the pages quickly as she searched for a certain spell.

"That's why we're willing to handsomely compensate you for the work," Jack replied. "We'll pay whatever it takes to save our friend."

"Keep your gold; I'll do this for the sake of my kingdom and my princess. Marie saved me once; I owe her whatever aid I can offer. But the point still stands: you're askin' me to break an item made by one of the most powerful fairies in all the lands. That sort of magic is hard, and always comes with a cost mere gold can't pay."

Jack chuckled under his breath. "You'd be amazed the things gold can buy."

Lily stopped flipping the pages as she found what she was searching for. "You two are in luck. The woman who taught me had some old tomes, the sort that aren't commonly found even among other witches. I think I can make a potion that will break Godric's necklace, assumin' you're able to provide the proper ingredients." She turned the book around to show them the recipe. Most of it was simple enough: herbs, incantations, bits of certain animals. However, at the bottom of the page was the largest entry; someone had even circled it in what appeared to be old blood or cheap ink.

"Sacrifice of the flesh," Frank read aloud. "I presume that has to come from us, not from some Nivelle guard parts we may or may not have kept on hand just in case?"

"You presume right. Breakin' fairy magic is tough, even for witches. If you want to do it, you have to give somethin' up. There's nothin' more personal than your own body, so if you want this potion to have the necessary punch then you'll have to pony up."

Reaching into his bag, Frank produced a small blade with a sharp edge. "I assume the eye of a dragon will be adequate."

"Hang on there; I said it had to be *your* flesh. That eye doesn't belong to you, it's stolen goods," Lily said. "Not much of a sacrifice if you can just pop another one in."

"Why am I not surprised that witch magic has to be pedantic about these things?" Jack held out his hand. "Frank, I'd rather your blade for this than mine, given the delicate work. An eye seems like a good choice though. I'll miss it, but I can manage with one."

"Be warned, adventurer. I can see the wisps of death magic still clingin' to you, and the stench of your body is that of one recently healed, but this is more than just a maimin'. This is a magical sacrifice, and those are not easily undone. Whatever has healed you in the past, don't expect it to bring back this eye. If you give it freely, then it will remain taken. I told you, the cost for a spell like this one is high."

"And I told *you*, we'll pay whatever it takes to save our friend." Jack motioned for the blade again.

Frank started to hand it over, then thought better of it. "Wouldn't you rather have me do the work?"

"Can't risk it. I don't want it counting as you stealing my eye then tossing it in, or whatever other arbitrary rule the magic decides to throw on us. Just get me something very alcoholic and prepare to stitch me up when it's done. If this is what the magic demands, then so be it."

With no more arguments to offer, Frank handed over the blade to Jack, who began to twirl it between his fingers.

"You may want to wait a while before doin' that," Lily advised. "I still have to get the rest of the potion ready and cookin' before I add that ingredient. I just wanted to be sure you'd be willin' to give it before we started."

"Rest assured, you'll get your sacrifice of flesh." Jack stopped twirling the knife, instead looking into the shiny reflection of his face staring back. "But I'm going to take a lot of eyes in return. They might call Nivelle the country of the blind when I'm done with it." A sharp laugh escaped his lips, and he looked away from the blade. "Only joking, of course. After what they've done, there won't *be* a country of Nivelle left when we're finished. Not one with a proper king, anyway." This time, he didn't laugh afterward, and the gleam in his smile betrayed how serious he was.

Frank didn't object or try to correct Jack; it would have been a waste of words and he knew it. For one thing, no one dissuaded Jack when revenge was on his mind. And for another, Frank had considered the possibility that only one of these kingdoms would be left standing long ago. Tactics such as this were not the sort to be forgiven. Either Godric would succeed in taking over Villeneuve or his attempts would spark a true war between the kingdoms. Such an outcome seemed unlikely, and not only because of the politics.

Finding a witch who happened to have the spell they needed, and by coincidence owed Marie a favor, was a little more than Frank could abide as mere chance. Few were that lucky, and certainly not them. No, this stunk of the Narrative pushing them forward. Why the Narrative would choose to back people like them was difficult to discern. His best estimation was that they represented the greatest chance to save Villeneuve. A grand final confrontation would suit the Narrative better than a quiet takeover, and they were merely vessels to deliver that outcome. Frank was at peace with being caught up in the Narrative's flow for the moment.

What concerned him was who it would back when this attempted coup reached its climax.

* * *

Marie had only dreamed about her wedding day in childhood. Once puberty hit and her beastly curse manifested, such notions were put away. Instead, she focused on fantasizing about what it would be like to not fear at any moment she would sprout fur and have her secret betrayed. So it had been a long while since she paid more than a passing thought to what her wedding would be like.

Even still, this felt off. The decorations were lovely, the food looked sumptuous, and the grand hall was positively stuffed with aristocrats from both Nivelle and Villeneuve. It should have been a nice, cheerful event celebrating the union of two kingdoms and the ushering in of a lasting peace, yet Marie couldn't shake the feeling in her gut that something was wrong. Perhaps it was the contingent of Nivelle soldiers seated in a back section of the hall. Godric had explained that he needed them for protection until the union was official, and it made sense at the time, but she couldn't remember *why* it had made sense. Another factor causing her discomfort may have been that the grand hall's great windows were open, as was the door to the balcony, so that the teeming masses of people gathered in the courtyard might be able to look up and catch glimpses of the ceremony. As royalty, Marie was always destined to be married in front of a crowd, but this felt a tad excessive even by such standards.

As her eyes turned to one side of the marriage pulpit, where King Adam and Queen Belle both stood waiting on her, Marie knew with certainty at least one reason this didn't feel right. Frank and Jack should be here. After everything they'd been through, after all the near-deaths and narrow escapes, it felt wrong to have such a major life event arrive without them. On that account, there was nothing she could do. No one made Frank or Jack do anything they didn't want to. Apparently that even included attending her wedding.

The music began to swell, and Godric stepped out from one of the many doors leading into the grand hall, flanked on either side by his guards who were now wearing formal tabards. As for the new king of Nivelle, he had donned a set of armor polished so finely it was like a mirror, with a royal sword at his hip and the ever-present blue necklace fastened around his throat. Curious, it didn't match the rest of his outfit well, although Marie couldn't seem to focus on why that would matter. He and his guards stepped to their positions and looked down the aisle at Marie.

When the music changed, her foot moved automatically, leading her onto the red carpet that was waiting for her. For reasons she couldn't quite pin down, she didn't want to look Godric in the eyes as she made her walk, so she glanced about at other things. Her mother, beaming with pride, her father, who was already tearing up and would no doubt enter full sobs before the ceremony was done. The smiling faces of Villeneuve's guests, the dour stares of the Nivelle soldiers, the fleeting shadow moving beneath the pews where the soldiers were seated.

Marie nearly faltered in surprise. *That* wasn't supposed to be there, surely. Or had she merely imagined it? Now that she looked closer, there was no sign of any movement under the wooden pews. Perhaps it had been a mere trick of the light; she wasn't used to getting by just with human senses anymore, not after having her curse for so long. She could still halt things and make a fuss, but she didn't. Whatever was going on, Marie didn't want to stop it, even if she couldn't find the words to say why.

Eventually, her walk drew to an end as she arrived at the pulpit next to Godric. The officiant, a duke from a nearby region renowned for his public speaking talents, stepped up to address the crowd.

"Friends, family, citizens of both Nivelle and Villeneuve, today is a grand occasion. We have gathered here to join two royal families, two kingdoms, together. This ceremony marks the end of our ages-old conflict, and the dawn of a new era for peace within these lands."

"Peace? You're mistaken good sir. What you have here is not peace, it's servitude. When one man says do and all must obey, unable even to protest in their own minds, that is not peace for anybody but the one in charge."

All eyes turned toward the ceiling, where a cloaked figured was stepping nimbly into view atop the rafters. Most chattered in surprise and anger, while a few whispered with fear. Marie, on the other hand, felt her heart leap from the pit of her stomach where it been sitting for days. She knew that brash, dangerous voice as well as she knew the half-mad smile poking out from under the cloak.

Across the room, the Nivelle guards began to rise but Godric waved at them to stay seated. "Be at ease, you fools. He wants to goad you into action, to disrupt the ceremony with chaos so he has an opportunity to strike. This is a cunning snake, you see. One who apparently knows how to play dead."

"Dead?" Marie whipped around to face her future groom. "You told me he and Frank vanished in the night."

Godric's face creased in brief annoyance before he mastered his expression. "I wanted to spare you the truth, my dear. We caught them trying to rob the place, and in the scuffle they attempted to kill my men, who were forced to defend themselves. Both men were believed to be dead when it was over, but I couldn't bear to hurt you with such news."

"I know that necklace of yours compels belief, but you could at least put some effort into spinning your falsehoods." Jack was still walking the rafters, looking down at the sea of confused faces watching his every motion. "You and your half-trained goons killing me and Frank in a real fight? That's ludicrous. If not for the poisoned body of your brother we could have gut you all before the first man had enough sense to break and run. But I'm not one to deny credit that's been earned; you did manage to trick and stab us, so well done on that. Unfortunately for you, thrifty a man as I am, I always believe in repaying my debts."

"Oh? Will you leave the safety of those rafters and come try to do it, or shall we call in the archers to shoot you down?" Godric was paying no attention to the crowd now; he was so absorbed in dealing with Jack. From the corner of her eye, Marie caught movement, someone in a dark robe drawing closer.

Jack reached a set of ropes tethering one of the many chandeliers in place and hunkered into a squat. "I'll be down shortly. There's just one thing I have to do first." From behind his back, Jack produced a torch wrapped in dark rags in one hand and a small device in the other. Instantly, Marie recognized it as one of the contraptions Frank built to hold flint and steel in a single hand, allowing one to create a spark with ease. Sure enough, in a moment Jack had lit the torch, which was burning brightly among the rafters.

"A torch? You think a torch can defeat me?"

The smile under the hood, now lit by the eerie flickering glow of the torch, widened to an inhuman level. As soon as she saw that, Marie knew things were about to about to get very violent, very quickly. Rearing back for a long throw, Jack's grin turned to Godric for only a split second in response.

"Whoever said you were *my* problem to deal with?"

The sparkle of glass reflecting sunlight caught Marie's eye as the vial twisted through the air, thrown with the expert coordination that only Frank could manage. Unfortunately, she wasn't the only one to notice something amiss. Godric either saw it coming or took Jack's taunt to heart, as he tried to turn away and curl up into his armor. Moving without thinking, because she no longer trusted her mind, only her instincts, Marie wrapped her left hand around the necklace on Godric's neck and yanked it forward, putting it directly in the path of the glass projectile. She no longer had her cursed strength, but between surprise and determination she just managed to drag him the necessary few inches forward.

With a surprisingly soft tinkling sound, the vial shattered against the blue stone in the center of the necklace, coating it in a yellow-green potion that stank like rot. Marie jerked her hand away, which turned out to be a wise move. The gem started smoking first, then cracks spider-webbed through it, until finally the whole thing shattered just as the vial had, sending out a final burst of blue light.

For a split second, all Marie could feel was a blinding pain in her skull. Then it cleared, and with it came the clarity she'd been denied since first speaking to Godric. All around her, others were shaking off the effects, angry faces glaring at the king of Nivelle as understanding of what he'd done set in. It might have come to a head right then and there, if not for the sudden blasts of noise that shook the hall and sent most diving to the ground.

Whipping around, Marie saw the remains of the pews where the Nivelle soldiers had been sitting, right next to the burning torch Jack had thrown while all eyes were on Frank. He'd clearly hit the mark, lighting the fuse to the bags of exploding powder Frank had snuck under the pews. There hadn't been enough to wipe out all the soldiers, but their numbers were greatly reduced and confusion ran rampant among the ranks. If the royal guards of Villeneuve struck quickly, the force could be put down without much of a fuss.

The sharp ring of steel echoed just as Marie started to call for the guards, a dagger against her neck seconds later. Chaos quieted quickly as the people saw the princess in danger, all eyes on Godric and his blade as he began walking her away from the pulpit.

"Do you have *any* idea how much work those two just destroyed? The amount of gold, promises, and sacrifices I had to make to get the Blue Fairy's backing for this? That necklace was going to be a royal heirloom, so that the king of our united lands would forever rule uncontested, leading to an age of endless peace."

"Jack's right, that's not peace, it's slavery." Marie struggled, trying to push his arm away and finding her strength lacking for the first time since childhood.

A dark laugh escaped Godric's throat. "Did you forget, my bride to be, that you no longer have the power of a monster to rely on? You got your wish, and now you're just a human. One who is going to accompany me back to my kingdom as a hostage to ensure we leave these lands safely. I doubt the king is willing to trade his daughter's life for simple vengeance."

Standing on the pulpit, King Adam looked as though he were about to tear the stones from the floor in fury, yet he held his position, not daring to risk Marie to a twitch of the blade. Queen Belle stood next to him, stone-faced in her anger, which made those who knew the couple well even more afraid than the king's fuming.

Carefully, lest he notice, Marie took the ring in her fingers and tried to pull it off. The trinket didn't even budge, no matter how hard she pulled it stayed in place, as though she were trying to rip off the finger itself. If she'd still had the strength, she might have tried to do just that, however she was no longer capable on calling on the beast.

Godric soon noticed her efforts and pulled the blade a hair closer. "You really think it's that easy? That's fairy-made, of the highest quality. I wasn't lying about what it does, Marie. The ring grants the truest wish of your heart. You can lie to yourself, pretend that you want it off, but the truth is you don't. This is what you always wanted: to be a normal princess like so many others scattered across the lands. Even now, you can't deny it's true."

He roughly dragged her further down the aisle, his pair of guards trailing by less than a foot. She could see Jack still in the rafters, and Frank standing off behind the crowd. Both would pounce the instant there was an opportunity, if she could only create one. Until then, they waited patiently, the murder in their eyes begging for an outlet.

As she and Godric neared the balcony where they were to have greeted the world as a couple for the first time, he turned her slightly, so that she could look out to the sea of faces staring up from the courtyard. Fearful shouting soon filled the air as they noticed their princess in peril, too far away to do anything but watch in horror.

"See your people, so worried for you, and know that even their concern is still the ring's doing. After all, how would they feel if they knew I was threatening a monster instead of the woman they adore? This is why you can't get it off, silly girl. To be royalty is to rule, and all secretly burn with that desire. You're no different. Look at them and be honest with yourself: would you rather be fighting me off with a curse that would make them turn away in revulsion? Or isn't this better? The way things should be, properly. Be honest with yourself, Marie, in your heart of hearts, would you rather be a princess, or a monster?"

Confusion was drifting up from the crowd near enough to hear Godric's taunts, though Marie paid them no mind. She instead did as Godric suggested and looked out to the crowd. Good people, living simple lives, whose peace could be easily shattered by those with ambition like Godric. In her time on the road, she'd met so many of them, been able to help so few. Only from the seat of a throne could she make lasting change, truly turn the kingdom into something better for all of those people. Godric had tried to steal that from her and her family. And if she'd learned nothing else from her time with Jack and Frank, it was that his kind would always try again. Until they were stopped for good, they'd keep coming, not caring how many of those nameless faces were hurt in the process. Godric was right; in the deepest part of her heart, Marie knew exactly what she wanted to be.

"A princess." The words fell heavily from her lips, lifting a great burden as they came away. The victorious smile that split Godric's face was short-lived, however, as another sound soon filled the air. Metal on stone, the gentle clatter of a ring slipping easily from Marie's finger, as though it had never belonged there in first place, and tumbling to the ground. Godric barely had a moment to consider what was happening, and that turned out to be too bad for him. Because Marie was already in motion.

Her hands wrapped around Godric's wrist and tore it back so violently she heard the bones creak, shoving the dagger away from her neck. Sights and scents came flooding back to her as her true senses returned, the sounds of tearing fabric filling the air thanks to her swelling body and muscles. All around, the guests were scrambling away in fear and shouts of terror rose from the courtyard, but Marie only had eyes for Godric.

"How… You just admitted that you wished to be a ruler rather than a monster. How did you get the ring off? *How*?"

"I said I wanted to be a princess." One of the guards lunged forward toward Marie, thrusting with his blade. Barely paying attention, she slammed a still-growing fist into his stomach, denting the armor, and then tossed him unceremoniously over her shoulder, and the balcony, where his screams echoed until he landed, then cut off instantly. "To lead a kingdom doesn't mean we are more important than our subjects, it means our lives belong to them. They trust us to care for them, watch over them, and keep them safe from would-be conquerors. No matter how much I might want to be human, right now my people need me to be a monster, because a monster is what can stand against someone like you."

Her tone was thick now; the proper voice of a beast had returned once more. Godric and the remaining guard continued to backpedal, and from the corner of the grand hall she could see the surviving Nivelle soldiers scrambling into formation. From the other side of the hall, however, the royal guards were pouring in, eyes on the towering creature standing in the center of the aisle, menacing Godric.

"Guards of Villeneuve, the king of Nivelle has tried to steal this land via trickery and enchantment. He and all of his soldiers are to be dealt with as bloodily as the need demands. But anyone who touches so much as a hair on the head of that creature in the center will see only the inside of a dungeon for the remainder of their days. She is very much on the side of our kingdom." Queen Belle waited only a moment after giving her order, noticing that no one jumped into action as the madness of scene caused them to hesitate. "I said deal with the people of Nivelle, *now*!"

The force in her voice spurred them forward, and the Nivelle soldiers hurried to get between the royal guards and Godric. For his part, the king of Nivelle took the opportunity to turn and sprint away as fast as he could, lunging into his crowd of soldiers and working to disappear in the confusion. Many of the soldiers turned to Marie, spears and blades at the ready.

Flexing her claws, she hunkered down, preparing to charge. The sound of a sword being unsheathed was all the warning they got before a figure swung down from the rafters on a freshly chopped rope, sweeping over them and slicing into every exposed neck he saw. Jack let go of the rope at its lowest point, tumbling across the ground with rapier still in hand until he sprang to his feet and stabbed a Nivelle soldier. The motion caused his hood to fall back, revealing that above Jack's violent smile was only a single eye, with the other now covered by a dark patch.

While she didn't yet know the details, Marie understood that whatever Godric had done, he'd cost Jack an eye in the process. Her righteous anger, already at a boiling pitch, burst over as she ran toward the cluster of soldiers. They learned very quickly that while Jack could be distracting, it never paid to take one's eyes off the beast.

Frank darted in, helping her carve through the ranks, but Jack didn't turn back. Instead, he ran off in another direction, out of the grand hall. She didn't know what he was planning, and that was fine. Marie trusted these two, more than she had even before today.

Jack would go where he thought he most needed to be, and based on past experience there was a good chance that he'd end up right.

* * *

What seemed like inevitable victory only an hour prior had now spiraled into a desperate race to escape. Nivelle's soldiers were a loss. Godric counted himself lucky one of his personal guards had managed to keep up in the mad dash through the chaos. Still, all was not lost just yet. The necklace might have enhanced his talent for deception to magical levels, but he'd been making people do his bidding long before acquiring such a trinket. If he could just get away, out of the castle and into his own lands, Godric could spin the whole thing as a devious trap devised by the kingdom of Villeneuve. He'd say they'd lured him with the promise of peace, only to discover that the princess was, in fact, an evil monster meant to devour him. There were holes in the story, but the peasants would be too stupid to spot them, especially once word of Marie's transformation spread across the land.

While it was an unquestionable setback, Godric might be able to use this as a reason to marshal his forces and lead a proper attack on Villeneuve. It was their own fault, really. Godric had tried to conquer them peacefully and they'd rejected his kindness, so now he'd be forced to do things the bloody way.

Turning down a hallway that was mercifully empty, Godric kept on sprinting, listening closely to the sound of his guard following steps behind. The man had been at his side for years, but if he grew too slow Godric would leave him for dead without hesitation. Escaping from an enemy castle was a stiff enough task as things stood. Thankfully, as a man of preparation, he'd laid a few exit strategies just in case. If they could just get to the courtyard, they'd have allies waiting to smuggle them back to Nivelle.

Another turn in the hallway, but as Godric took it he realized that the footsteps behind him had suddenly halted. Glancing back to check for enemies rushing them, Godric instead found himself staring at the unmoving body of his guard, looking entirely normal with the one large exception of the blade sticking out of his neck. In a flash the steel withdrew and the guard tumbled to the ground, revealing Jack's violent smile as he flicked specks of blood from his rapier.

"Fleeing from your own wedding? As a friend of the bride, I hope you'll understand why I can't let you get away with that." Jack stepped nimbly over the corpse, advancing as Godric carefully moved backward. His own blade was pulled out quickly, a true longsword befitting a king that had been crafted just for him.

"Be warned, mercenary. I don't know what trick you pulled to survive that last blow, but this time I'll take your head from your shoulders to be sure the job is properly done. I grew up with five brothers and the knowledge that we'd one day fight for the title of king, so I am well-acquainted with how to use my weapon. However, time is of the essence here, and I am a reasonable man. If you aid me instead of forcing me to kill you, I will happily pay an inordinate sum of gold. For saving the life of a king, I think nothing less than fifty thousand gold pieces would suffice."

Another step forward from Jack, and this time Godric didn't retreat. "You know, if I was the only one you'd killed, I might actually take you up on that. The price is fair, well more than what I spent, and I'm a practical man at heart. I don't particularly care which kingdom comes out on top in any given conflict, and I owe no special allegiance to Villeneuve." Jack halted, lifting his rapier as his weight shifted to an offensive stance. "But you also stabbed Frank, and put a dagger to Marie's throat. I'm afraid there's no amount of gold that can buy my forgiveness for that."

"So be it." Godric didn't wait for the attack; instead he lunged forward, hoping to push through Jack's guard with the greater weight of his blade. The thrust struck only air, as Jack turned out of the way, whipping his own sword forward on a crash course with Godric's neck. A clang of metal filled the air as the rapier struck Godric's wrist guard instead, adding a scratch to the dents Marie's grip had left, and the two backed away momentarily.

"You wore real, functional armor to a wedding? I hate to admit it, but you're not bad at this."

"I am a man of strategy and thought over brute force. That is why *I* am the king of Nivelle and my brothers are either dead or subjugated. A mere criminal like you could never understand such complexity of thought."

Godric attacked again, this time not settling for a single strike. His sword shone in the light from nearby windows, dancing through the air as it tried in vain to cut the man known as Jack. Some thrusts got close, yet he was always a touch too quick. It didn't help matters that Jack was counterattacking the entire time, his rapier flashing as Godric did all he could to block blow after blow. When they finally parted once more, neither man was injured, although Godric's wrist guard was scratched all over.

"Scoundrel, actually." Jack still had his blade raised, ready for another assault.

"What?"

"You called me a criminal, and while that's not untrue it's more a general term for anyone who breaks the law. I prefer the term 'scoundrel'. Carries more of an uninhibited air than someone who just holds up carriages for gold. Scoundrels aren't better, *per se*, just more focused. We know what we want and aren't above doing what's necessary to get it. It doesn't mean we're evil, just not particularly good."

Godric adjusted the grip on his blade slightly. He was wasting too much time with this; if escape was to happen he needed to flee soon. "The Blue Fairy told me about you. Not as much as I might have liked, but enough to plan my trap and a little more. She told me you're a man who has had the chance at countless happily-ever-afters yet refused them all, and that means you're someone who's hard to predict. How do you fight a man who seemingly has no objective? Me, I think it's simpler than that. You're not some grand riddle, you're just a reckless idiot who knows how to fight, but has no idea what to do when the battle is done."

Leaping forward, Godric let loose his most furious attack yet. Jack was too quick to defeat through sheer might, so Godric's only hope was to shake his enemy's confidence. Get in his head, fill it with pointless thoughts, take even a small fraction of his edge away. It was a tactic Godric had used to great success many times before, but as his sword swung about uselessly through the air it became clear that the gambit hadn't succeeded.

"Well, you're right that I'm not a grand riddle." Jack didn't even bother to stop attacking this time, continuing the conversation even as he deftly avoided Godric's strikes. "It's very simple, actually. For a proper scoundrel, there is no happily ever after. The next journey, the next adventure, *that's* where my happiness lies. If my adventures came to an end, be they atop the throne of a kingdom or in a mud pit with pigs, I'd be equally miserable. Riding on toward the next horizon or dying sword in hand, those are the only true endings for a man like me."

More strikes to Godric's wrist guard, but now it was starting to feel as if Jack was hitting it on purpose. Was this… Was he toying with Godric? This whole time, had there been a fight at all, or just an elaborate stalling tactic?

"Why won't you fight me properly!" Godric's swings were getting wilder, frustration and desperation overriding the cool head he prided himself on.

"Because you're a king and I'm a scoundrel. We both know I can't kill you. The Narrative would never permit someone as lowly as me to end a man like you." Jack's smile was getting wider with every dodged blow; each bit of tooth he bared felt like a mocking dagger in Godric's gut.

"Then why did you bother to fight me?"

"So that someone who *could* kill you, perhaps a wronged princess, would have time to catch up." With that, Jack leapt out of the way, revealing the massive, furry form of Marie at the other end of the hallway.

The *bastard*, he'd kept Godric too distracted to notice the approach. Worse, he'd baited the king of Nivelle into the center of the hallway, much too far from a door to run. With no other option, Godric raised his sword to fend off the charging beast. It wasn't even past his shoulder when he felt a stinging pain in his hand, dropping the longsword to the ground with a clatter. Sticking out from between his fingers, through the chainmail glove, was a small, strange blade not quite like any he'd ever seen. Glancing up, past the barreling monster bearing down on him, Godric was just able to make out the cloaked figure at the other end of the hall, similar blades clutched between his fingers.

"You people are the *worst*," Godric said.

"The absolute champions of it," Jack agreed before ducking out of the way.

Marie slammed into Godric so hard his armor dented around his chest, making it hard to breathe. The issue became compacted further as she slammed her fists into his limbs, cracking them through the protective metal. When that was done, she began to squeeze, crumpling the armor in on itself until Godric was little more than a twisted mound of shattered bones and bent metal.

"What do you think? Keep him as a prisoner, or finish it here?" Jack asked.

"He's got a slippery tongue. I don't think we need more of his lies." Hefting Godric up, Marie stared into his bruised face. "How did he try to get rid of you two?"

"Stabbed us through the heart and tossed us in the moat." Frank had approached quietly during the scuffle, arriving more for support than aid. It was clear Marie already had the task well in hand. "I should also mention that, given his injuries, there's a minimal chance he won't die of internal bleeding."

Marie looked Godric up and down once, then broke into a toothy grin that nearly rivaled Jack's. "Guess that means we can skip the stabbing part." With one punch, she shattered the nearest window and looked outside, to the moat below. "Can't imagine he'll be a good swimmer with all that armor and those shattered bones."

"Almost seems unfair," Jack noted. "Are you okay with taking these actions, as a princess?"

There was a moment of hesitation, and then Marie tossed Godric unceremoniously out the window, watching as he crashed in the moat with a sizable splash. No sooner had he landed than the water began to roll, the moat's inhabitants grateful for an unexpected meal.

"My whole kingdom just found out what I really am. There's no going back to the deception, so if this is my last day as a true princess, I think it's only fitting that I spent it taking out a major threat to our kingdom."

From down the hall, they could hear armor rattling and footsteps bounding, and soon the royal guards of Villeneuve burst into view. One of them, the bravest by no small measure, took a step forward to address the trio. "King Adam has requested you meet him in the throne room."

"We'll need to stop by my chambers first," Marie said. "That dress wasn't enchanted to change with me, so I'm going to need to pick up some new clothes."

"The king expressed his desire for you to come immediately." The guard's resolve on carrying out that order lasted less than five seconds under the withering glares of the Bastard Champions. "But it would hardly be appropriate to ask a princess to attend a formal summons in the nude, so we will of course wait while you fetch new clothes."

Slowly, Marie turned away from them, pausing only briefly to address her friends. "I'll get my enchanted ones. Something tells me I'm going to need them."

* * *

In contrast to the madness and panic that had swept through the grand hall, the throne room was a peaceful sanctuary. King Adam was seated in the throne, with Queen Belle at his side. The royal guards were dismissed as soon as they'd brought their charges. Jack, Frank, and a once more human Marie all approached the king slowly. But before they'd made it within ten feet of the throne, King Adam had leapt from his seat to wrap his daughter in a tight hug.

"I am so, *so* sorry. Not only did we allow ourselves to be taken in by an enchantment, but our mistake forced you to reveal your secret to the public. Our error is unforgivable, and I know you may never—"

"Be quiet, Father." Marie hugged him back, long enough that Jack and Frank both looked away uncomfortably. Neither was especially familiar with paternal love, and they weren't quite sure how to react to it. Finally the two parted and King Adam walked back to his throne.

Queen Belle motioned to the three of them. "Approach." They did as they were told, until they were only a few feet from the royal couple. "Marie, your father is right. What happened here today is our mistake, yet the consequences will still fall heaviest upon you. There is no way to hide what happened; word is already racing throughout the kingdom and not even a royal edict would halt such whispers. Now, you are our daughter and this is your home where you will always be welcome, but I fear the people of this land will not tolerate being ruled by someone they see as a monster. Your father already learned that lesson firsthand."

"With respect, your majesty, if Marie showed them anything today it's that she *is* fit to rule," Frank said. "She sacrificed her own desires for the kingdom's greater good. What more do they want from a princess than that?"

"If all of them knew what we know, could hear what we heard, then it might be a different story. *Might* be." Queen Belle shook her head, a tinge of sadness peeking through the veneer of authority she was visibly struggling to hold in place. "There was a time when I was one of those people. I know how they think and feel. To them, the world is already full of magic and monsters that threaten to upset their lives with no warning. It is a life of perpetual fear they must endure. Having their own ruler be one of those mysterious, magical elements…it is asking more than they can give."

"There is hope, however." King Adam had composed himself, power returning to his voice as he spoke like the ruler that he was. "We already have messengers out there spreading a new rumor. They will say that Godric was the one who laid the curse upon you when you refused him. If it takes hold, it opens the door, because even the lowliest of peasants know that curses can be broken. Should you decide to continue seeking a cure until you find it, you might one day be able to return to Villeneuve and claim your royal birthright. We will not send you away though. If you can let go of your title as princess then you're free to remain here for the rest of your life."

With a theatrically loud cough, Jack stepped slightly forward. "Begging the king's pardon, but I feel there's something that needs to be mentioned. Godric claimed to have the Blue Fairy lending aid to his scheme, and given the items he was using it seems likely that was true. That means we just thwarted her plan and destroyed at least one magical tool she created. These are the sorts of actions that invite retribution. As king and queen of a prosperous land, the Narrative will likely offer you both some measure of protection so long as you don't make any poor fairy bargains or give cause for attack. Once she is no longer a princess, Marie will not have such a luxury. None of us will. It might be wise to take this chance to set out for new lands, ones with new magics that might be powerful enough to break her curse. If nothing else, it might take us beyond the Blue Fairy's reach."

"We can't go back across the Endless Sea," Frank said. "What lies there is not magic as you know it, and would be of little aid to Marie."

"True, but there are more waters to cross. The Ocean of Certain Death always had a promising ring to it; I'd like to see what lies on the other side. Or the Waters of Doom. I'm open to ideas; I only bring this up because we would need a boat. Strong, fast, and well-provisioned."

The king and queen exchanged uncertain looks as Jack stepped back in line with the others, until King Adam finally addressed the obvious issue. "Moving goods up and down the coasts is one thing, but to wander into the open waters is a suicidal journey. You want to run from a fairy who *may* want to do you harm by embarking on a journey that will inevitably lead to death?"

"The oceans are named in a way that makes people not want to cross them," Frank explained. "However, they can be navigated, albeit not easily. Perhaps the Narrative pushed some ships away from successful voyages, but Jack has already crossed the waters. He found me on the other side of the Endless Sea, where people tell different stories about all the ways to die on the open water. We are likely not meant to move between these lands, but that doesn't mean it cannot be done."

"I'd also like to add that we're not fleeing outright, more giving the Blue Fairy some time to let the edge fall from her anger. Who knows, in other lands we might even find better ways to deal with the fey." Jack quit talking as he noticed the king and queen looking at Marie, who had fallen largely silent during the discussion.

It was Queen Belle who spoke this time, addressing her daughter directly. "Your friends make good points, but the choice is yours. We have missed you dearly, and would welcome the chance to have you back in our lives. In the end, though, you must choose the path that is true to yourself."

Marie ran her fingers along the spot where the ring had been, a small, fading indentation below her knuckle the only sign it had ever been there. "Godric was right about one thing: I can't lie to my own heart. What I said today was true; I want to be a princess, and then a queen. I want to lead my people, to watch over them, to protect them. If that means crossing deadly seas and dealing with unknown magic, then so be it. I will return one day, cured and human, in hopes of ruling this kingdom half as well as you two have."

"On the subject of the ring, did anyone recover that?" Jack asked. "Sorry to break up the moment, but given how powerful it was that might be a useful trinket."

"Though we searched when the fighting was done, there was no sign of it. Someone doubtlessly made off with it during the chaos, and I'm sure it is a headache we will have to deal with down the road." King Adam rose from his throne once more, as did Queen Belle, and they both walked over to Marie. "But it will be our headache, as I think by then you three will be far gone from this land. We will have a ship purchased at the nearest harbor and outfitted with all the supplies you could possibly need. If there is a way to send word across the oceans in these other lands, please let us know that you are safe."

"And you two." Queen Belle moved slightly away from Marie, approaching Jack and Frank. "Thank you for helping protect our daughter. I have no right to ask it, but I pray that you will continue to watch over her in the future."

"We don't watch over each other, Your Highness," Jack corrected. "We're all in it together, side by side. But we'll always be in that position, guarding each other's backs, no matter the fight or the enemy. That much, I can promise without hesitation."

Queen Belle turned away from them, embracing her daughter for what she knew would be the last time in a long while. As they hugged, she leaned in and whispered softly, "You have made strange allies in your time away. Strange, but loyal. Take care of them. Such bonds are not easily found, even in a land of magic."

* * *

A servant slipped out from the royal courtyard, easily overlooked in the franticness of the day's attack. She made her way past the gates and onto the road that led toward a small village, pausing only when she was far enough away to stop seeing other travelers. Slipping into the woods, she climbed a hill with inhuman speed until she'd reached the very top. There, surrounded by a grove of dense trees, she could look out onto the castle from a distance.

From her pocket, she produced the ring Marie had been wearing, cradling it carefully in her palm. Her fingers flexed, forming a fist that squeezed the enchanted object, and when they parted there was nothing but dust remaining. She smiled as she tossed the dust into the wind, letting it blow from the hill and away from the castle. As the wind ruffled her hair, the woman's appearance began to change. Her hair lengthened, her skin grew clearer, and her face shifted until it was the unmistakable visage of the woman known as Lily, at least to the trio of Jack, Frank, and Marie. There was one large difference, however. Today, she didn't conceal the true appearance of her eyes, the shining orbs that glowed blue with overflowing magic, nor the magical aura that naturally manifested around her.

A dragon's eye could see through much, especially in the possession of a walking corpse, but she was no minor fey weaving mediocre veils. She was the Blue Fairy, one of the most powerful beings in existence, peer to almost none and second only to the true Fairy Godmother. Yet even as a being of unimaginable power, boredom was one of the few things she couldn't simply magic away. Perhaps that was why she'd taken up the hobby of learning witchcraft, despite what the other fairies thought of such arts, or dropped the occasional curse on an unsuspecting mortal. Diversions, all of them, to keep life a little more interesting.

So when she'd first heard about the group of three wandering the lands and assaulting lesser fairies, her best hope had been that they might make for an entertaining afternoon. But once she met Marie and saw the other two storm the cave, she realized they could be more fun than expected. Yet not even she had expected the trio to make for such a lovely diversion. It had been a thrilling few weeks, baiting them into following her trail, twisting Godric to her uses, and walking the Bastard Champions right into a trap designed just for them.

True, she could snuff them out with a thought and a flick of the hand, but it would be a waste. There were so many other traps to make for them, so many ways her new toys could entertain her. Although she knew they were planning this very moment to flee, the Blue Fairy could tempt them back. It might not be easy from so far away, but sooner or later they'd return to these shores.

And when they did, she'd make sure to squeeze them for every drop of amusement they had to offer.

Some Tales Later...

"...and you see, even if the words I overheard work and we gain entrance to the cave, there is a band of thieves that would cut us to pieces if we were caught. To take on this robbery is a great risk. I cannot in good conscience ask you to lend aid without making sure you fully understand the danger involved."

A gust of wind blew sand in through the tent's poorly closed flap. There were many fine buildings to meet at in the market, yet these three kept only a small tent on the outskirts of town. He would have never come here, except that rumors said the trio could accomplish any job they were given, assuming they were well-paid for the work. They did not betray their employers or stop until the task was done, and for something this dangerous that kind of trustworthiness was vital.

"I'm willing to split whatever we can haul away. Down the middle, equal parts. I do not know how much we may find, so this is the only fair offer I can make."

All three figures seated across the table wore hoods, masking their appearances. Rumors conflicted on what they looked like. Some said one was hulking and huge, others detailed a terrifying man with scars all over his body. The one in the middle spoke at last, his voice calm yet with a hint of dangerous laughter.

"I've also heard rumors that these thieves have stolen quite a bit, from many merchants across the sands. I think, perhaps, it may be a matter of what we can carry, not what we find. To that end, let me make a counteroffer: if we find more than we can take, then we keep what we haul. You will have your share, and we will divvy ours up. If that is not the case, then we go down the middle just as you suggested.

The man nodded, more than happy to accept such a condition. "That sounds fair."

A small chuckle escaped from the hood of the man in the middle as he leaned forward, revealing a wide smile that felt out of place in a mere negotiation.

"In that case, Ali Baba, I believe we have come to an arrangement."

About the Author

Drew Hayes is an author from Texas who has now found time and gumption to publish a few books. He graduated from Texas Tech with a B.A. in English, because evidently he's not familiar with what the term "employable" means. Drew has been called one of the most profound, prolific, and talented authors of his generation, but a table full of drunks will say almost anything when offered a round of free shots. Drew feels kind of like a D-bag writing about himself in the third person like this. He does appreciate that you're still reading, though.

Drew would like to sit down and have a beer with you. Or a cocktail. He's not here to judge your preferences. Drew is terrible at being serious, and has no real idea what a snippet biography is meant to convey anyway. Drew thinks you are awesome just the way you are. That part, he meant. You can reach Drew with questions or movie offers at NovelistDrew@gmail.com Drew is off to go high-five random people, because who doesn't love a good high-five? No one, that's who.

Read or purchase more of his work at his site: DrewHayesNovels.com